© Boris Vallejo 1977

BORIS

"Golden Wings" by Boris Vallejo
FROM THE BOOKS OF

Gene Fisher

'Ware Hawk

'Ware Hawk

ANDRE NORTON

A MARGARET K. McELDERRY BOOK

ATHENEUM   NEW YORK

'Ware Hawk

Estcarp, the last-held land of the Old Ones in the latter days, was ruled by the Witch Women with the Power that had once been the heritage of all those from whom they had sprung. The land had been caught between two enemies—the new peoples—those of Alizon in the north, and Karsten in the south. To the east lay the mysterious land which, by the Power, was closed to the people of Estcarp, as protection against ancient evil. Then, from the sea in the south, came the Kolder who were rapers of men's minds, who used strange machines to create armies of living dead. Determined to rule the world, they had come through one of the Gates. They hated the Witches mightily, for their minds could not be overborne by the Kolder machines.

They captured Gorm and the city of the Sulcar sea people who had been long allied with Estcarp. In Karsten they made Duke Yvian one of their mind-dead. So they moved upon Estcarp as though it were a nut to crack between two stones.

Then, out of another space and time, came Simon Tregarth who swore liege oath to the Witches. With Koris, exiled from Gorm, and the Witch Jaelithe, as well as Loyse of Verlane (axewedded to Duke Yvian whom she had never seen), he moved to mighty action, rousing all the land.

The Kolder were driven back to their Gate, and it was closed by Simon and Jaelithe (who had wed with Simon against all the custom of her people and so lost the Witches' favor but not her own powers). Then, because Duke Yvian was dead without heirs, there was war in Karsten.

Before Yvian's death, by the Kolder orders, he had outlawed—or horned—all of the Old Race who lived within the borders of the Duchy of Karsten. There was red massacre and much horror, but some escaped, to flee north to their distant kin in Estcarp. There they became the Borderers under Simon, and, with the Falconers, held the mountain passes.

Now a "new man," called Pagar, appeared, and he united the quarreling lords of Karsten by giving them a common goal—the invasion of Estcarp. The Estcarp forces were too few to resist. To save Estcarp, the Witches gathered all their might and, in a single night, struck at the land itself, destroying the mountains, turning and twisting rocks and earth into chaos. This came to be known as the Turning. Many of the Witches died in the backwash of the Power and the few left were reft of much of their strength, but Pagar and his forces were annihilated.

Jaelithe Tregarth had borne her lord three children at one birth—a thing hitherto unknown. In their childhood she went seeking her lord who had never returned from a scouting trip. The three young Tregarths held fast to each other, though the sister was torn away to be trained by the Witches. It was on the very night of the Turning that her two brothers brought her out of imprisonment. Together they fled east, for the old barrier did not hold against them who were of half blood. So they came into Escore, the forgotten homeland, and there they warred with evil stirred to new life by their coming. To them, little by little, were drawn many of those who had once been of Karsten and then had defended the border, together with their kin and clans—moving into the same country from which their ancestors had fled.

Karsten, after the death of Pagar and his army in the mountains, was in a chaos of warring lords. The turned and twisted mountains gained an evil reputation and only outlaws sought refuge there. Also, from Escore, now awake and seething with magic, came strange other beings to prowl this new territory.

Estcarp, exhausted by years of war, first with the Kolder, and then with her neighbors, was under the rule of Koris of Gorm. He was joined in time by Jaelithe and Simon Tregarth, returned through the aid of their children and choosing to defend the west and not the east.

Alizon, to the north, having been tricked by the Kolder into invading the western continent where lay the dales of High Hallack, was badly defeated there. Now it held an uneasy peace, though there were frequent raids south to test the defenses of Estcarp, and on that border the forces of Koris centered.

These later years were a time of many perils, of the wandering of masterless men, especially those exiled from Karsten by the Horning. Some settled in Estcarp, though they did not accept that as their true home, others took service wherever they might.

The grim and deadly race of Falconers, forced to flee their Eyrie in the mountains at the Turning, became marines on Sulcar ships or sought employment where they could, their tight organization scattered. Their once-great hold was a pile of stones. So the years sped and there were no firm roots for most men. Estcarp, under a new type of rule, was unsure of the future.

The wind blustered through the gray dawn. There was a crash as one of the slates from the inn roof shattered in the courtyard. Once Romsgarth had been a major town where far-traveling merchants met—the last Estcarpian hold before the overmountain way to Karsten. It was very old and worn, with perhaps a third of the stone-walled, ancient building falling in, to become weed-grown rubble. The days of those merchants, with their busy going and coming, were nearly two generations ago, banished now into the past. Karsten—who went to Karsten by mountain roads now? There *were* no roads since the turnings for the mountains themselves had set up new barriers unknown to any save outlawed men, skulkers and raiders, drawn from afar to seek refuge in holes and dens.

The pickings hereabout for such outlaws must be scanty. Three years of severe winters would have reduced even the most lawless to a small threat.

The girl standing by the inn window, holding the edge of a shutter against the push of the wind, looked out upon the not-yet stirring town, the tip of her tongue showing between her lips. This nervous habit, of which she was not aware, betrayed her anxiety, though none now were left to care what troubled Tirtha of Hawkholme.

There were many roaming along the broken border who, worn by long years of war, sought aimlessly for some refuge or had some business they held secret, lest it be taken from them, as so much else had been. Questions were not asked of travelers in these broken, dying towns. Such life as had returned to Estcarp now lay in the north—in those rich lands once more to be set under plow in a week or two, and in the ports where Sulcar ships nosed in, those hardy traders already seeking their old sea tracks.

Within this room, where a twisted rag—anchored as a wick in a bowl of oil—gave more smoke than light, hung the sour smell of too many wayfarers, too little pride in the inn, too long a span of years. Time weighed on the cracked walls, made the floor uneven, its thick boards worn by the passing of countless booted feet. Tirtha breathed in deeply of the cleaner air outside, then closed the shutter and slipped the bar into place. She moved swiftly to the uneven-legged table with the lightfootedness of one used to dangerous trails.

There she sought, for the second time since her awakening, the purse carried within her jerkin, part of the belt clasped about her waist beneath layers of drab clothing. Made of serpent skin, it was supple enough—as well as tough—for her to feel its contents without opening it. There was money there—gathered slowly, painfully. She need only to look at her calloused hands, feel the ache rising from a sudden shift of her thin shoulders to remember how most of it had come into her keeping. There was also a small hoard of ten irregular discs of gold—so old that all markings had long vanished from their surfaces—the gift of fortune itself. This she had taken as a sign that what she must do had advanced from wishful dreaming to reality.

She had hacked away a fallen tree to free a path for the plow, thus revealing in the turn of its roots a shattered bowl—and in it—this hidden treasure! Fortune had been with her also that she was alone at its discovery. The surly garthman who had hired her as a harvest hand had seen fit to send her out alone on the roughest job he could find—merely, she believed, to teach her that as a woman she was of little use.

Once more Tirtha's tongue touched her lips. Service at the hearth or with the wash paddle along a streamside was not for her. She wore men's clothing; a sword hung at her belt, though its blade had been so nicked and thinned she feared any use of the weapon might break it. On its pommel was still the tracing she treasured—the head of a hawk, its bill a little open as if voicing a cry of defiance. That was all of her heritage unless . . .

Karsten—Karsten and a dream. Since the Witches of Estcarp had wrought their magic in the Turning, upheaving the mountains and making the land walk and so destroying the invading forces of the Pagar, who had risen to rule in the southern duchy of Karsten, no one knew what lay overmountain in these days.

The bits and pieces of knowledge Tirtha had gathered so avidly from any wayfarer (and most carefully, lest curiosity be aroused as to why this sun-browned, hard-featured female was interested in anything beyond the earning of her bread) made clear that the duchy had been split into many small holdings often at war with one another. No lord since Pagar had gained power enough to make the broken duchy whole again.

This present state of Karsten might well serve her purpose in one way, hinder it in another—she had no way yet of knowing. With the discovery of the hoard of gold discs, which she took as an omen, she had come to find out that one did not venture south without a guide. In the rending of the mountains by the Power of the Witches, all landmarks had disappeared and she could not wander alone.

Hence—the hiring fair.

Tirtha buckled on her sword belt and swept up a hooded cloak of stout weaving, lined with hareskin—an extravagance to one slim of purse. Yet the garment was a necessary protection against the weather, like the winds that howled outside now, as well as a sleeping nest for the night. There was her shoulder pack also and her bow and quiver of arrows. She had worked a whole season to learn the making of those, practicing thereafter with dogged patience. She had no dart gun. Those were for the wealthy, heads of households and their guards or for the Lord Marshal's own forces, which kept such law as now ran in Estcarp.

Down in the stable there was a rough-coated but sure-footed mountain mare—used to living off scant grazing—a mount with a rolling eye and a wicked temper. However, that temper was also a good protection against her being stolen. She was as gaunt and ill-looking as her mistress, her rusty black coat matching the short-cropped hair that hung in scallops across Tirtha's forehead.

With calloused fingers Tirtha pinched the wick of the lamp, before moving noiselessly out into a hall where the stink of too-close living made her nose wrinkle as she descended use-hollowed steps into the common room.

Early as it was the innkeeper, a woman with a sagging fat belly beneath a sack apron, sleeves rolled up over arms that were thick enough nearly to match Tirtha's thighs, was at the hearthside, a long-handled iron spoon in one hand, the other rolled into a fist which she had just used to cuff a girl who had been watching the pot. A smell of scorching worked its way through the other odors, and Tirtha guessed at the sin of the younger cook.

Scorched perhaps, but it was food. She had long since learned not to be dainty—if food was hot and filling it would do. Also she had no money to waste by calling for any special dish. She scooped up an empty wooden bowl from the table, picked out a horn spoon, which looked as if it had been at least wiped clean after its last use, and advanced to the scene of conflict.

The serving wench scuttled away on hands and knees, snuffling, seeking a safe distance from her mistress who was stirring the pot with a vigor that sent bits of its contents slopping over the rim. Now her attention switched from what she was doing to Tirtha.

"Porridge—you can have a chop of beef—" Her small eyes had already valued and dismissed this visitor as not being worth urging to eat a more varied meal.

"Porridge," Tirtha agreed, extending the bowl into which the inn-mistress ladled an even six spoonfuls with the ease of very long practice and an eye for profit.

The smell rising from it was not only of scorched meal, but musty as well—the end of the winter grinding. No lumps of chopped bacon, not even a shaving of onion, cut the dusty taste. Still it was food—energy to see her through the morning, and she was not about to add to her reckoning. There were supplies that she must buy. Game did exist in the mountains, yes, and she was adept with a snare—not even wasting an arrow unless she had the fortune to meet a pronghorn. Also, she was countrywise, and with the beginning of the growing season, there were a number of newly green sprouts that could be boiled, not only as food, but for their tonic.

There remained salt and some other things that she must reluctantly lay out money for, and she had the list ready.

The inn-mistress glanced Tirtha's way now and then, as she methodically emptied her bowl, doubtless ready to answer with a quick tongue any complaint. That this woman was wary of her, Tirtha had known from the beginning. She was neither bird nor hare in this land. A woman who rode as a man might, who had no proper place. She was marked, yes, but there were other strangers, some as odd as she was. If they tattled among themselves about her for the space of a day or so, there would arrive some other to make them wonder and surmise. She had nothing to fear this side of the border. On the other side—well, even her face might condemn her there, if the old stories were true, and she was certain that none of their grimness was the matter of a songsmith's imagining. Her own kind—the Old Race—had been thrice-horned, outlawed, hunted, slain—sometimes horribly—when Duke Yvian had ruled, and those days were still unforgotten.

Those who had escaped into Estcarp had formed the Borderers, to ride a blood-stained trail back and forth, providing the first wall of protection for the north. Men and women of the Old Race, who had seen their dead, did not forget. The sword at Tirtha's side had been a part of that time, though the fighting was over when she was but a child not as tall as the table at which she now sat. Still, hatred was bred into her. The Old Race was long lived—unless death cut them down prematurely in war—and their memories were even longer.

Others were stirring in the inn now—tramping down into the common room. There were at least three, who, she decided, were bound for the same place as drew her—the hiring fair held here in the early spring. They were better dressed, fuller of face than she was, as if they did not know the gauntness of late winter. They were garth stewards, perhaps, sent to pick up a herdsman, a dairy maid, even a weaver, if they were lucky.

Her own seeking was different, and only rumor had brought her here. Though many of those who had served in the wars had been granted lands to the east, and others were still attached to lords to whom they had given shield oaths (and some were outlaws because raid and rapine were all they knew), a trained fighting man down on his luck could still be hired. With the better sort, who still had their pride and kept to the old customs, sword oath might be given in return for hire.

She needed a man who knew the mountains, was not an outlaw, yet might be a guide into Karsten. For such she was willing to give a good weight of what now lay snug about the upper curve of her hips.

Tirtha scraped the last unappetizing morsel from her bowl, dropped the licked spoon into it, and rose. The hiring lines would be gathering now where the long-ago guild merchants had had their principal market. With the wind still shrieking, those seeking employment might shelter in the pillared and roofed alcoves, which had held stalls in the old days.

She fastened her cloak throat buckle, jerked the hood well up over her head, and pushed out into the courtyard, to the street beyond. It took only a few moments' quick walk to reach her goal, but the wind cut and pulled, leaving her gasping when the full strength of it hit against her face. There were few to be seen on the street. It was a foul day, and by a new lowering of clouds overhead, like to be fouler. She turned into the square and saw that she was right—those who waited huddled in the alcoves.

Each wore in his hat or her hood the small symbol of the trade offered—a whittled staff for a herdsman, a tuft of wool for a shepherd, a miniature paddle for a dairy maid. Tirtha gave only a quick glance as she strode by. Perhaps she faced disappointment—what she sought might no longer be offered.

It was in the last of the alcoves, as the rain began—carried in fierce lances by the wind—that she saw what she hunted. There was only one. He was alone, as if he were indeed an outlaw—some venturer whom none of these peaceful serving folk wanted a part of, a hawk dropped into a flock of domestic fowl.

Hawk—

Tirtha halted, her hand seeking the half-effaced insignia on the pommel of her sword. This one was as out of place as if he had been painted brilliant crimson and hung about with gem chains.

He leaned against a pillar until he saw her stop. Instantly he straightened, to match her stare for stare—cold-eyed as something that was more of the Dark than the Light. Where she wore leather beneath her cloak, he was mail-shirted, his own cloak cut about at the hem so it came only to his knees, two rents in it badly cobbled together with large stitches. Though he had on a horseman's boots, they were spurless, showing signs of heavy wear. But it was his headgear that left her astounded.

Instead of the plain helm of a Border fighter, he wore a far more ornate one, which masked him half-face. It was badly battered, and there had been a clumsy attempt, even as there had been to repair his cloak, to restore it. Its form was that of a hawk, or a falcon rather, and the right wing had been riveted back into place so that it hung slightly askew.

A Falconer!

This was the legend indeed. Had those men, born for no other life than that of fighting, been so reduced through the mischance of chaos? Their Eyrie had stood in the mountains—but Tirtha had heard that the warning, which had brought the Borderers down from the heights before the Turning, had been relayed to them also, and surely they must have survived. Yes, in the months past she had heard of some serving on Sulcar vessels as marines—even as they had done centuries ago when first they had come to Estcarp.

They were not such as to find any favor with the Witches of Estcarp, even when they offered their well-trained force to augment the badly depleted army of Estcarp. Their way of life was too alien. To those all-powerful women, it was also hateful and perverse. For the Falconers were a purely male clan—holding females in contempt and revulsion. They did have their women, they bred their own kind, yes. But those were kept in an isolated village to which selected sires went at ordained times of the year. Also they were ruthless with their own get—killing any child not whole and perfect at birth. To the matriarchy of Estcarp they were totally opposed by custom. Thus they had settled in the mountains, built their great stronghold—the Eyrie of

Falconers—and border watch towers and carried on a service of protection—first for the merchants who would travel the roads, and then as a barrier for Estcarp against Karsten in the latter bad days.

The Borderers claimed them, though not as sword brothers, and held them in respect. They served together in good accord. Supplies were sent, first secretly since the Witches forbade it, then more and more openly to both the Eyrie and their village of women. In the last days of all there had been very little barrier between the male fighters of Estcarp and these strangers who had come originally from some disaster overseas.

Not only were they expert at arms, but their prized falcons, fitted with devices that were part of their secret, formed a network of aerial spying, which time and time again had proved to be the deciding factor in many skirmishes and mountain battles.

Now Tirtha instinctively looked for that bird—black with the white vee on its breast, its dangling red tresses—which should be riding on its master's wrist. But there was none. Also there was no hand on the arm that would have offered perch to such a bird. Instead there protruded from the fine mail of the sleeve a thing of bright metal. The man kept his mail, his dilapidated helm, and doubtless his sword, well polished and honed. This thing he wore was not a hook; rather it split at the end into five narrow prongs, resembling a bird's tearing talons. Tirtha thought that it was a formidable weapon, nor did she doubt that he knew well how to use it.

But a Falconer—and she could not deny her own sex. This was the tool she had been seeking, but whether he would consent to her service might depend upon how desperate he was. She wished she could see more of his face—but the half-masking helm turned it into a mystery. Well—Tirtha squared her shoulders as she faced him, taking two steps forward to be out of the fury of the swiftly rising storm. She raised her voice to outbattle the wind as she asked:

"You are a blank shield?"

Such were for hire, though she had never heard of a Falconer who proclaimed himself so. They were a clannish lot, and, though they hired out their services, it was always as a troop or a squad—their commander making the bargain for them. Nor did they then mingle with those they served.

For a moment she believed that his inborn contempt for her sex would keep him silent, that she would have no chance at all to suggest hire. However, he did break that almost too long moment of silence.

"I am a blank shield." His voice was emotionless. He had not raised it to outvoice the storm, but it carried well.

"I have need of a guide—a mountain guide—and a fighter. . . ." She came directly to the point, shifting her position a little, not liking it that he could stare at her through the eye holes of his helm and yet deny her a similar view of him. As she moved, her cloak loosened, fell a little open, so that her leathern riding dress, that of a Borderer, though she lacked the mail overshirt, was plainly seen.

"I am for hire. . . ." Again that level voice. It was as if she spoke with a man of metal, one lacking all emotion or purpose. Had what brought him here made him only a husk of the fighting man he had once been? She could not waste her small funds on any such. Still, he kept his armor as well as he could. Her glance returned to that claw hand. It was, to her mind, more dangerous every time she saw it.

She looked out into the storm, then back to where he stood so statue-like by the pillar.

"There are better places to talk of this. I lodge at the inn—the common room is not private—but the stables . . ."

He made his first real movement, a nod of his head. Then he turned and stooped to pick up a bundle lashed into a blanket, which he shouldered, steadying it in place with his claw. Thus they returned to the inn stable where she had left the mare. It was by the latter's stall that Tirtha seated herself on a bale of hay, waving her companion to a similar perch.

With this one it was best to be direct, she believed. There was something about him that reassured her instinct, which she had come to rely upon through the past four years. She dealt with a man who had faced the starkness of ill fortune, but not one who had betrayed himself because of that. This one might break, but there was no bend in him—nor perhaps much breaking either. The more critically she surveyed him, the more she was aware that he was a fighting man still to be reckoned with.

"I need to go through the mountains—into Karsten," she said abruptly. There was no reason why she should explain her mission there. "The old paths and trails are gone—there are also masterless men abroad. I am not ignorant of the use of arms nor of living off the land. But I have no desire to be lost and perhaps make an ending before I do what I desire to do."

Again he answered her with a nod.

"I shall pay two weights of gold for a service of twenty days—half in advance. Do you have a mount?"

"There—" He was certainly sparing of speech. He gestured with his claw to another stall two away from where Valda crunched hay.

Another mountain pony, slightly larger and heavier than the mare, was stabled there. Its mane had been clipped and over the edge of the stall hung a riding pad with the forked horn that should have given rest to a falcon. But there was no bird here either.

"Your falcon?" She dared now to ask that.

There was a feeling of chill; she might have walked into some forbidden place of the Power where there was a walling against her and her kind—so it seemed for an instant. She feared a second later that her question had indeed put an end to any bargain that might have been struck between them—natural though the question was under the circumstances.

"I have no falcon. . . ." His voice came a note lower.

Perhaps that lay at the root of his exile from his kind. She knew better than to pursue the subject any farther.

"The terms suit you?" She made her voice as cold as his to the best of her ability.

"Twenty days . . ." He spoke as if he mused upon something in his own mind. "And at the end of that time?"

"We can see what comes." The girl got to her feet and held out her hand for the bargain grip. At first she believed he was going to lay that cold metal claw across her flesh, his arm twitched a little as if that movement came the more natural to him. Then his other true hand clasped hers.

She had reached under the shadow of her cloak during their walk here and loosed a disc of gold from her money belt. Now, as he speedily broke their clasp, she gave it to him. He held it for a moment, as if weighing it against her offer, then nodded for the third time.

"I have supplies to buy," Tirtha told him briskly. "But, in spite of the storm, I would be out of town this day. Do you hold with that?"

"I have taken shield service. . . ." He began and then stopped as a thought seemed to occur to him. "What badge do I now raise?"

The old custom still held, it would seem, with this Falconer. A blank shield taking service put on the new badge of the House employing him. She smiled a little grimly and slid her sword out of its sheath, holding it into the rays of a stable lantern that some groom had lit against the storm dark and left hanging nearby.

Though the device was faint it could still be seen, the head of a screaming hawk, voicing defiance to both man and world.

"The House of Hawkholme, Falconer. It would seem that we share something in common, though Hawkholme has been rubble for more years than I would waste now to tally."

He bent his head well forward, as if to see the better. Then he looked to her.

"Who speaks for the House?"

Again she smiled, and her smile was even more bleak and bitter. "I speak for the House, Falconer. For I *am* the House, and the Blood, and all the kin there is in this world—and no one yet has learned the trick of summoning ghosts to answer any rally. Thus you ride for Hawkholme and I am Hawkholme."

So saying, she turned and left him, to carry out the rest of her bargaining, the beginning of what she had planned for so many hard-lived years.

2

The storm's fury lasted half a day, forcing them to brace their bodies, huddle into their cloaks, and urge their unwilling mounts onto an upward trail that became only a bare trace a half-league out of Romsgarth. From the first, the Falconer took the lead as a matter of course, moving with a self-confidence, which assured his employer that he did indeed know something about the twisted lands of the heights.

However, that faint trail did not hold him long. Within a short time of turning into it, he paused for Tirtha to draw level with him, speaking the first words to break the silence between them since they had ridden out of town.

"It is your will to go with as little notice as possible?"

He had asked no questions concerning their reason for heading south, nor did she intend to supply any. However, now he appeared to guess part of her purpose.

"You know another way?"

She resented once more, with a growing spark of warmth, that he could look plainly upon her and she could not view him unmasked.

"It will not be easy, but I do not think anyone moving along the path I know will be overlooked. There was a hosting hereabouts two months ago. The Marshal's men swept out a nest of raiders and their lookouts."

"Well enough." Tirtha had no mind to ask him how he had become familiar with a raider path. Falconers did not turn outlaw—or so she had always heard. Also, she had her own way of recognizing danger. The Old Race—yes, a measure of their heritage still held, even for such draggletailed roamers as herself. She did not claim even a shadowing of true Power, but she had that sense which she could also use with animals in the wild, knowing where lay peril and where was only common hardship, such as she had long faced. This man would be true to his oath; he was no turncoat.

Thus they struck farther west, and the way *was* rough, leading up slopes where it was necessary to dismount, urge their snorting ponies to tread delicately over chancy footing, winding around drifts of season-old avalanches, halting at regular periods to rest their mounts and themselves.

By night they emerged upon a ledge half-roofed by an overhang. This certainly was a former camp, for at the back of the shallow cave was a smoke-blackened half-pit in which were charred ends of wood.

By all the signs, there had been none nighting here for some time. In the windblown ash Tirtha could trace the clear marks of paws. The gorex of the heights—and they were timid creatures—had padded freely about since the last fire. There was room enough at the far end of the cave to shelter the ponies. Pulling off the riding pads, they rubbed down the beasts with twists of coarse rags carried for such purposes. There was no herbage here, but both carried bags holding supplies Tirtha had frugally bargained for—grain out of Esland which she had found in Romsgarth market.

She divided portions scrupulously between the two ponies, though she must scant on what she would give them, since they had passed little grazing during the day's trailing—sighting no valley or slope that gave root to fodder plants. Nor had they found water, so that this also must be rationed.

Having seen to their animals, they returned to hunker down on either side of the fire pit. Tirtha, willing enough to be guided by one she was sure knew this land, looked to her silent companion for a lead. Was it wise to risk lighting some of the small stack of wood? He had said that this portion of the country had been cleared by Estcarp forces. Still, during two months, another band could well have descended upon an empty territory, setting up its own holdship.

The wind, which had pushed and punished them in gusts throughout the day, died down, while the clouds lightened, turning gold and crimson to mark a sun that had been sullenly veiled. There was a clean, fresh taste to the air here. Oddly enough her spirits felt a lift— as if, having taken the first day's journey successfully, she sensed that fortune was smiling. Yet she also knew that same fortune was fickle and had seldom favored her.

Tirtha's fellow traveler fitted wood carefully into the fire pit, using his claw with dexterity now and then to snap some longer piece into place. Thus they had fire, a comfort to the eye, as well as for its limited warmth, as the dusk closed in.

They whittled sticks to spear pieces of the dried meat Tirtha had added to their provisions, toasting them between bites of journey bread, sliding the hot morsels directly from the improvised spits into their mouths.

Having finished, her new shieldman slid off his helm for the first time, so she could see the full face of the man she had taken on trust. He was neither young nor old—she could not have set any age on him. Though there was a gaunt youthfulness about his chin and thin-lipped mouth, there were also lines between his eyes and a great weariness in those eyes themselves.

His hair was as dark as her own, clipped tight to his skull like one of those woven caps the Hold Ladies wore abroad. For the rest, she thought he looked much as any man of the Old Race might—save that his eyes were not the dark, storm-gray of her people, but rather held in their depths a spark of gold—as might those of a bird of prey.

She learned this by quick glances, not wishing to reveal open curiosity. He seemed unaware of any regard from her, smoothing his forehead with his one hand as if to rub away an ache caused by the weight of the helm, his hawk's eyes on the fire between them. He might be reading some message in those flames after the fashion of a Wise Woman, learned in far- or foreseeing.

"You have traveled this path before." Tirtha made of that more a statement than a question.

"Once . . ." he returned absently, his attention all for the flames toward which he now stretched his single hand. "I was scout two years ago when there was some thought of return. . . ." His voice trailed away—still he did not look at her. "There was nothing left."

The finality of those last words came harshly, and for the first time, he raised his eyes to meet hers. In them the yellow sparks might be the fire of long controlled rage.

"We were caught by a mountain fall. These ways are still unsettled. That which the Witch Women stirred into life does not yet sleep. I was to the fore and so—" He made a small gesture with his hand, not enlarging on it but leaving it to her imagination.

"You have ridden alone since then?" Tirtha did not know just why she wanted to force him into some personal disclosure. This was no man of easy words; to pressure him at all might lead even to his withdrawal. All she knew of his race and kind argued that they held strictly aloof from those not of their blood.

"Alone." With a single word he made answer and in such a tone as left Tirtha well aware that she must press no farther. However, there were other questions she could ask now, and those he could not deny answering, for they were no part of his own inner life.

"What do you know of Karsten? Men talk, but I have had only rumors to shift and those can be less than half-truths."

He shrugged, setting the helm beside him on the rock, once more smoothing the band of furrowed skin immediately above the well-marked line of his brows.

"It is a land of battles—or rather petty skirmishes, one lordling against another. Since Pagar, their last overlord, fell, there have arisen none who can impose their wills—or the weight of their swords—enough to bring a binding peace. The Sulcar come, under arms, to deal with some merchants. The iron out of the Yost mines, the silver of Yar—those can pay any captain. But trade is near dead, while there are those who die for lack of food because none dare tend fields which may be at any moment trampled by raiders. The riches that were once here are plundered, hid, scattered to the winds. Thus it is, along the western coast and below the mountains. What lies farther east . . ." He shrugged. "There are not even rumors that seep back from that region. When Duke Yvian horned the Old Race, he began the rot and it spread, until now the whole land is half-dead and the rest forsaken."

Tirtha wet her lip with tongue tip. "The Horning then began it—" Again she did not question, for her thoughts were quick and alive. Did the secret, which had brought her here, have such a root?

He shot her a measuring look, and she thought that, for the first time, she had shaken him out of that deep preoccupation with his own concerns which had held him since their first meeting. A fighting tool and an efficient one he had hired himself out to be, but he had shown no curiosity at all concerning what drew her south.

"The Old Race"—he paused, put out his claw to snap another

length of wood and feed it to their fire—"they had their own secrets. Perhaps one of those was keeping a firm peace. It is said that, before Duke Yvian was possessed by the madness of the invading Kolder and turned into one of their mind-dead, men held the Old Race in awe, and their being there—few as they might seem—was a check upon lawlessness. Then the Duke proved that the Old Race could be killed—like any others—when he ordered their Horning, and there were those who had always hated and envied them. They wanted to appease that hatred. Also the Kolder, possessed, rode to push the slayings. But why do I say this—it is your blood that we speak of—is that not so?"

"Yes." She could be as laconic as he. In her mind, Tirtha weighed impulse against prudence, not quite sure as yet which might serve her best. Then she added, "Hawkholme was of Karsten. As you see, I am of the blood Yvian strove to erase from a land where he and his were, to begin with, intruders and invaders."

"You return to no easier a fate than was granted those who were horned. That still holds. Too many seized and killed and profited by that blooding." He did not seem greatly moved, rather he spoke as if merely pointing out that they were two travelers united only for a limited purpose.

"We have learned something." Tirtha bit off each word as one would bite upon a binding cord. "There is no such thing as trust in Karsten for us. Still, I have that which takes me there."

Further than this she would not go. He had hand-grasped for his allotted time in her service. There was no reason to think that any further quest beyond the mountain-crossing would draw him. Nor, she thought, was he one with whom she would willingly share secrets, being who and what he was.

So Tirtha spread out her cloak and rolled in it, pillowing her head on one of her saddle bags before she resolutely closed her eyes, saying:

"We share night watch. Rouse me at the time the red star shines."

He inclined his bare head, accepting, as she had wondered if he would, that they would share, as if they were comrades, the needful duties of any camp. While she settled herself to sleep, summoning that nothingness of mind as she was able to, he made no move to reach for the rolled blanket that was part of his own gear, only sat beside the fire which glinted red on his claw, alternately revealing and hiding his well-cut features, their emotionless mask as complete as that of the helm he had worn during the day.

Though Tirtha had willed herself to sleep, it was not a dreamless one. What followed was that vision, or series of visions, which had haunted her for years, until each detail remained so engraved even on her waking memory that she could have recited all she saw and something of what those sights meant. She knew that there was true dreaming, which was part of the Farsight. She might not be a Wise Woman, but she was a full daughter of the Old Race, and she never believed that all vestiges of the Power had vanished from any of her blood, even though her kin had not held grimly to such knowledge as had their cousins of Estcarp.

There the Power had made the race thin. For the Witches gloried in gifts that they would not surrender for any man. So, fewer and fewer children had been born, until the race came near an end through their pride. However, since the Witch Women had united in the Turning, their last great battle, and most of them had died of it (their bodies unable to hold and project the forces they summoned and still survive), there had come a change.

He who ruled in Estcarp now—Koris of Corm—was only remotely of the kin. There were also the Tregarths who guarded the marches of the north as once they had held these very mountains where she sheltered this night. Simon Tregarth was an Outlander, not of the kin at all. His Lady was a foresworn Witch who, in her day, had been outcast because of her choice of him, and who, by some quirk of strangeness, had NOT lost her Power when she married him. These three ruled Estcarp, and their influence was felt. So there was no longer any recruiting of Witches, save among those of such manifest talent that they withdrew from life by their own desire. There was more mingling, more wedding and bedding. Those from the Border shared blood with Sulcar and with their kin of Estcarp. There were more children in the holds, and also there was some traffic with the mysterious east—that Escore where the children of Simon Tregarth and his Lady had gone to seek the ancient foundations of their line. There was war there still, but it was with old evil. Had Tirtha not been who and what she was perhaps the east would have drawn her also.

Drawn her! She walked again easily down a hall—wide—only half lighted by dim, wall-set bars of light, the secret of whose ever-burning had been lost long since. There were shadows that moved among shadows, had a sometime life of their own. But what they did, when, or why, had no meaning for her.

Though she had never come this way except in a vision, still it was better known to her than many of the places into which her actual wandering had taken her. This was a part of her as no other place, waking or sleeping, could ever be. She had come here in dreams since childhood, and always it remained the same, save that its hold on her grew stronger and deeper, more real than all else in life.

This was the hall of a hold—a place near as long established as the ancient walls of Estcarp itself. There at the high table were the tall chairs of a lord and lady. Those shades she could not see clearly were tenuous, forming a company around her. Tirtha knew that this was a time of formal meeting, that though she could not hear, yet there was deep meaning in what was being discussed.

Most of her attention was for what stood on the table, midway between the two tall-backed chairs. *That* was real and fully visible! A casket gleamed with a light issuing from it, for the cover had been raised and thrown back. The carvings on it did not seem set or sustained as they should have. Rather they possessed a life or purpose of their own, appearing to change shape, to crawl and move, so that she could not ever be sure of them. Some, she realized in the moments when she could catch them at rest, were words and symbols of Power.

Nor had she ever seen what the casket held, for its lid was raised at an angle which prevented direct sight. Only—this was the very heart and substance of all she witnessed here—it was more alive than those who had cherished it.

Now the dream followed its set pattern. That wisp of half shadow which was the left hand of the lord and the one which was the right hand of his lady moved forward as one. Together they clasped the lid of the casket, closing it.

Tirtha felt the old and familiar rise of cold fear in her. Now was the coming of the evil. She could not escape it—ever—because for some reason it was necessary that she see—see and know—see and remember!

That shadow, which was the lord, held its grip on the lid of the casket for a long moment. The glow of life, which the girl had felt dwelling within it, dimmed. It might be that by some warning a flow of the Power had been alerted, was taking certain steps of its own for needed protection. Reluctantly—Tirtha always sensed that reluctance as sorrow or foreboding—the lord pushed his treasure toward the lady.

A pillar of mist she was, with only a round ball for a head, extensions which were not hands or arms, but served her as such, no more than fragments of fog. Yet she took up what her lord passed to her, arising while that flitting company stirred about the far edges of the wide hall as if hurried, pushed into action—and the lord stepped from his place to join them, moving out of the range of Tirtha's vision.

She never followed him. No, it was the casket that was of importance and that drew her now as the mist woman raised it, pressed it to her unsubstantial form, close to where a human heart might beat. Then she, too, turned and went.

It would seem that Tirtha then also became a specter, a thing without body or form, for she followed that other as if she floated— shadow herself—in this half-and-half world. Down the hall they went to the space behind the high table. And the pace of the lady wraith was swift—she might have been running, time itself her enemy now.

Thus they came to a paneled wall against which the shadow flattened herself oddly—as though releasing a secret lock. A narrow opening was revealed, and she squeezed into a dark place—the power of the thing unseen drawing Tirtha with it.

This was a place where Tirtha felt, even though she possessed no body in her dream, the touch of Power—Power which had built up and lingered—drawn and fed by talent used for years, perhaps centuries, to guard the casket.

There was a stone table in that small windowless chamber; the walls were tapestried by misty hangings. The aura of this hidden chamber was enough to make known to any who came what it was, a place into which only the talent trained might come. Still—even though that be so—Tirtha in the dream was not walled out, forceless and empty-handed though she was.

The shadow lady, still holding the casket against her breast, freed one misty hand and raised it high, making a gesture that seemed to bring the edge of her palm and fingers to strike against the center of the stone table.

That massive block appeared to quiver on the very spot which she had struck. Now the lady looked as if she must free herself of any touch speedily, moving up her hand—or that wisp of mist which served her for such—into the air above. Tirtha, though she had never witnessed otherwhere any such ritual, knew well that this was mastery of an ancient kind in which mind controlled matter and made it obey.

The casket, set in place on the table, quivered as had the rock—

rooting itself there, the envisioned girl believed. Still the shadow woman stood and wove her ensorcelments—she might have been locking and bolting unseen doors, making very sure that this place might not be breached.

And—

Tirtha stirred, the silence of her vision-dream broke—she was being touched, and she was again in the flesh, able to feel, even as she was able to hear a whisper very close to her ear where her cloak hood had fallen or been pulled away. There was a faint puff of breath against her cheek. She opened her eyes upon darkness, but she did not move, for a hand kept her pinned where she lay.

"Quiet!" The whisper came again.

She had been shaken so suddenly out of that other place that she was not yet truly aware she had returned to the camp on the ledge. There was no longer any sign of the fire. She roused enough to realize who knelt by her, holding her in place, perhaps even ready to slip his hand across her mouth to muffle any sound she might make, being so summarily aroused.

Tirtha was too well trained a rover to do that. She remained where she was, her ears straining now to pick up sound. He must have known she had been awakened, for his hand left her body speedily, and she had a flash of thought that to touch a woman, even for such a reason, would be difficult for a Falconer. But he did not move away.

One of their ponies stamped and blew. Then the man was gone in a flash of movement. Tirtha realized that he must be on his way to make sure that no sound from their two mounts might betray them. Still she listened.

At last a sound came from a distance, though she could not judge how far away. There was a scrabbling as if something strove to find a path across none too secure gravel or loose earth. She remembered that not far distant there was one of those mounds of debris left from a slide, such being still only too common in this shaken hill country.

Tirtha sat up, throwing off the enfolding material of the cape. She had her well-worn sword, her bow lay beside her, but night did not favor an archer. Slowly, with caution, she reached out, feeling for a pile of stones she had noted near their fire hole. They were still warm from the heat of the vanished flames as her fingers curled about the top one, which fitted well into her hand. It was heavy, and she had used just such a rough weapon before to good purpose.

The Falconer wore a dart gun at his belt. However, unless he was one of those legendary fighters trained to fire correctly at a sound, that weapon would serve him little better than her bow could aid her. He had a sword also, and she had little doubt that it was now in his hand. There was his claw also, and that—Tirtha could not suppress a small shiver, stupid though she knew any shadow of distaste might be—that was as able a weapon at close quarters as anyone could wish.

The scrabbling had stopped. Yet Tirtha was certain that whatever sniffed about had not gone. No, it had another way of locating its prey.

She did not gasp, she was struck too hard by the new attack to do more than reel back against the rock. The thing hunted with its mind! She had met that blow, which was meant to locate them, with the instant instinctive mind lock that was part of her heritage. But was the Falconer able to counter such a seeking? She knew very little of how his race thought or what defense he could raise against such a questing.

Unfortunately, a mind lock of this kind worked two ways. She dared not relinquish her tight mental cover to seek out the nature of the thing waiting in the dark. That it used mind-send at all meant that they had not been tracked by any outlaw raider, for it was only the Old Race who could seek thus. She herself could handle beasts so, but she had never attempted to trail one of her own kind. That was an abomination which was of the old evil, against which all her blood had stood since they had come into Karsten or into Estcarp.

Now there arose something else, wafted by a rising breeze—a thick animal odor. Not an honest one, such as any beast she had ever known would give forth. This was foul, as if dregs of filth had been stirred or some utter rottenness had breathed a great sigh.

No snow cat, none of the rare verbears rumored to have come into these mountains since the Turning, would so befoul the night air. This was something different. She sent a fraction of her thought to the ponies—surely all their instinct and fears would be speedily roused by that stench. But her would-be soothing thought met a barrier, and she was no longer left to wonder what the Falconer might do. Perhaps the long years in which his kind had schooled and lived with their birds had sharpened a native talent. He was holding a mind wall about their mounts, and to that Tirtha speedily lent her own strength of will.

3

Since that thing below trailed by thought-touch, then the barriers they both had raised must have alerted it to the fact it was discovered. Tirtha arose noiselessly. The thick soles of her boots were soft enough not to crunch as she inched to the lip of the ledge, listening, striving also to see, though the moon was under cloud and starshine could not aid her. She had only nose and ears to serve her.

A second rattle of loose stones sounded. She judged that the stalker had been able to avoid a misstep. The sound was certainly closer—just as that rank stench was stronger.

Then—

There was a dull yellowish glow—two such on a line. Eyes! And a kind that did not need any reflected light to betray them, possessing within themselves that which was perceptible in the dark.

Perhaps the lurker had better than human sight, an ability to pierce the night for its prey. Still, the eye-gleam betrayed it in turn as it climbed. She could now hear a steady scrabbling, as if claws searched out irregularities in the wall up which it must come to reach them.

Tirtha laid aside her stone, reaching for the pouch on her hip. She had had a chance to renew its contents back in Romsgarth, and she knew well how to use one certain packet among the rest. This might not work against the unknown, but that was not certain until tried. She located it by touch, an envelope of the same supple serpentskin as her belt. Through that skin she felt the grating of grains inside, and with care she shook some into the palm of her other hand.

Those eyes never blinked nor broke a steady stare—they only drew closer. She watched carefully for a second pair—or a sound revealing that the climber was not alone. She was well aware that what strove to reach them was wholly of the Dark—a thing such as the Songsmiths averred dwelt in the halls of Ever-Night. There came the faintest of sounds on her own level. The Falconer had left the two ponies, was coming to stand ready at her side. Tirtha longed to ask if he knew what manner of creature threatened them, but she hesitated to speak while she held the thought barrier.

Her cupped hand ready, she reached through the dark with her other hand until her fingers touched a mail-sleeved arm. She squeezed, hoping that he was astute enough to recognize it as a signal. Then, leaning farther forward, watching those evil, pale discs now raised to hers, sensing that her mind barrier was under assault, Tirtha turned over her palm, releasing the coarse dust it held. There was no breeze to hinder what she would do. Thus she could hope that fortune would move to favor them.

A moment of waiting was followed by a squall such as could not break from the throat of any known animal. The evil eyes blinked and blinked again as the thing hurled itself up at their perch.

The Falconer had jerked out of her hold. Her own worn sword was drawn. Something as large as a pony hooked appendages over the edge of the ledge while it screamed and spattered a foul moisture, which burned her skin as might fire sparks.

Tirtha stabbed outward, felt her blade strike a hide so tough that ancient steel could not penetrate. Beside her sounded the snick of a dart gun. One of the blinking eyes vanished. There was another scream, a last heave of the misshapen body. Then their attacker lost its hold, to fall outward, its cries tearing the night. They heard a heavy sound, which must have marked the striking of a body against some projection on the down slope. A rattling of stones followed, as if the falling creature had started another landslide.

Though the noisome smell remained, plainly the thing was gone, and there were no more cries nor any sound of struggle as a last shift of sliding stones died away. One of the ponies cried out now—in the throes of a great terror. Tirtha was quick to add her talent to that of the Falconer, suggesting to the beasts that all danger was past—and she judged it was, that nothing was left to fear.

As their mounts quieted, Tirtha dared to go and run her hands along the ponies' rough coats, dank with sweat, using touch systematically to convey peace, soothing the distraught animals. Once her hands slipped across her companion's only hand, and she realized that he was aware of this need also.

With their mounts reassured, Tirtha returned to the edge of the ledge. It would appear that the Falconer did not expect another attacker, at least not yet. Still he knew that this was a time for strict watch. The creature they had defeated might be only a scout for more of its kind. She glanced up at the sky, guessed that dawn was

not far off. There could be no move until they had more light. Once
more her companion joined her, and for the first time, she dared a
question: "What was that?"

Tirtha was half surprised at his answer.

"I do not know. There are rumors that things have drifted from
the east, that, with the death of Pagar's invaders here, such a great
slaughter drew what had not been seen hereabouts before."

"The east," Tirtha repeated. "Out of Escore—the barrier being
broke . . ."

She felt cold, but it was not the night air and the absence of her
cloak that chilled her. It was the fragmented tales she had heard of
that eastern land so long barred—by choice—to her blood, where
death walked in the guise of monsters with unknown powers. Many
of her kin had since returned there, engaging in a war being fought
against the Shadow, it was said. Could that war—or at least some of
its evil—be slipping westward? The barrier had been broken in Estcarp with the passing of men into Escore. Might it have been cracked
here as well when the Witches of Estcarp had summoned all their
Power to rive this country? Perhaps in that act they had also destroyed defenses they had not known existed.

Against men, against animals, Tirtha was willing to take her
chances. That was the price of living in these darkened days. Only
what could she do if faced with a Dark talent when she had none to
raise in turn?

"It was not an animal," she mused aloud, "and certainly not a
man—not even Kolder-ridden—if such still exist. Yet it had Power
of a sort."

"Yes." His answer was crisp. "The Power—always it is the
Power!" There was anger in his voice as if he would deny the talent
and yet could not.

They sat side by side, Tirtha drawing her cloak about her, waiting
for the light. This had been a harsh warning against her journey, but
one she could not heed. Nor had the Falconer said aught about
turning back. Once having been given, his sword oath would hold
him to the end of what she demanded from him.

The sky grayed, a few stars, showing through ragged rifts in the
clouds, faded. She could see the ledge, the ponies, their gear piled by
the sunken fire pit. However, Tirtha was more interested in what lay
below. At first true light she must see what had crept upon them in
the dark, learn the nature of this enemy.

It would appear her companion shared that need for he swung

over the lip of the ledge, with her close beside him, down the scar of the attacker's slide. Protruding from the debris was something Tirtha first thought to be a broken branch of a winter-killed tree, then saw it for what it truly was—a hairy limb rising out of the mass of stone and gravel.

Working together they shifted the rocks until they laid bare most of the night hunter's body. Tirtha drew back with an exclamation of disgust. They had uncovered only the head, the upper limbs, and a wide portion of a distended paunch. In color those were near the same gray-white of the stones about them. The skin was matted over by a coarse growth of thick-fibered hair or fur.

From one of the large eyes protruded the end of a dart. The other had wept tears of mucous, oozing down to a mouth that formed the lower part of the face, if it could be termed a "face." In that much her own action had succeeded in their night battle.

Though they did not bare the entire body, Tirtha believed the creature would stand equal in height to her, and she surmised that it had gone erect, two-footed, for the upper appendages ended, not in paws, but in handlike extensions possessing talons as thin and cruel as the Falconer's claw.

Tirtha had never seen or heard of its like before. But if such as this had spilled into the southern mountains, she wondered that even the hardiest or most desperate of outlaws would choose to shelter here.

The muzzle gaped open, but even closed, the fringe of teeth within must have interlocked outside, and those fangs were as long as her middle finger, sharp-pointed, able to tear any body those talon hands could drag down. Her companion knelt, hooking his claw about the butt of the dart he had aimed so well, to pluck it forth, following the sensible action of not wasting any of his small store of weapons. He flipped it away from him to lie in sand, and not touching it with his hand, rubbed it back and forth there to cleanse it.

But he did that mechanically, looking to her the while.

"You also fought," he said abruptly. "How?"

Her hand sought the bag at her belt. "There are herbs of the fields which, when powdered and mixed by those who understand their essence, can blind a creature. I tried such—I think it"—she nodded to the body—"was a night hunter. Blind them and they are as easily brought down as a snagged hare."

"To do that," he commented, "you must be close, closer than a warrior would choose."

She shrugged. "True enough. Yet one learns the use of many weapons within a lifetime. I have trudged the fields—and worked them also—there is much to be learned there. My sword"—she half drew that blade from its sheath to show him the too-often-honed length—"is not such as I would willingly use in battle, though it is mine as Holdruler. I have my bow and arrows." She would not boast, considering her skill. "And I had no credit or favor to purchase a dart gun. Thus I must study other ways."

He said nothing. Since he had resumed his helm, she could not read his expression unless there had been a small tightening of his lips. However, she thought she could guess his reaction, and she resolved not to allow that to anger her. To each his own—let him fight with steel and dart since that was what he was bred to do.

However, she well knew what had schooled and tempered *her* during the past years. She had her own code of honor and dishonor, and as Holdruler (though that was only a name and one she had never claimed) she held to it. Tirtha begged no bread, sought out no fancied kin for roof and shelter. Her two hands earned her that, and if she employed weapons that seemed to him beyond a warrior's code (for perhaps he looked upon her blinding dust as a kind of poison) then she would answer herself for such.

A gift from the earth was free to all. If a discovery was not used in a mean or dark way, then it was as true a defense as any steel forged five times over. If he wished to quarrel with her over that, let him say so now and they would break bargain.

Apparently he was not moved to do so. For, having run his befouled dart into the sandy ground several times over, he brought out a rag and wrapped it about, setting it into a loop of his shoulder belt. A scuttling noise aroused them both.

Tirtha saw a small brownish creature—it might have been scaled, certainly it moved on several pairs of legs. She guessed it to be a scavenger eager for such bounty as was seldom found in this barren land. They left the night hunter behind with no more words between them, climbing up to the ledge again, where they gave their ponies another limited measure of feed, watered them sparingly, ate their own cold rations, and moved on. Her companion was again to the fore, leading his mount, tracing a path where it took all her sharpness of eye to mark any trail at all.

They reached a ridge top by sun-up, and here there was indeed a narrow way, scored by old hoof prints, as well as the slot tracks of what must be the smaller species of pronghorn which had withdrawn centuries ago to the heights. Those were wary game, but Tirtha kept her bow to hand, hoping to bring one down to replenish their stores.

The trail dropped from the heights before midmorning, ushering them into a cupped valley where greenery grew about a stream trickling from a spring. Snorting, the ponies made for the water, and Tirtha was content to linger there a space to give the beasts forage and thus conserve their supplies.

There were signs here, too, that they were not the first to find this campsite. A lean-to of piled rocks, roofed by poles overlaid with thick branches (their lengths and dried leaves weighted down with stones), stood there. Before its door, a fire pit had been dug. Tirtha hunted for wood, sweeping up any dried branches she could find. She was exploring what appeared to be the wreck of a mighty storm, for dead trees lay in a crisscross maze, when she chanced upon more recent evidence that they might not be alone.

Here a patch of soft earth held the impression of a boot—recent enough that the rain two days earlier had not washed it away. She squatted down to brush aside dried leaves, examining it carefully.

She herself wore the soft-soled, calf-high, travel gear known in the border land—supple, with many layers of sole, the bottom one of which was made of sac-lizard hide, which wore as well as or even better than any thicker covering known in northern lands. They could grip and anchor on shifting ground, and in her pack she carried extra strips of the sole-hide for repairs.

This was plainly a northern boot and one, she thought, in excellent repair, which certainly meant that its wearer had not tramped for long among the rough mountain trails. She was still studying it when the Falconer joined her.

He stretched out his hand above the impression, being careful not to touch the earth.

"Man—perhaps a soldier—or a raider who has had some luck with loot. Perhaps yesterday morning . . ."

Tirtha looked back at the shelter, thought of her plans for resting the ponies. With such plain proof that they were not alone here, would it be wise to linger? She was beginning to weigh that when he spoke again. "He rode with trouble."

She saw that his nostrils were expanded showing wider below the half-mask of his helm. Now he gestured to where a mass of half-buried bush leaned crookedly. She saw the flash of wings. Here again were scavengers—bloated flies that sought filth even in the lowlands. They clustered and fought over gouts of blackened blood that bespattered the withered leaves of the bush and formed an irregular splotch on the ground.

On his feet, dart gun in hand, the Falconer moved forward with that soundless border tread. Tirtha was in two minds over following him. Manifestly, someone wounded had come this way—an outlaw forced to lie up because of some weakening hurt might well shoot from ambush any who searched him out. Thus she wondered at her companion's instant attempt to trail. Or could he believe that this stranger might be one of his own kind, lost and needing aid?

Standing in the shadow of a larger mass of brush, Tirtha deliberately opened her mind. She had done this before on the road, seeking to make sure that she was not walking into danger, and it seemed to her that each time she used her small talent so, it grew stronger.

Only now she met with nothing.

She returned to where they had left the ponies hobbled and grazing. Swiftly she brought in the reluctant animals, resaddled them, and looped their reins well within hand reach. When that was done she studied the valley in which they had found this campsite. The water was hardly more than a small brook, spouting out of the ground between two rocks and then pouring along ice cold—perhaps snow-born—to run into a screen of green brush. The spring season touched here early.

There was a colored scattering of small flowers under the shelter of outstanding bushes, and she saw bees at work among them. This valley was a cup of renewed life amid the desolation of rock walls. She put aside her cloak to give freedom to her arms, strung her bow, and held her head high as might a pronghorn buck on herd sentry, listening.

The rippling of the water, the hum of bees, the crunching of the ponies who now pulled leaves from the bushes to satisfy their hunger —that was all her ears picked up. If the Falconer made any sound along the path he had taken, it was too slight to reach her ears. Nor did her other senses find anything to alert or warn.

Her companion appeared again abruptly. He still had his dart gun in hand, and what she could see of his weather-browned face was set and cold. She was beginning to know him perhaps as well as she ever could one of his race, and there radiated from him a chill anger such as she had not felt before.

"You have found . . . ?" She determined that he was not to consider her the less as was the manner of his kind toward women. What they shared here in this debatable country must be equally faced.

"Come—if you will then!" She believed there was still a tinge of contempt and suspicion in his voice, as if he thought that she was of no consequence, save that he needs must serve her whims for a space. Bow in hand, arrow to string, follow she did.

There were other patches of blood, about which the carrion flies crawled. Then they reached the other side of the brush wall. Before them spread a wider strip of meadowlike open land. At the far side of that was a horse, bridled and saddled, with such trappings as she had seen lowlanders use. This was no mountain pony, but instead a Torgian—one of those beprized mounts that might cost a holdkeeper near a year's crop in price. They were not large or imposing as to looks, but their staunchness, their speed and endurance, made them the choice of any who could raise such payment.

It stood above a body lying in the trampled grass, and when they came into view the horse drew back its lips, baring wicked teeth as it moved from side to side as if planning to charge. Some of its breed, Tirtha had heard, were battle-trained, specially shod on forefeet to cut down a dismounted enemy.

She strove to beam toward it such soothing as she would have used with the less intelligent ponies she knew and believed that the Falconer also was trying to so reach the uneasy and angry beast. For there was anger in it, more than fear—the radiation of that emotion was easily detected.

It lowered its head twice to nose at the body in the grass. Then, with a lightning swift swerve about that limp bundle, it made to charge. That she had not reached it mentally surprised and alarmed Tirtha. The mount might have been truly enraged past sanity. She did not want to shoot the horse—and she was sure that her companion had no idea of loosing a dart to bring it down.

Into her attempt to touch the beast's mind Tirtha poured all her strength. The Torgian swerved again, not stampeding directly at them, rather turning to run back and forth across their path, keeping them from the fallen rider. They stood where they were, concentrating, striving to project that they meant no harm, either to it or the one it defended.

Its run became a pacing, then it stood, snorting, a ragged lock of its mane falling forward to half cover white-rimmed eyes, while with one forefoot it pawed up chunks of turf that flew into the air.

Though neither spoke to the other, it would seem that Tirtha and the Falconer could communicate after all, for at the same moment they walked toward the aroused horse, shoulder to shoulder. The

Falconer's arm had dropped, his dart gun pointed barrel to the ground. She did not put aside her bow, but neither did she tighten the cord.

The Torgian snorted again, beginning to back away. Its anger was becoming uncertainty. They had passed the crucial moment when it might charge them blindly.

Step by step, always striving to keep to the fore of their minds their good will, the two advanced while the horse retreated. It moved to one side at last, letting them reach the man who lay face down in blood-soaked grass. He wore the riding leather of a lowlander and over it a mail shirt, which had been mended by slightly larger rings, but was still plainly better than most one could find in any market these days. His head was bare, for his helm had rolled to one side. Still they could not see his face, only the tangle of his black hair, for he had fallen belly down.

There was a crust of blood along one leg, and more had flowed from his neck across the shoulder. The Falconer knelt and turned him over, and the body obeyed in one stiff movement as if frozen.

The face was that of youth—as the Old Race knew it—and it was pain-twisted from what must have been the agony of death. Only it was what was fastened heart-high on the breast of that mail shirt which caught Tirtha—stopped her and brought a gasp from her lips. The dead man did not surprise her. She had viewed death often and in more than one ugly guise—many worse than this.

But none of those bodies had worn a metal badge fashioned like a device from a coat of high ceremony. She was looking down at the open-beaked hawk which was her own single hold on the past. Hawkholme—*she* was Hawkholme! Who was this stranger who dared sport a badge that was all she had to claim in the way of heritage?

She leaned forward to study it, hoping to note some small difference. But the Hold badges were the proud and cherished possessions of each clan, and to copy or wear one that was not blood-sealed was so unheard of as to be an impossibility past all reckoning.

"Your kin?" The Falconer's tone was cold, measuring.

Tirtha shook her head. There was no denying that badge. Could it be that some refugee out of Karsten had brought it, then had it stolen, looted, had even given it away? A Hold badge with the hawk's head never would be given away! That was not to be even thought of!

"I have no kin," she returned, and she hoped that her voice was as cool and level as that of her companion. "I do not know this man, nor why he should wear what he has no right to. That is no kinsman's mark—it is a holdmaster's." She was sure of that. "And though there is no hold now in Karsten, yet I alone am of the Blood!"

She lifted her eyes from that unexplainable symbol and stared straight into the yellow-sparked ones of the Falconer. Perhaps he and his fellows believed all women liars and worse. She might not be able to prove the truth of what she said. Let him go then. But *she* was Hawkholme, and she *could* prove it when the time came.

4

They had searched the dead man. There was nothing about him that could not have been worn or carried by any blank shield riding out of Estcarp on some private errand. His wounds, the Falconer declared, were not from steel or edged weapons but were caused by tooth and talon. To Tirtha's surprise, the dead man had no weapons. There was a sword belt, to be sure, but the scabbard it supported was empty, as were all dart clip loops. He certainly had not ventured into this high, dangerous land bare-handed. Had he been stripped after death? If so, how had the looter passed the Torgian? And what enemy had traveled with a fanged and clawed hunter?

The mount snorted and pawed the turf at intervals, even though it kept its distance. Attached to its light saddle hung a pair of travel bags. It was to those Tirtha turned her attention next. If the Torgian would allow her to free them, they might just learn more of the dead.

He had lain there for some time, the Falconer averred, judging from the post-death stiffness of the corpse. Oddly enough, except for the clouds of flies, he had not been preyed upon by any scavengers, such as gathered elsewhere, no doubt because of the Torgian.

Since they had no tools, the Falconer used his sword to hack at the turf, loosening clods which Tirtha broke away and piled to one side. The grave they so dug was a shallow one, but they did the best they could. When they laid him in it, the girl brought forth a square scarf, such as she used in bad weather to cover her head under the folding of her hood, to lay over his face. She helped repile the clods of turf, then brought stones from the brook edge to add cover. When they had done, she arose from her knees, regarding broodingly the mound they had raised.

Tongue tip swept across her lower lip as she found words. They were not those formal ones she had heard said many times when she was not yet woman grown, but they were the best she could summon at this hour:

"May your sleep be sweet, stranger, may your path beyond be smooth, may you come to your desiring and it give you peace." She stooped, picked up one white stone that was nearly round, fashioned so, she thought, by water's rolling, and which she had laid aside for this purpose. As if she were indeed kin-blood and close kin, she placed this above the hidden head of the dead man. It bore no symbol of the old Power, nor could she breathe into it any spell of releasing. But through the last hard years, Tirtha had come to believe that such formalities were intended to lighten a little the grief of kin left behind rather than touch one who had already taken the Long Road and who, perhaps, had already forgotten this world, impatient for what lay beyond.

She knew nothing of what the Falconers believed concerning this life or what lay beyond it, but now she saw her companion take his sword, holding it by the blade, its hilt high. Then he turned the length of steel so that the hilt, as he moved his arm, traveled down the length of the grave while he chanted, in a voice hardly above a harsh whisper, words that held no meaning for her.

Afterward they looked to the horse. It would seem that the sealing of its master into the earth had, in an odd way, broken the anger that had made it so wary and wild. It had wandered away, and was now cropping grass awkwardly, the bit in its mouth manifestly bothering it. Slowly, with care, Tirtha approached, stopping short when it lifted its head to stare at her.

There was no longer any emanation of fear or hatred. She went ahead coolly, lifted the two saddle bags from their place while the Falconer busied himself with the horse itself, stripping off saddle and bridle, rubbing down the rough coat on which there were matted splotches of dried blood.

Within the bags were a packet of trail bread, another of dried meat, both very meager, a twist of coarse woven stuff which contained a mass of dried huk-berries squeezed into an uneven ball. Below those was a flask, battered, with its intricate plating scratched and dented. Tirtha forced the stopper out and sniffed the odor of the fiery corn spirit which could not only inwardly warm a man in the cold, but was equally useful for treating wounds so that they did not mortify.

Turning the flask around, she studied the style of ornamentation. It was Old Race work plain enough, and indeed out of Karsten, from the aged look of it. However, there was no particular part of its patterning which made it unique—no crest on this anyway.

The other bag yielded a shirt, which had been poorly washed and then rough dried, creased into as small a roll as possible. There was a honing stone and a small amount of oil for the tending of any edged weapons, though the dead man had not managed to keep his. But, last of all, there was a tight-capped cylinder about the length of her palm—also old metal—with only faint traces of some engraving to be detected along its sides. Such she had seen once or twice. They were fashioned to protect parchments, which were precious things—records to which hold-lords and songsmiths clung.

Each had a trick to the opening of the cap. It could not be forced lest it and perhaps its contents be destroyed. She turned it around now, its smooth surface slipping in her grasp as if oiled. This might be the answer to their mystery—to her mystery. But as yet she was in no hurry to pursue it. Tirtha sat back on her heels as the Falconer loomed over her, looking down at the result of her rummaging. She knew that his attention centered on the thing she held, so she made no attempt to belittle her discovery. "It is a record holder—very old."

He could see that much for himself. Though she did not in the least want to let the thing out of her hands, Tirtha held it out to him as if her own curiosity was only nominal. Since the sighting of that badge-crest she well knew that he must believe she kept more than one secret, and she had no wish to add to his suspicions.

"Open it!"

That was an order and she stiffened. She was right, his suspicions *were* aroused. Had he some idea that she had come into these mountains perhaps to meet with the dead man? But she owed him no explanations. When he took sword oath for a stated time, he must serve her in everything save that which would dim his own honor as a warrior. What stood between them now was the aversion of his race toward any female, their refusal to accept that a woman had truth in her. She had heard enough of the Falconers in Estcarp to be aware of their belief and what it had cost them.

"If you know anything of these"—she gestured to the rod he now held—"you also know that they are sealed secretly and that only those who carry such and perhaps their close kin—or a sword brother, a shield mate—know the trick of the fastening. This man was no kin to me—I cannot loose his secrets."

It might become necessary to try, at some point, Tirtha thought, even if it meant destroying the container. Though again that could well threaten any contents. She wanted very much to know who the stranger was, why he rode these mountains. Had he also been headed for Karsten? Would it advance her case with this other, whose distrust now appeared so tangible that she could feel it, if she were to tell more of her story? She shrank from such a self-betrayal. Her quest was hers alone, a precious thing to be doubly guarded because, if she told the story properly, he might well consider it either part of an hallucination spun for some dark purpose or think it the dreaming of a stupid woman, such as he was already certain she must be.

He was inspecting the faint line of cleavage at the top of the rod closely. Certainly there was no lock or fastening there. Now his eyes sought hers again through the helm slits.

"You call yourself Hawkholme—perhaps so did that one." He used the rod itself as a pointer to indicate the mound they had built. "Yet you say he was a stranger. I know the Old Race well. They are closely kin-tied as a part of their heritage."

Tirtha shook her head slowly. "Yes, we are kin-tied—just as securely as you are tied to your sword-brothers. Still I found you alone in Romsgarth and you answered to Blank Shield—is that not the truth? Where then are those you shared comradeship with?"

Those yellow sparks in his eyes blazed. She saw his lips move as if he wished to lash out at her with words of hot abuse. What *had* brought him without his bird—in such a sorry state—into Romsgarth? She had never heard that it was in any Falconer born to leave his company, to drift alone. It was as if they held a wall against the whole world and could not see past that barrier into any other way of life.

Tirtha had no wish to force an answer from him. What lay behind him was his own concern. But he must grant to her the same dignity of no questions. However, she could yield a little, without laying bare all that had driven her through the years.

"We were horned in Karsten, hunted without warning, as the farmers sometimes hunt hares in the spring—beating the fields to bring them into a circle where they can be clubbed and killed. So was the Old Race hunted. Though we"—she raised her head proudly, meeting him stare for stare—"fought and did not cower and scream beneath the clubs. It was death and blood from the hunting packs for us or any who dared to give warning.

"Some of us got into Estcarp. The Borderers were Karsten warriors. You must know that—your own people rode with them. But there was a breakage of kin lines. Some holds were overrun, none of their folk escaping. From others a handful might flee safely. I . . ." Her hand sought that well-worn sword, brought it out of its scabbard into the light. "I am of the Blood of two who fled so. Hawkholme went down, but the younger brother of the Lord and his newly wedded wife were not within its walls. They had gone to a guesting with her kin and so were closer to the border—to freedom. There was a farseeing—for in my mother there was some of the talent—and she saw death. I am the last of Hawkholme." She slammed the sword back into its scabbard. "Who this stranger was—that I cannot tell you. For farseeing does not lie and it was plain—Hawkholme went into the fire and with it all those of the Blood."

"Farseeing . . ." he repeated and paused.

She nodded. "Witches' trick—would you call it that, Falconer? To each race its own secrets. You have talents, even if they are not of a Wise Woman's summoning. How else could you have trained your birds, kept so well the watch in these mountains before they were moved? I do not disdain what you have of your own; see that you do not try to lessen what my people possess either. I have not the real talent, but I have seen it work, and well, many times over! Now," she reached forward, and before he could prevent it, she had plucked the record rod out of his fingers. "What do you say that we move on? You have said that the dead died of . . ."

Something glinted behind his shoulder. She caught sight of it and stiffened. He must have read her expression, for he slewed about, sword ready. Only what he saw was not moving, certainly had not yet presented any threat. It was visible on the valley wall above this strip of meadow, and no living thing could perch on that perpendicular height.

The angle of the sunlight now brought a definite pattern into sharp visibility. Without conscious volition Tirtha moved forward, brushing past the Falconer, her full attention claimed, as if she were indeed ensorceled by those shiny lines which spiraled, outward, becoming more and more distinct.

As Tirtha pushed through a last screen of brush, unheeding when it caught at her garments, laid scratches across her hands, she saw that the whole face of the cliff must have been shorn away during the troubling of the mountains. But if that were so, then what was so plainly visible now must have been hidden deep before. For what purpose?

What she read was a sign she had seen only once before, when she had wintered in Lormt, that greatly revered and nearly deserted repository of truly forgotten knowledge. She had made herself useful in a barnlike barracks once dedicated to the use of scholars and legend-keepers, now inhabited by a handful of the very old, some still delving into rolls and records, others content to doze away the latter days of their lives—a haven for those withdrawing from the cold winds of the world as it was.

That symbol had been on a scroll unrolled on a table where one of the most forgetful of those Tirtha had come to look upon as her charges had left it. She had researched during scraps of free time, striving to learn anything that could be of service in the future task which she had set herself. So she had asked concerning that symbol, to be told that it was indeed very old, once a defense against any encroachment of evil where it had been pictured or inlaid or engraved after proper ritual. Now it shone out here, apparently set into the stone.

But why? Tirtha swung around to view the pocket of valley. What lay here, to be protected in days beyond modern reckoning? Or had it been intended for this valley at all? The churning of the mountains must have brought it into sight. What had it once guarded in hiding?

"What is it?" The Falconer came to stand shoulder to shoulder with her. He had not returned his blade to its sheath. Now, with his claw, he pulled off his helm as if he could so see those marks the clearer.

"That is a strong defense against the Dark—one used in very ancient times to hold safe a portion of the land as no wall or steel could—more witchery, warrior," she added, a fraction of mockery in her tone. "I wonder . . ."

That thing they had slain in the night—it was certainly not of Estcarp, nor Karsten either. There was that war which still raged to the eastward between the Shadow and the Light. Had such a conflict once touched *this* land? Mystery upon mystery. Yet below that mark on the wall, unless all she had ever learned was false, there lay safety.

Had the dead man fought to reach this valley because of it? Not wounded by dart or steel, but by claws and fangs. Had he suffered those wounds some distance away and headed for this small island of safety—reached it too badly injured to live?

"This is wild land." Now the Falconer sheathed his weapon, his helm swung in his claw. "Who would put such a safeguard here?"

"This is an old land, very old," she returned. "It hides years upon years of secrets. Perhaps the mountains, when they leaped at the Call of the Council, merely moved into a pattern once known before. At any rate, this is a protected place." She brought up her hand, stretching the fingers to form a sign of recognition. "Here we can be safe. He might have been," she glanced over her shoulder at the mound, "had he reached it unwounded. We cannot tell what may be abroad now. Would you still move on, or shall we give our beasts a chance of rest and good forage?"

He still studied the sign on the cliff side. "You speak of years—and I think those may have piled up beyond counting. Does any ensorcelment last so long?"

"By the legends it may. Let us see . . ." She pushed on until she could touch the stone of the cliff wall. The symbol was well above her head. Looking about, Tirtha caught up a branch half embedded in the earth, jerked it free. From her pouch she took the record rod they had found. There could be yet another reason why the dead man had fought so valiantly to reach this place, if he knew of the symbol and had not come here by mere chance or the wandering of the Torgian bearing a near-conscious rider.

In her belt pouch was a looping of leather for the mending of her boots, and she selected one strand to bind the record rod to the branch end.

"These holders," she explained as she worked, the Falconer watching her closely but plainly without understanding what she would do, "are made charged with certain powers. They cannot be fashioned in these days for their secret had been lost. But I was at Lormt two winters since, and one can learn *how* things may work, if not why—that being forgotten. The symbol there is wrought of charged metal—worked by smiths who had talent, who knew their witchery, as you would say. It is a very old knowledge that like answers to like. If the power still lies in these two workings, the cliff and the rod, different as they may seem, then we shall have proof of it. Now!"

Having tested her lashing, Tirtha stood on tiptoe, one hand braced against the cliff side, the other raising the branch as far as she could, so that the record rod did, indeed, reach the bottom-most looping of that inlay. She nearly cried out.

Feeding downward, even through the dead wood she held, came a surge of power, while both symbol and rod gave forth a thin bluish light. She jerked the stick away, afraid that perhaps such an awakening might consume the rod itself. But she had been right! Blue was the color of protective Power always. There were many accounts at Lormt concerning places of refuge which could be so identified, though those must lie in Escore since Estcarp boasted none that she knew of. And if the rod had also blazed blue, then what it contained held Power, was not just some simple message!

Her hand stung as a queer prickling ran along her fingers. Quickly taking the branch into her left fist, Tirtha flexed and bent those fingers. An exclamation from her companion brought her attention away from her own reaction, from knowing that she meddled with what she did not understand and had probably been too reckless in trying.

He had seized upon the branch above her own hold and nearly shook it free of her grasp in his excitement. Then she saw, also. The hair-thin line which had marked the sealing place on the rod was not only wider, but it was ringed by a slim blue line of fire, as if energy ate the old metal.

"Don't touch it—not yet!" Her cry came swiftly, as he was about to free it from its lashing. "Not unless you want, perhaps, to lose another hand!"

He loosed his hold to stare at her, suspicion again in his face. Tirtha laid the branch and rod carefully at the gravelly foot of the cliff and watched. It was true! There was an ever-increasing opening. She looked at her hands, at her sword. If that blue light did not continue, she might try to force it more. However, the reaction that had reached her even through the length of dead wood was a warning. They must wait until whatever had begun worked itself out.

She glanced up. There was nothing to be read now by the lines on the rockface. Their shining was as it had been at her first sighting. The influence, whatever it might be, had passed into the rod. Now that was failing also. At least the blue strip about the one end was losing brightness. As it failed she could see a dark space, and she was sure that the sealing had been sprung. That she had succeeded in such an act was as surprising to her as it must be to the Falconer, who watched the cylinder of metal intently, even as he might look into the eyes of an enemy, with the same wariness and readiness for battle.

It had been only experimentation, a wild guess on her part. That it worked . . . ! *Had* this been the reason to draw the dead man here with his last failing strength—that he might read a record as important to him as life itself?

The blue light vanished. Tirtha knelt, stretched out her hand, very cautiously, toward the lashing of the rod. She could sense no heat, nothing of that energy which had touched her before. The gap in the rod remained apparent.

Very carefully she worked at the knotted thong, moving gingerly when she had to touch the rod itself. When there followed no pricking, she took confidence, twisted it free. Gripping the cap in her fingers, she gave a sharp pull. There was resistance, but only slight. Then the small round of metal came free, the rod remaining in her other hand. She dropped the cap, upended the rod to shake it above her left palm. Nothing was forthcoming. When Tirtha inspected it more closely she could see a roll inside, tight against the wall of the small cylinder. That had to be worked out very carefully. If this scrap was old, it might well vanish into dust under rough handling.

She held a roll of what could only be several layers of the same reptile skin as formed her money belt, glued one to another to make a sheet akin to parchment, but infinitely more durable. She spread it wide to view a jumble of symbols that made no sense at all.

Her disappointment was so keen, she gave a little cry of disbelief. A thing of power this doubtless was, but as locked against any use by her as if she had never freed it from the rod! None of the symbols on it were familiar. Not even at Lormt had she come across such meandering lines, such swirls, as were inscribed here in red paint or ink. They did not even form lines as if they were some enciphered message—rather sprawled here and there, some large, some small, in no reasonable pattern.

"Perhaps it is a map."

Almost, Tirtha had forgotten the Falconer. He moved beside her again to stare at what she held, his slanting brows drawn together in a half-frown.

"A map!" Tirtha had reason to consult such in the past. Though nothing had been done since the writhing of the mountains to lay out guides for travelers into the borderlands, she herself had contrived to fit together bits of information which she believed would guide her to her future goal. She had set down, memorized, and destroyed them methodically. Nothing she had ever seen or heard of matched this peculiar scrawl. Yet it had not been done roughly, she could perceive that the longer she studied it. The pictured symbols must have definite meaning, yet it was a meaning that eluded her.

"Not of this." With a wave of his hand her companion dismissed the countryside around them. "I think it is a different kind of map—perhaps of a place, a hold even, rather than the countryside."

"But there are no lines for walls, no . . ." she began her protest.

His frown had lightened. "I think everything that might have been used in that fashion was deliberately omitted. So that the place could not be identified. This is a seeker's guide, one pointed at a special place, perhaps a treasure."

She did not miss that quick glance he had given her, before his eyes went back to the paper again.

"Also," he continued, "it is a part of that witchery." He raised his head toward the symbol on the cliff face. "It could well be that there is sorcery in what is written here, and only one endowed with your talents—you of the Old Race—can make much of it. He—this man you speak of as a stranger—was of your blood. He carried this, and it meant much to him. Could he have been seeking out just such an aid as that hanging up there to make it plain to him?"

So he shared that guess with her. Well, there was a good chance he was right. However, that dead seeker must have known much more than she did. That presented a new fragment of mystery. In Estcarp only the Witches pretended to any use of the Power. It was not given to any man to read such a puzzle as she held—nor would a Witch believe that in a man's hands the rod could ever have given up its secret.

Therefore the rider must have been instructed what to search for. Tirtha drew a long breath and rerolled the layered skin, pushed it back in its container. Stooping, she picked up the cap, but she did not restore it to the top of the rod. There might just be a chance that time and fortune would give her a means of penetrating the secret of what she had found, and she had no intention of sealing it away. Another time there might not be a way of forcing it open.

She stored it in her belt pouch, and they returned to the meadow. But as she went, Tirtha was busy with scrambled thoughts. The Falconer's guess—which could only be a guess, of course. Was this really some clue to the inner parts of—say—a hold hall such a one as she had envisioned? *Had* the dead stranger and she both been drawn by a stroke of fortune or troubling of Power past their understanding to make this journey at the same time and in search of the same thing? It was a disturbing thought, but she could not force it out of mind.

5

They chose to camp in the protected valley, returning to the crude shelter they had earlier discovered, turning their ponies loose, though hobbled, to share the meadow with the Torgian. Because of that symbol on the rock wall Tirtha dared a fire. Also, at the coming of dusk, the intricate design there began to glow blue, even as a portion had done at her testing. Whatever virtue it possessed was still locked in it, and Tirtha believed that this was indeed a pocket of safety where they need fear no monstrous prowler of the night.

The rations they carried were so limited she made a very careful division of what she had brought out of Romsgarth. However, the Falconer ventured down stream to return, swinging from a reed thong, a brace of plump water hens, which he rolled in mud and pushed well down into the coals of the fire. So they fared better than she would have thought, the feathered skin peeling away from this feast with the mud.

They did not choose to lie within that half-shelter. The night was not cold and somehow Tirtha wanted not to be pent in. It seemed the Falconer shared her desire for freedom. However, she agreed readily that, in spite of the glowing symbol on the rocks, it was well to keep watch turn by turn. This night it fell to her to stand sentry first.

Once the Falconer had rolled into his blanket, she did not remain long by the fire. Hearing the even breathing of the sleeper, she got to her feet, followed the faint path meadowwards. The three beasts grazing there paid her no heed. All the defiance and fear, she sensed, had gone out of the Torgian. He was perhaps ready to accept a change in traveling companions, and certainly he would be a welcome addition—a horse of his stamina and speed might well mean, in Karsten, the difference between success and failure.

Of course, the Falconer could bespeak an equal claim on that mount, but Tirtha believed she might buy him off by an offer of extra gold. Perhaps she might even add her mare whose worth was high in the border country. Now she turned her back on the grazing trio and stood, hands on her hips, looking up at the symbol on the cliff.

What it had been intended to guard was a mystery to both intrigue and disturb her. If it had been hidden until the quakes had revealed it so, then what lay or had lain under the land hereabouts? There were certainly no holds this deep in the highlands—only the Eyrie which the Falconers had built and which had been destroyed. Nor was this Falcon "witchery."

Never more than at this moment, she longed for the talent. One who possessed farsight—or even the smaller gift of water-seeking with a peeled wand—might have unlocked a little of the ancient puzzle. In spite of her winter at Lormt, Tirtha had been too lacking in early training to absorb more than the knowledge of what might exist—with no chance of making the smallest usage of what someone else could have put to the test.

What did she possess, in truth? Only her dream and the conviction that it drew her, that there lay before her something that must be done—the reason for her existence. It was that which had carried her through these years, worked upon her body and spirit as a smith works upon the metal he handles to fashion a cunning tool, a stout weapon. A tool, a weapon—to be used by whom and for what? She had asked herself that also, knowing that there would be no answer out of the heavens to make all plain.

There was the Power, and it did lie in all things that had life. However, it was comprised of many different energies, some of which served those trained in use, some of which could harm—and another, a larger part, that was beyond even the greatest adept to understand or know. Out of Power came birth and life—to it, after death, returned that which was the spark of all inner essence. Once there had been ritual and ceremony where kin gathered to warm their hearts at a summoned manifestation.

That was long gone. Tirtha could only stand and stare at lines upon a rock wall and wonder who had wrought them so carefully. Had the Power drawn her here? The Falconer had chosen the trail leading to this valley, but she was certain he had not known that it lay under such protection; if so he might well have sought another road. For his kind were not, they had often declared, to be caught in any spell laid by the Old Race.

Again, almost shyly since she was alone and had no need to impress anyone with the fact that she faced something of her own people, Tirtha raised a hand to sketch in the air the sign of peace and acceptance. Then she turned back to sit by the fire, feeding it stick by stick, listening to the sound of the running stream.

She realized that, save for the carrion flies, there had been no stirring of life in this valley. Though the Falconer had caught water hens, she had heard no calling of such fowl or sighted spoor of any beast. Yet in this wilderness of stone, the water, the meadow should surely have attracted some wilderness life. It was too quiet here. The girl moved restlessly, arose again, once more pacing into the meadow where the ponies seemed undisturbed. She listened for the wing-sound of any night bird. During all her roaming she had slept out many times, and she knew only too well the cries of the great hunting owls which were common in the lower border lands.

A quiet night . . .

There was a thin sliver of new moon showing, as well as stars. Moon Magic also—she had a fraction of it herself. It was special to the Wise Women—if not to the Witches—woman's magic. . . .

Magic—it was all magic! Tirtha's fingers balled into a fist that she pounded against the earth as she hunkered down again. She deliberately fastened her mind upon what she must do once they were cross-mountain, even though all would depend upon what they found there. Would she be wise to try to keep the Falconer past the time they had bargained, even if she must, in turn, then share something of her secret? There were no decisions she could make now—only try to think a little ahead so that she knew what decisions might await her.

The silence, the sight of that symbol, made her restless, ill at ease. She tested with seek-thought for any slinker, any life form that might dare the valley in spite of the guardianship. She caught the life essence, which came from the sleeping man; and farther away, that of the three mounts; also some smaller sparks—without anything about them of Dark threat—which she guessed might be wild life. Then . . .

Pain and despair—horror—need . . .

Tirtha was on her feet, running, her sword out.

She came to the cairn, stood staring wide-eyed at the mounded turf, the stones they had chosen and fitted above them.

Need—need! Such a wave of it struck at her that she was unaware of falling to her knees beside the mound, watching it in pure horror, which gripped and froze her whole body with waves of unknown force.

Need!

No! Death was a final gate through which all life essence passed. There was no imprisoning of self in rotting flesh that had been discarded. They had buried a dead man. He could not summon—demand—assault her with this desperate cry for help! She dropped the sword, put her hands to her head when the demand she could neither explain nor deny struck at her, set her swaying back and forth as if blows were being rained upon her.

The sword had clattered across the stones. Its Hawk-signed pommel touched the white stone she had added for the very old ritual of her people. Hawk!

Kin-blood—kin-blood to take up a burden, accept the need!

Kin-blood? There was none. She denied that fiercely. Dimly, out of the stories she had heard in childhood, Tirtha knew what sought to ensnare her now. There was the kin oath-laying, which could pass from dead to living and which could not be denied. But that was a true kin thing, accepted by the chosen as a duty coming before all else in life! She was not blood-tied to this stranger. What lingered here could *not* set its mark on her!

"Peace . . ." She got out that word with great effort, as if she must speak past a constriction in her throat. "Peace to you, stranger. I am not kin-blood. Go you on into the Power's way. We choose not our endings; we choose only the manner with which we meet such. Your task may have ended, but it was the body that failed you, not. . . ."

Tirtha gasped. The sword and the stone—above them where they touched forming something that might well have issued from her abiding and commanding dream—save she was not asleep. There, in a faintly blue mist, was the casket even as she had seen it carried into hiding by that hold lady whose face she had never viewed. *There* was what she must seek and find—and it grew sharper, more distinct.

Need . . .

Fainter now, as if the last vestiges of whatever had summoned her were fast fading, as if the call she heard came only from a distance, growing ever more immeasurable.

And that need—it was hers also! Stranger—no! In some way past her understanding, this one *had* been kin-born. However, the dead did not have to bend her to his fading will—that geas was already a part of her.

"Hawkholme—!" Tirtha said. "I go there, yes. And what lies within that"—the casket was merely a wisp of vapor again—"is to come forth. I knew you not, kin-blood. But your need is already mine."

The haze vanished—also that other—that remnant of will which had outlasted death itself. She was bound, but no more tightly than she had been before she entered this valley. Save that it seemed, in that moment, that when she took up the sword again from where it had fallen, there passed into the hand gripping it a new kind of energy, a strength she had not hitherto known.

Tirtha was still trembling, fighting down the raw fear that had touched her, as she returned to their camp. The night had swung by. She roused her companion, wrapped herself in her own cloak. Almost, she was afraid to surrender to sleep. Would the dream enfold her now, or would something else—a last lingering trace of that demand—strike at her? She closed her eyes with determination and willed herself to rest.

No dream came this night, nor did she confront, as she had more than half feared, that other presence. Instead, her sleep must have been very deep and heavy, for when she was awakened in the morning, she felt a reluctance to move, as if weakened.

They discovered the Torgian now biddable enough, standing quietly so that he might be saddled with the riding gear from which the Falconer had scrubbed the blood stains. But neither of them wished to mount in the place of his dead master; rather they put him on a leading rein and kept to their own sure-footed ponies.

Tirtha hunched her shoulders a little as she passed both mound and symbol, glancing at neither. In the brightness of this new day she could almost believe that illusion had enfolded her last night, and she kept her hand well away from sword hilt as she rode. Let the dead lie in peace—and might she ride so. She owed no debt to anyone—carried nothing but the purpose that had brought her here.

There was a thin trace on the far side of the meadow, a shadow trail such as only the very sure-footed mountain ponies could follow, and one they must take unencumbered. Both riders dismounted to lead their beasts, the Falconer hooking the Torgian's halter rope to the empty perch on his own saddle pad, thus securing the horse in line.

The climb was one to be taken slowly and with care. When they at length reached a split in the valley wall, Tirtha stared eagerly ahead, hoping that they were not to be faced by another such ordeal. She was heartened to see that the trail beyond widened and when it did descend, the angle was far less sharp. Also there was greenery to be sighted in pockets ahead, as if they had now passed through the sharp rock desert which had been the outer forbidding part of the mountain ways.

Shortly before midday she brought down a pronghorn—a young buck—and they stopped to skin and butcher the kill. When they broke their fast at nooning, it was with good meat, fireroasted. Nor was there any lack of life to be seen hereabouts. The fresh slot tracks of other pronghorns, the calls of birds, even a lazy scattering of well-fed quarewings out of a patch of fresh standing law-leaves—the crops of the birds so stuffed that they seemed too weighted to take to the air—all testified to that.

This was good hunting land, and Tirtha wondered if it might be well to try smoking some of the meat, halting for a day or so to add to their supplies. Oddly enough, along this particular trail, where she would have thought it more natural to find snow still lingering, spring growth was more advanced than in the lower valleys from which they had come. There were flowers in pockets of earth, wild fruit trees in bloom, so that the perfume blended on the air, bringing back memories of those farm garths where she had labored.

They were two days crossing this gentle land, and there was no trace in it of any evil. Sometimes Tirtha felt a freedom of spirit, in short flashes, as if nothing pushed at her. To live here in peace and quiet, depending upon the bounty of the earth alone, troubled by no dreams, no need—she wondered dimly now and then what such a life might mean.

If her companion had such thoughts, he never voiced them, any more than she revealed hers. They traveled mainly in silence, and she believed that he was intent upon accomplishing their journey as swiftly and with as little danger as possible. They still kept night watches in turn, and he rode ever, she noted, with the attention of a scout invading unknown territory.

Strangely enough, she no longer dreamed. That visit in her dreams to the ghostly hold had been for so long a part of her nights that Tirtha felt disturbed when it was not repeated. Several times she had drawn out during their camping that "map," as the Falconer would call it, studying the symbols set on it to no better purpose than she had done the first time she had looked upon it. Was it a map at all? There were patterns for calling of Power; hastily she pushed that dangerous idea out of her mind.

On the afternoon of the fourth day after they had ridden out of the protected valley, the vegetation grew sparser, their path once more led into a barren country as it climbed. Just before nightfall they sighted a fall of stone. The Falconer halted, staring ahead—not as one who faced some to-be-expected barrier, but rather in bemusement, which showed openly on his usually expressionless face, for that day he had ridden bareheaded—a strange choice for one who had always kept to his mask.

Tirtha could see no reason for this sudden halt, but here the path was so narrow that she could not push ahead, but must wait on him to move. When he did not, she broke what had nearly been a full day of silence.

"There is no way beyond?"

For a long moment she believed that he was so lost in what thoughts filled his mind that he had not even heard her. Then, haltingly, his claw swung out, gestured at the river of broken stone.

"The Eyrie . . ."

Some trick of his voice, its pitch, awoke an echo from the rocks around them.

Eyrie. That was like the wail of a mourner at a Sulcar burn burial.

Tirtha stared. There was certainly little to show that this had been the site of the centuries' old dwelling place of his race—at least nothing she could distinguish. She had heard that the Eyrie had been so well designed that it had the appearance of a hollowed-out mountain, and that very few, if any, outsiders (and those only the Borderers and males) had ever crossed its one-time drawbridge.

Here was nothing but river stone resembling any other slide they had skirted or crossed during their travels. Her companion held his head well back on his shoulders, gazing up the line of that heap of rocks, as if he hunted desperately for something that should still exist. In turn, she imagined a mist out of the past come to cloak that slide, to show for a heartbeat or two the fortress that had been. Yet she could truly not trace anything at all.

He called, the words she did not know spiraling up, then running into a single sound that might be the scream of a hawk. Three times he uttered that cry. Then he was answered!

Tirtha clutched her reins tighter, her mount shifted foot to send some small stones rattling. The answer was thin, not full-throated— yet she could not deny that she had heard it. Ghosts—the vanished dead who should be peacefully at rest—was she not yet done with them? Had *his* kin a call for blood vengeance and was that demand strong enough that it could manifest itself in the full light of day? The Falconers had been well warned; surely they had taken refuge down in Estcarp before the churning of the heights. Certainly also her companion could not be old enough in years to have been sword-oathed to one who had lived here before the end of the Eyrie.

The Falconer shouted—for a ringing shout was what he uttered this time, echoing and reechoing—something in the pitch of sound making the ponies snort, the Torgian whinny, and her own ears hurt.

Once more an answer. Then she caught sight of a speck in the sky overhead. Down it struck, as if it would bear with it from the air some intruding prey. She watched with some awe the swiftness of that descent out of the heavens. The flyer passed from sunlight into the more shadowed air of the half-choked cleft into which they had headed.

Now the strike eased, wings flapped, a black body circled, and circling, came closer and closer until it passed above them. A falcon settled on an edge of rock, its wings still a little spread, as if it would take to the heavens again once its curiosity was satisfied.

Black of feather, with the white V marking on the breast, a falcon of the Eyrie—or else the descendant of such a one—wildliving, for it did not wear the scarlet jesses that marked the partnership between man and bird. Bright eyes regarded the unhelmed man. From his lips came a series of birdlike notes, scaling up and down. The falcon answered with a scream, mantling, appearing ready to lift again, be away from this creature of another species who strove to communicate with it.

Still the Falconer forced out sounds, which Tirtha would not have believed any human throat or lips could have shaped. He made no move toward the uneasy bird, simply spoke to it, Tirtha was now convinced, in its own language.

There was no scream; rather the sound the bird uttered in return was not far different from those made by the man. Its head was slightly to one side. Tirtha could believe that it was considering some proposal or striving to come to a decision of its own.

Then, with one more cry, it took to the air. Not to approach the waiting man but to rise steadily with all the force of its wings into the heights from which it had come. There was no disappointment on the weathered features of the man, he simply sat and watched it go.

It was only when it winged to the west and was fully gone from their sight that he seemed to remember he was not alone and looked back at Tirtha.

"This is no road, not now." His voice was steady, as cool as it had always been. "We must go back and take a northward turning, and that before the dark closes in."

Tirtha asked no questions, for there was that about him which said he was entirely certain of what he was about, and she had learned to trust his sense of mountain ways. Turn north they did, and in the end found a basin that was clearly the work of men, into which ran a runnel of water, falling out of a pipe made to handle thrice the amount that now trickled through. There was forage of a sort—tough clumps of grass growing along the overflow from the basin—at least enough graze for overnight.

They had no fire. Though there were sticks enough among the stones of the stream's banks for the feeding of one, the Falconer shook his head when Tirtha would have gathered them.

"This a place of watchers."

"Falcons?" she asked. "But fire would not rouse them."

He shook his head again emphatically. "Others have come into this country."

His exchange of sounds with that bird—what had he so learned? She felt she had a right to demand such information, when he continued: "Such are not outlaws—nor those from Karsten. They are others from the east."

From the east! That snout-nosed monster out of the dark! Things on the move from Escore over-mountain! With that in mind Tirtha glanced quickly about their camp. It was as well protected by its situation as any place she might have picked, she thought. As soon as the mounts had had some grazing, before the dark closed in, they could bring them up here and tether them, satisfy them with handsful of the grain together with a strewing of salt across the gritty stuff. To reach here any attacker would have to approach along a very narrow way that either one of them could defend alone. It was not the stoutest fortress in the world, but it would have to serve tonight.

They ate sparingly, then brought in the ponies and the Torgian. It was Tirtha's turn for the first rest period of the night, but she was not ready yet to try for sleep. Instead she found herself casting out thought loops, as a cattle herder of the plains might spin his catch rope, striving to pick up any trace of a Dark mind which might be lurking even now to spy upon them.

Dead by tooth and claw—that was what he had said of the stranger. Perhaps that unfortunate invader of these haunted hills had been trailed, preyed upon, by just such a night-running creature as they had faced with greater fortune. Tirtha searched in her pouch for the small packet of herb dust that had served so well during the attack, bringing it out to hand. Twilight was already gray within their refuge. The ponies stamped and whickered, straining a little at their halters, so now she went to share out the handsful of grain with the trace of salt to keep them quiet.

She realized that to sit staring into the growing dark would avail her nothing. The Falconer was on watch and upon his skill she depended with unbroken trust. These were his homelands after all, and he knew best what need be feared.

Tirtha sought to empty her mind and sleep. For a space the dreamless rest that had recently been hers settled down upon her.

When she awoke it was to the summons to take her place on watch. He answered her question before she asked it.

"Nothing."

Nothing but the night, and the memory that picked at her, of what had crept upon them in the dark before, and of that other night when she had been caught by the cry from the dead, shown something which she thought was hers alone. She sat cross-legged, moving now and then to the animals to smooth her hands across their rough-coated hides, sending soothing thoughts into their minds. For she did not believe that it was hunger alone that kept them restless.

Far keener than the senses of her own kind were those of the beasts. They could measure danger at a greater distance than even her thought-sweep might reach. She no longer wished to try that—knowing that any creature of the Dark could seize upon it as a guide and so be drawn to them.

Yes, out there somewhere, things moved that were not of the world she had known. Legend and the chronicles of Lormt—neither had made such real. One had to confront them for one's self, sniff the foul stench of evil, see it—then one accepted and understood.

The falcon—what had it seen prowling about these ruined heights? It must be a descendant of those that had once been the pride of the Eyrie. Perhaps such birds, too, had their own legends of another time —one in which they had been companions to men and ridden out to war on a saddle perch. A legend that today had drawn the winged scout to give its warning.

Tirtha wondered if the Falconer had longed for that free flyer to join with him. Or was it only once in the lifetime of each that bird and man united into a fighting, living whole, and when one died there was no second such coupling? There was so much Tirtha did not know and could not ask. For she was certain her companion would count it an intrusion such as might even be strong enough to break his sword oath. His secrets were his, just as hers were hers.

6

If evil did run that night, it did not seek their camp. Nor did the mounts show any increasing uneasiness. However, Tirtha was not in any way lulled into believing that her fellow traveler's warning had been exaggerated or false. With the morning light she roused from an uneasy sleep to see him carefully checking his dart gun, slipping his small supply of its loadings in and out of their loops on his shoulder belt, as if he would make certain they were ready to hand at a moment's demand. There was only a limited number of them, and Tirtha realized very well that they would be used, if it were necessary, most sparingly and with all the skill he could summon.

She sat up, shrugged aside the folds of her cloak, to thought-listen. There was the essence of life forces which marked man, ponies, Torgian. Nothing else abode here. Caution limited her to a very narrow sweep, but even so fleeting a touch had alerted the Falconer, for his yellow-fired eyes were sharply on her as he turned helmed head in her direction.

"That is folly." He spoke with cold precision. If they had fallen into slightly easier ways with one another during the days past—very slightly easier—that had changed. Perhaps sight of the ruins of his people's hold had fastened on him the bonds of their long training. She was not of the kin, and she was that distrusted, even hated thing —a woman.

Tirtha refused to be irritated by such change in attitude. All knew the Falconers and their ways—what else could she expect?

"There was nothing during your second watch?" She made only a half-question of that, knowing well that, had there been invasion of the camp territory during her rest, he would have aroused her, even as he had on that other night.

He finished with his examination of his ammunition. Now he drew sword to inspect its edge, his attention seeming more for the steel than for her.

"It is out there, perhaps watching, spying."

"You know because your falcon would have it so?"

Again he swung a cold and quelling gaze at her. "I have no falcon." The words were like icy pellets hurled across the small space between them. "The free one and his brood have scouted afar. There are movements through these heights. One needs not touch to know."

She must not provoke him. Instead Tirtha nodded. "Yes," she agreed and went to wash her face in the chill water gathered in the basin. The sting of it, like a swift slap, awaked her fully.

They allowed the mounts another short period of graze while they broke their own fast, eating most frugally. Having filled the water bottles, watered their horses, and saddled up, they moved on, the Falconer riding ahead, Tirtha bringing up the rear.

It did not take them long to get beyond the stream and the ragged growth about it, picking a careful way around rock falls. As far as Tirtha could determine they now headed southward. She had no way by which she could calculate how much longer this mountain travel would take. All roads and known trails had been destroyed with the army that had marched along them, on the day the mountains had been moved.

They had been on their twisting trail, having to backtrack sometimes to seek another route (for hereabouts the ravages of the overthrow were far worse and more apparent to the eye), for a period of time well into the morning when they came across the first signs of that drastic wiping out of the invaders a generation ago.

Their discovery was signaled by one of those harsh cries that Tirtha associated with the Falconer, though the sound had not issued from the lips of her companion—rather it echoed from some point ahead. There was a division of possible ways here, and at that sound, the Falconer turned unhesitatingly into the one from which that cry had come.

Ahead, after they had wound their way around another slide of jagged and cruelly broken rock, was a space nearly choked with a fall, even as had been the site of the Eyrie. On a boulder that overtopped Tirtha's head as she rode, perched a bird—like the one that had answered her companion's call the night before.

The sun-struck gleams from metal caught in and among that tumble of cracked and broken stone. There were red stains of rust streaming down from some of these twisted and crushed weapons. Other scraps had remained oddly untouched by the years and the weather, as if they had lain ensorceled during the time since the disaster. A roundish yellowed stone, when touched glancingly by the mare's hoof, rolled over to show that it was a skull.

The falcon screamed again, and the man he appeared to summon slid from his mount, leaving reins dangling. He went to climb that crumbling hill toward the waiting bird. Tirtha watched them narrowly. There was certainly no open path across this battlefield between men and the unleashed Power—why then had they come here?

She saw him reach a rock that brought his head on a level with the waiting predator. Then his hand shot forward as he jerked at one of those bright bits of metal, its surface showing no rust. There was resistance, which his strength bested. What he drew into the open was a hilted blade—not the length of a full sword—nor yet that of a long dagger, but somewhere between the two.

The bird was watching him intently, its head forward as it looked down. Now, as the man pulled forth that weapon, it again uttered a cry—a scream that might be one of fierce triumph—and rose into the air a fraction with a beat of wings. The Falconer held out his arm straight and still, and the feathered hunter came to perch on his wrist. It settled there as if it had chosen a resting place it liked well. So it remained for a long moment while the eyes behind the mask-helm and those within the feathered skull met and held a gaze Tirtha knew was silent communication of a kind unknown to her race.

Once more the bird took to the air, this time descending to the pony which the Falconer had ridden. The mount jerked up its head sharply, but the bird came to rest on the empty saddle perch. It folded its wings, and the sound it now made was soft, such as Tirtha thought could never have come from the throat of such a fierce hunter and fighter of the skies.

The Falconer climbed down the rocks, taking the last step as a single leap, for stones began to shift, the knife-sword swinging in his hand, his claw out for balance. Then he looked, not to the waiting bird, but at her.

Something momentous had happened. Tirtha believed that as if it were part of the life-sensing that could reach her at times. There was a change in the man that was not physical, but lay within. Now for a moment he gazed down along the blade he held and then again to her, holding out the find to which the falcon had drawn him.

"A thing of Power . . ." he said slowly.

Tirtha did not attempt to touch it, but she leaned well forward to study it as well as she might. The blade was not smooth, as it had seemed from a distance. Rather it was deeply engraved with a pattern. She saw thereon such symbols as she knew were of the long forgotten elder knowledge, and where the blade widened near the hilt there was also the image of a beast inserted in another metal—blue like the symbol on the valley wall. This was a creature such as she had never seen, though it might not be even a living entity, but rather a dream vision of some adept, used as a chosen mark for his blood and house.

The hilt, which was revealed through the loose clasp of her companion's fingers, was of the same blue metal as that inlay, ending in a bulbous globe of murky substance like a huge dull gem, smoothed but unfaceted. Tirtha put out her hand slowly, not to touch it, no. The tingling in her fingers was enough. This was indeed a thing of Power, perhaps never meant to be a slaying weapon at all, rather a focus used by someone who would command forces. Yet who in Karsten would have dabbled, or dared, to meddle with *the* Power?

Those who had hated and hunted her people professed to believe that any such contact was evil, that they might be blasted out of life by it. They had done all they could to stamp out any contact with it. All with talent had been slain—or else, as in the case of witches, rendered helpless. Witches did not lie with men, but if a man took one by force, then her talent was drained and lost.

Tirtha drew back her fingers. "It is alive—there is Power," she agreed. "But from *Karsten?*" There was no denying that what they had come on must have aided the destruction of the invading force. Who among *them* would have dared carry a weapon charged with Power into a country where that force ruled?

"From Karsten . . ." He spoke musingly, glancing around at the tumble of stones that must hide many dead. "Yes—who and why?"

"And how did the falcon know?" Tirtha dared then to ask.

"The feathered brothers have their own ways," he answered almost absently. "This would attract such a one."

He drew the long hunting knife out of his belt sheath, leaned over to slip it into the top of his riding boot. Then he slid his find into its place. It seemed to go easily, though a part of it projected above the edge of the sheath.

"A thing of Power . . ." Tirtha repeated his words. She had no desire to handle it. The energy that had reached her even though her flesh had not touched it was enough to warn her off. Yet if the Falconer had felt that same surge, it did not appear to turn him against a thing that his own people had feared as much as those newcomers in Karsten who were not of the Elder Race.

"It came to me." He said that evenly, and Tirtha remembered another tale—that story of the Axe of Volt and how it had come into the hands of Koris of Gorm, from the hold of Volt himself, long dead and entombed. Volt's Axe had chosen. Was this once more a case whereby a weapon charged with unknown life had chosen to fit into the hand of a new owner?

"Volt's Axe," she blurted out, caught in amazement that such a thing might happen a second time. Yet this blade had no such history, no name, and he who had taken it was of a race without the talent.

His head in the bird helm moved as if he had taken a blow.

"It came to me," he said slowly again. "There will be a cause and that shall also be revealed in time."

Then he swung upon the pony and pulled at the reins, bringing the mount around so that once again they retracted a way, out of that rubble- and death-choked valley into the second passage. Tirtha found her attention turning often to the blue knob of gemstone where it rode at his belt, shifting a fraction now and then, since it did not fit the sheath. She could not believe that chance had led him to it. Now she, too, moved uneasily on her riding pad from time to time, discovering a desire to watch their back trail or the walls of the mountains about them. Still her companion displayed no uneasiness, nor had he appeared to question the fact that the falcon now occupied what had been the empty perch on his saddle. It was as if he accepted all that had happened as a necessary part of what was meant to be.

That night they advanced into a more open section of a valley that sloped upwards at the far end in the direction of what Tirtha believed must be a pass. The jagged peaks guarding either side looked as if sections of the earth had been slashed out by sword strokes, turned edge upward against the sky. There was a brutal savagery about this entrance to the land ahead that posted a warning against further advance. She fought down such thoughts with a firm hand. Perhaps it was the ravaged look of this country that added strength to her feeling that they were always under observation.

Twice more during that day they passed evidences of the slaughter that had ended the army of Pagar and pushed the southern land back into barbarism. There was rusted metal, once the pole of a standard, planted upright among stones, the width of its banner now only a few threads windwhipped and knotted about the pole. There were bleached bones. They were well content to skirt such traces of the carnage that must have filled these ways.

However, they could not attempt the pass until morning, so they made a dry camp beneath heights where the wind howled and whistled until one could almost believe that it echoed cries of the dead. Their supply of water was so limited that they wiped out the mouths of their mounts with wet cloths and allowed each only a small cupping of water in one of the eating bowls from Tirtha's saddlebags. They scanted themselves even more, and it was very hard to choke down the now crumbling journey cakes which stuck in the throat.

The falcon had taken to the air as they had come to camp and perhaps found some forage in the heights above. It did not return until the dusk neared night, and then it communicated again with the man it had chosen to accompany in the same series of notes they had used at their first meeting.

As the bird settled down on its saddle perch the Falconer spoke. "We are within perhaps a day's journey of the foothills. I have served more than a quarter of my oathed time. What would you have of me when we are down from the heights?"

It was a fair question. She had set his service as twenty days simply because she had wanted to make sure of his guidance and company through the mountains. Did she now want him to accompany her further? Tirtha was faced at last with a decision that she must make, and then abide by the results of the making.

Hawkholme lay to the east. She had—her hand went into the front of her jerkin seeking to finger the money belt. In one compartment of it she had a map, the only one she had kept, though it could hardly be an accurate one, drawn as it was from bits and pieces of information she had managed to assemble.

Her simple plan as far as she had made it, not knowing the country except by repute, had been to angle along the foothills themselves, not venturing far down into the open country, until she believed she could strike fairly straight across to the hold, or what remained of it. It was certainly not a plan that carried any certainty. Now she was silent a long moment.

Well, she had very little to lose, she decided. Perhaps she had answered the question without being conscious of having done so during these days of journeying. The Falconer would be no more welcome in Karsten than she herself, having harried the borders with his own kind.

To whom could he betray her? And what did he have to betray, save that one of the Old Race sought to return to the land that had once been held by those of her blood? She herself could not tell him exactly what she sought there, or why she was driven into that seeking. Let her tell him what was most of the truth, then let the decision be his whether he asked oath release or not.

It was dark in the valley, and they had lit no fire. He was only a blacker dot of shadow against the wall of rock behind him. It made little difference as even in the light of day she was not able to read anything from his expression. Let him use his voice to answer her aye or nay.

"I seek Hawkholme," she began. "It is the land anciently bound to my blood, and I have waited for long to go there. I have thought to travel east through the foothills and then strike over land."

"You know the road you must go?" he asked, as she paused.

Tirtha closed her eyes. In a way, yes, she knew—or felt within her that she would know when the time came. The dream—whatever had sent that—it would guide her. How could she speak of dreams to this one? Or—she considered that point. Since his finding and taking of the odd sword-knife, she had somewhat revised her first opinion of the Falconer. Reputed as he and his kind were to be bitter enemies of all her own people prized and revered, why then had he put that weapon in his belt? He should by rights have hurled it from him, if he set hand to it at all!

"I know it," she returned now firmly. There was, she decided, no reason for her to explain how tenuous was her foundation for that assertion. "But I do not know the length of such a journey. It may run far longer than your bind-oath. I asked for guidance through the mountains. When we reach the foothills, you will have fulfilled your part of that bargain. If the days are not accomplished, the purpose is."

When he made no answer through the dark, she licked her lips. Why was she disturbed? She had never intended, had she, that he should accompany her on the whole of her mission. Why was she waiting now, with an eagerness she did not understand, for his reply?

"I am oath-bound for twenty days." His voice held its usual cool and steady note. "For twenty days I ride, whether it be through mountains, foothills, or Karsten."

Tirtha could not understand her feeling of relief. What had she to do with this man? Their whole lives were alien to one another. Yet had he chosen otherwise, she knew, it would have been a disappointment. This was so new and strange a thing for her who had built her life upon her own silence and aloneness that she pushed it from her foremind, telling herself that there might well be trouble in the foothills, and two fighters were better than one if that came. Also the falcon seemed to have taken up service with her companion, and the scouting ability of those birds was legendary.

"So be it," she returned, and thought that her voice sounded overly sharp. Still, she had no intention of allowing him to believe that she had nursed a strange hope he would answer exactly as he had.

In the morning they climbed to the pass. The way upward was longer than it had looked from below, for the footing was rough, and they dismounted several times to lead their beasts. The falcon took to the sky early, returning periodically to perch on some higher portion of the trail and await them, always then exchanging sounds with the man.

It was past midday when they stood in the notch of the pass itself to look down upon the outward sweep of the over-mountain country, which was no longer one land but a number of quarreling fiefs in which war and pillage had ruled for years.

The foothills were tree-crowned—it would seem that the fury of the Power had not reached here to uproot and crush. Tirtha, looking upon them, was pleased, for it seemed to her that this was the type of country that would best serve those who needed cover. She turned a little to gaze eastward and saw that there were the dark lines of what could only be woodland in that direction.

In the old days, the plains of Karsten had been most fertile and open to the west. There had been the garths of the farmers and the landowners among those younger, newer people who had spread inward from the sea. The cities and the holds of some pretense of importance had all lain there.

The Old Race, her own people, had withdrawn gradually from those settlers who had come overseas in days now shadowed into legend. They had established their own holdings to the eastward. In some places the advancing newcomers had proved hostile, and there had been no intercourse at all between the old blood and the settlers. In other sections there was friendliness and sometimes a trading of skills, neighbor aiding neighbor. So it had come about that some of those neighbors had suffered death and worse in the day of Yvian's Horning because of aiding the escape of her own kind.

It would be mainly in the plains, where the land was rich and there were cities, that any struggle centered now. Farther south lay other provinces (from one of which Pagar himself had come) where the new people were even more firmly established and occupied the whole of the area.

However, these foothills, just like those on the other side of the border, might give refuge to outlaws and masterless men who had become pillagers and raiders. It was the kind of country to attract such.

Tirtha mentioned this, and the Falconer nodded. He swung out with his claw. The sun glinted on metal as he pointed.

"It is true there are others here."

She saw it now—a column of smoke rising from between two of those hills. It was far too thick a pillar to be born from a campfire. Something of greater consequence, perhaps even the buildings of a farm, burned there. Though what farmer would choose such a setting for his holding? Or did that mark an outlaw post raided by whoever stood for law and order here—even as the Marshal's men strove to clean out such vultures' nests to the north?

In any case that billowing smoke was warning enough that they must travel as secretly as they could. There was no reason to throw away all she had struggled for these past years by being too bold now.

An afternoon of descent brought them into wooded land. Then the lead pony snorted and quickened pace, the Torgian pushing up beside, the mare quick to follow. It was plain that the animals scented water. They found it in a stream that ran fast and clear at an angling path from the north, where it must have been born among the mountains, toward the west and south, perhaps to join the river on which Kars stood.

There was cover in plenty—a copse of trees growing closely—composed of that mountain pine which flourished in these upward lands. The falcon returned twice, each time with a young hare in its talons. Tirtha set about a craft she had learned on the trail long since, rolling up stones under one of the trees to form a wall about a fire pit, the branches of the tree to break up any trail of smoke that might arise. She grubbed under the trees while the Falconer hunted the stream side, each bringing the driest sticks they could find for a fire large enough to broil the meat, which they ate eagerly. Then they allowed the flames to die down.

Tirtha went to the stream and along to a thicket. It was still light enough to see as she stripped off her trail-worn clothing, waded resolutely into cold water, which brought a gasp from her, and bathed, putting on fresh shirt and under-pants from her small supply, washing out those she had taken off, wringing them as dry as she could and returning to hang them not far from the warm stones of the fire's back wall. The Falconer watched her, then took up his own saddle bags, disappearing in turn to do likewise, she guessed.

It was good to feel clean of trail sweat and dust, and she had rubbed her body with the dried leaves of a scent herb—an affectation she seldom allowed herself, but which she had done now as a small celebration of triumph that they had actually done what she had been told so often could never be accomplished—come safely across the accursed mountains.

Wrapped in her cloak, she found herself once more listening. There were sounds here as there had not been in the twisted lands through which they had just passed. She could pick up life sparks of woods creatures about their night business. The falcon stirred on its perch, eyeing her with the same feral fires as appeared in the man's eyes upon occasion. She made no effort to touch its mind in her own imperfect fashion.

The bird was surely wholly his, one of the things which Tirtha and he could never share. Eat the same food they could, feel discomfort (though they did not reveal that to each other), perhaps share some of the same fears and dislikes, if not for the same reasons. But a barrier existed and always would.

Tirtha leaned forward and on impulse dropped into the very small flame before her a pinch of one of her herb packets. There was a puff of whitish smoke and then scent. She inhaled as deeply as she could, striving to draw it into the full expansion of her lungs. Tonight she must dream!

But she must not allow herself to be pulled into the same old vision. Rather now, while she was still desired and needed—a guide to the road ahead.

This lore she had had as a child from a Wise Woman, though she had never dared to use it before, in spite of the promises she had been given concerning its effectiveness. Because she must remain always in command of herself, she feared such aids to farseeing, if farseeing could be so summoned. Then, too, she had been alone and she had not known how long the visionary state would last or whether it would affect her in some other way. Tonight she had to discover what she could while she was not solitary. She inhaled a second time, feeling an odd lightness rising within her. This was not power—no, she could only hope that what summoned the vision could be induced to work in another way.

7

Tirtha enfolded herself in her cloak, having refused any more food, since what she desired was better accomplished fasting. Had she followed the proper ritual, she would have fasted for a full day while clearing her surface mind of all thought. Now she must take the Falconer into her confidence—what she practiced was the "witchery" he distrusted, but there was a need for it. Tirtha used flat and decisive words to settle the matter. After all he was an oathed shield man; thus what she did, unless it threatened them both, was beyond his questioning.

Already Tirtha floated in and out, half aware of their bare camp, half into gray nothingness. Then she slid entirely into the gray, like a feather or leaf tossed by air, without substance and with no control, though she tried firmly to keep her purpose to the fore of her mind.

No Hawkholme lay before her this time, though she emerged from nothingness into sharpening clarity. Before her, smoke trailed upward in rank, standing amid trampled earth beds of heat-withered or broken plants. She recognized some of those as sources of balms she well knew. Whoever had dwelt here had cultivated the gifts of earth.

The rankness of spilled blood was foul through the acrid stench of fire. There was another odor also—a sickening one. For a moment or two she thought perhaps this was Hawkholme after all, that she viewed it after the vengeance of Yvian's attack.

Only this was surely much smaller, even though she had never been granted a complete vision of Hawkholme in its full pride. No, this was not the remains of any great hall or lord's hold, rather more the garth of a small landholder.

A hound sprawled on the crushed herbs. A ragged wound had

ripped its side to bare the white arch of its rib cage. Beyond the dead beast lay another body, small, crumpled together, as if flung contemptuously aside. Because Tirtha knew that she was being shown all this for a reason of importance, she willed herself to approach the dead.

A child lay face down, her unbound dark hair swirled, mercifully hiding her features, but there was no mistaking the brutal usage which had been given that fragile broken body—discarded in death as a worthless bit of refuse. In Tirtha awoke a flame of deadly anger. She had seen much in past years of pain, death, and hardship; she had believed herself immune to easily-aroused feeling. Now some part of her, long hidden and buried, was aroused to life.

This dead child, she knew—perhaps by virtue of the drug that had awakened her talent to its utmost—had not been the only one slain. Within the fired building lay others, as hardly treated, as ruthlessly used and slain. There had been those here who had played with their victims, relishing the cruelty they employed—who might call themselves men but were no different within (save perhaps less strong and powerful) than the beast thing she and the Falconer had killed in the mountains.

Why vision had summoned her here, Tirtha could not tell. She strove to master her anger, to loose herself, that she might be guided into learning what meaning this held for her. For she did not believe that the single purpose was to warn her. There was another and far more powerful reason to summon her for a viewing of murder and ravishment.

She moved, not by her own volition, but as if she rode a mount she could not control. Past the burned-out house that compulsion carried her, on into a stone-walled field where a stand of young grain lay beaten into pulp in ragged paths as if riders had crossed and recrossed it. Riders—*hunters!*

That impression of a deadly hunt struck her full on. She could view those tracks and visualize the action that had taken place here. What prey had they ridden down?

The need that drew her, now drove her toward a pile of stones at one corner. A break in the wall about to be mended—those stones were piled ready to hand. Behind them, crouched in so narrow a space that Tirtha would not believe any body could exist there, was another child. Dead?

No! This one lived—with a mind filled by overwhelming horror and terror. The one in hiding had been driven near to the point of complete withdrawal and denial of life by what had happened, but there was still a faint spark of identity remaining.

Tirtha had asked guidance for her own purposes. It would seem that the knowledge she had sought was not of importance to whatever force she had so hazily called upon—but this was. She had been summoned, she was being used, and to the demand there could be no denial.

She opened her eyes upon the night, their handcup of fire, the Falconer seated cross-legged beside it. In his hands was the dagger-sword, its pommel beaming with a fierce, demanding light, his head downbent as he stared at the now living gem, bemused.

Out of her vision, she had brought urgency.

"We must go!"

His head jerked as if she had startled him out of a vision of his own. Tirtha was already on her feet, hurrying toward the picketed ponies. A full moon above provided brilliance stronger than she had ever seen, the better for the task that must be done.

"What is it?" Her companion was at her heels, his weapon in sheath.

Tirtha pivoted slowly, struggling to pick up the trace which must exist. Time might be against her. No! This duty was a part of her, as compelling as that other search had been through all the years, only much more immediate.

Fire! That smoke they had witnessed from the pass! That must be the place! She was suddenly certain.

"A garth they burned." She spoke out of her vision, not caring if he could not follow her thoughts. "It is there!"

Swiftly she loosed the mare, girthed on saddle pad. He did not question her, only followed her example, and the falcon on the saddle perch, mantled, raising wings, then took to the air, up and out into the dark. Perhaps the man had dispatched it without audible command.

They angled toward the west, yet farther south. Where the land opened, they went to a fast trot. As they rode, Tirtha gave a terse account of what she had envisioned. The Falconer listened without question; when she had done he made comment. "Raiders or some lordling's men who had reason to loot. This is a riven land." There was harsh distaste in his voice. For all their somber reclusivenss and their well-tested fighting ability, those of his race did not kill wantonly, nor ever amuse themselves with such nastiness as she knew had blasted the garth. Falconers dealt clean death when and if that were necessary, risking always their own lives in the doing. But for the rest, no man could ever declare that they were merciless barbarians, no matter how much the Witches of Estcarp disliked their private customs.

Down from the night sky spiraled the falcon, alighting on the saddle perch to face the man. Tirtha heard what sounded like sharp clicks of its beak. The Falconer turned his head.

"It is as you saw—the burning, the dead. There is no one there." She shook her head determinedly. "Not at the house, in the field. They hunted but they did not find. There is still life. If there is not" —she hesitated—"then I think it would be given me to know that there was no reason for us to go on."

He said nothing. Perhaps he thought that as a shield man there was no reason for him to contradict her. Still she believed that he thought her wrong—that only the dead awaited them.

It was graying for dawn when they picked up the odor of the burning and that sweet stench of death which was a part of it. Then they came to the edge of open land, and she saw before her a wall of logs deep set to make a barrier. This had not been a part of her vision; but just ahead of them a gate swung loose as if, for all their guard, those who dwelt here had relaxed vigilance for some reason, allowing entrance to the very wolves they prepared to defy.

Tirtha's mare snorted and shook her head vigorously, not liking the smell. But she did not resist when Tirtha urged her on, and with the Torgian trailing behind them on a lead rope, the two rode into this once guarded place.

Facing her stood the smoke-blackened ruins she had seen, the trampled garden. The fire had burned itself out. She could sight the dead hound, the other pitiful body beyond. The dead did not need them now; the living did.

Tirtha pulled rein, sending the mare circling to the left, away from the destroyed house. Yes, there was the stone wall—high here, built as part of that protection which had proved so futile. Another gate stood open as she pressed on into the field where signs of the chase were so deep printed.

Straight across pounded the mare at a harder pace than Tirtha had pushed her before. While they were still some distance from that neat pile of rocks, Tirtha pulled up, slid from her riding pad, and ran, throwing her cloak back across her shoulders lest it impede her speed.

As she went she mind-sought. Life essence—yes! They were still in time! She reached the neat pile of stones, looked around it. There was nothing wedged there! Tirtha swayed, so dismayed by the evidence of her eyes that she could almost believe she was again not here in body, but rather caught up still in sleep-vision.

Once more she sought mind touch. There *was* life essence, faint, wavering as if almost drained away—yet still here! Only she *saw* emptiness. Tirtha pulled away some of the stones—letting them thud outward into the field. Then she knelt to stretch forth both hands. Where her eyes could see nothing her hands felt what her vision had told her was there—a small body huddled into such confined space it would seem that there was no room for breath to enter the lungs of the compressed form she could feel.

She spoke over her shoulder to the Falconer as he joined her.

"Can you see . . . ?" she began.

His bird helm, easy to mark in this growing half-light, turned from side to side in denial.

"Then come here." She reached out, caught his hand, pulled it and him closer, dragging him down so that his fingers might tell him the truth. He jerked back, freeing himself from her grasp, and she could tell that he was aware of the same mystery.

"There—it is there, though we cannot see it!" She was triumphant.

"Witchery!" She heard the word as a half-whisper. Still he loosened stones with his claw, hurling them afar with his hand. Now the falcon perched on the wall to watch them, leaning forward to peer into the small space they uncovered, much as it had looked upon the knife-sword it had led her companion to find.

Slowly, carefully, Tirtha ran her hands along that body they were freeing though they could not see it. This was another thing she had read of in Lormt—the strength of a hallucination whereby one could hide safe from danger, though in the accounts she knew, such had consisted mainly of form-changing. To achieve complete invisibility was another matter of which she had not heard. Still, anything was possible with the Power. Who had hidden the child here so successfully?

By those marks in the field the hunters had pursued prey back and forth, played with a victim after a brutal and beastly fashion, prolonging the terrible fear of the one who had fled. A woman carrying a child—who had had something of the Talent brought perhaps to the highest level because of her fear for her own blood, who had managed to so conceal son or daughter and then had herself fallen prey to ravishers and murderers?

All Tirtha knew of such matters had firmly stated that any building of illusion was a weighty exercise, for which one needed time and knowledge of complicated ritual. Certainly there had been no such time granted the hunted here.

Cautiously, with the utmost care, because she could only use her hands to aid, Tirtha drew out the small body, held it against her so she felt the weight of an invisible head against her shoulder. The flesh she touched was very cold, and she quickly drew the edge of her cloak around it, the bulging of the material proving that indeed she held substance, not shadow. With fingertips she sought to examine the face, feeling against her own flesh a faint surge of breath, just as a faltering rhythm of heartbeat could be distinguished. How they might aid a child who remained invisible, she had no idea.

There was a sound from the falcon. The man's head whipped around, his helm tilted as he looked up at the bird and listened to the sounds uttered by the feathered scout. Then he turned to Tirtha, where she still knelt, cradling the child.

"The Brother can see it," he said quietly. "What witchery holds for us does not curtain his eyes. He says that it is not wounded, but in deep hiding within itself, that there is great fear in it."

Tirtha remembered other lore. Deep fear, terror could strike so into a mind that there would come afterwards no reawakening of intelligence. Had this small one retreated so far that they could not draw it back? She had some healing knowledge, that was so, but nothing to handle such a problem. In Estcarp this victim could be taken to one of the hospices set up by the Wise Women to be treated by those specially trained to seek out the inner essence of the mind, draw it carefully back once more. Even those trained to do so had failures when a case was too severe. She had nothing save the belief that she would not have envisioned the plight of the one she held unless that vision meant she could aid.

They could not remain here. The raiders had gone, yes, but that did not mean that their own small party might not be sighted. There was nowhere she might deliver what she held into safety; she must take the fear-bound child with her. For all her cultivated hardness, Tirtha recognized that truth.

The Falconer dropped his hand to the butt of his dart gun. Now the bird took off in the sky. Tirtha's uneasiness at remaining was obviously shared.

"There is no place for . . ." She indicated what she held. "We must take it with us."

She half expected a protest. Falconers knew nothing of children. They did not even own those they fathered. In their villages of women, men impregnated selected females, perhaps several of them, within a stated time, but they were never true fathers. When they were six, the male children went into the Eyrie, or they had in the old days—to be housed apart, trained by selected fighters who were old or maimed and unable to serve in the field. They had no true childhood, and it would seem that the custom served their way of life adequately. To be saddled not only with a child, but one invisible and perhaps catatonic, would be an experience none of his kind had faced before.

Yet he made no comment, only went for Tirtha's mare, bringing the pony to her. She loosed the throat latch of her cloak, wrapped its folds about the limp body of the child. She passed the bundle to the Falconer, mounted to accept it back. Then, with nearly the same speed with which they had come, they recrossed the field to pass by the ruins. To bury the dead—she nearly checked her horse by that other small body, then realized that her first charge was the child she carried and that their own safety might depend upon a swift withdrawal.

Back they rode into the forested hills; again the Falconer led. They went more slowly, while he took the precautions of the hunted, dismounting at times to draw a leafed branch over ground where they had left too plainly marked a trail, winding a way that took every advantage of the nature of the country and any cover offered.

The falcon made periodic flights, reporting back at intervals. Though the man did not translate for her any messages it brought, Tirtha guessed that they were in no immediate danger from any other travelers in this land.

In her hold the child lay unmoving, inert. She tried at intervals to break through the mind barrier terror had set, longing fiercely to know more, have the ability to help. There was, she feared, a very good chance that if the conscious mind was lost forever, the will to live might follow. Death would then ensue. Such an end might be merciful, but she knew she would fight for this life with all her strength.

They reached a place before noon that the Falconer appeared to believe spelled safety for a while, and there they halted. There was no water, but a tough growth of grass satisfied the ponies and the Torgian. There was a half-shelter formed by some rocks to conceal them from any but the most intent search.

Tirtha sat, holding the child across her knees. The small body, still invisible, which had felt so cold when she had first taken it up, was now warm—too warm. Her cautious hand brushed aside fine, sweat-dampened hair to rest on a forehead where fever heat burned. She located a small mouth, which hung a little open, was able to dribble into it some water from her saddle bottle. There came a faint gulping noise, the first hopeful sign she had received, and she eagerly gave her charge another drink.

At the same time her mind was busy. To break an ensorcelment as strong as this—no, she had not the power. On the other hand there were spells of the shape-changing kind that possessed their own time limit. She gritted her teeth against hot, hard words she had learned in her tramping, which could be a release for her frustration and anger.

Having done what he could to establish their camp, the Falconer returned to squat on his heels beside her, pulling off his helm as if he felt his sight too limited by its half-mask.

"What holds it so?" he asked.

"Illusion, I think." She could be sure of nothing. "It could have been carried there for hiding—you saw the tracks in the field—they were hunting someone. A mother might have possessed some talent. If she feared enough, she could have cast a spell to cover a child, hidden it away, even allowed herself to be taken. . . ."

"Those now of Karsten have no witchery," he pointed out. "And the Old Race . . ."

". . . were long since damned and doomed here, yes. But that is not to say that some of the old stock could not have remained in hiding. Also, we can wed with others and prove fruitful. Some of us have mated with the Sulcars who have no witchery in them, their power lying in their sea knowledge only. There is also Simon Tregarth, the outlander. He bedded with one of the Wise Council. They outlawed her for it, saying she was none of them but a traitor to their beliefs. Yet it is true that he had something of the talent, and neither did she lose hers for being wedded as they had sworn she would.

"Three children she had at one birthing, which was never known before. And all three have the Power—still have—for it is they who, they say, now lead the war in Escore and have opened that land again to the Old Race.

"Thus it could be that one of my blood bred half kin here, who had talent. If that lies within one, then it can be summoned when the need is great. Still . . ." She paused.

"Still—?" he persisted.

"Even Lormt held no such secret as this. No"—she shook her head vigorously—"I am of the Old Race, but I have very little talent. I am a healer of sorts, and I can use the vison-seeing. That is the best of my learning. As you know, I can sense life essence and communicate with animals after a limited fashion. But all that I know or have heard of illusion is that it must be summoned by ritual, and that is not done swiftly or with ease. I do not see how one pursued, as those tracks showed, could have so wrought to hide this child in that way."

"Then how else—?"

She had considered that all morning, striving to fit this and that answer to the same question. What was left was only a suspicion and one that seemed near impossible to believe, though she had long ago learned that the world was full of strange and awe-filling things.

"The child itself," Tirtha replied slowly. "In Estcarp, girl children were tested early—sometimes when they were no more than five or six. The power can be recognized even at so small a score of years. Here in Karsten there would be no such recognition. Suppose a child of the full old blood—even of mixed blood—was born with full power. Such a one might see the world differently from the way we view it, and that early enough so that it would learn to hide what it was and what power was in it or be taught to so hide it by one close to it. There would be no formal training, but if danger—fear—were great enough, that fear in itself might open a door to the full talent, such as comes usually only after a long training.

"Uncontrolled, frightened by great terror, then a child's instinct for survival might react as a protection, overriding the need for ritual that a trained Witch or Wise One would have as a barrier to betrayal through their own emotions."

He nodded. "What you have reasoned sounds sensible. I know little of witchery. But fear which is strong enough can give a man physical strength past his own potential; this I have seen. The will, which is the inner core of a man, if it is determined, can lead him to accomplish more than his fellows would believe possible. Given this talent you speak of and fear great enough—yes—it might be so. But if that is the truth, how can we then help? Is this one so lost within itself that it cannot be summoned forth again?"

"I do not know." Tirtha looked about her. If she was only sure they were safe here—perhaps the same drug that had sent her into the vision . . . But she could not herself seek within the child. That was an art far beyond her. "I know so little!" she burst out, her frustration banking down the anger that had been in her since she had gazed upon the work of those worse than brutes, making her voice rough and hard. "Mind healing or touching is a chancy thing."

"I wonder . . ." He rubbed one of the prongs of his claw along the side of his thin cheek as he might draw a finger. "The Brother in Feathers can see where we cannot; can he reach farther than we may hope to?"

"The falcon!" Tirtha stared at him in open amazement. "A bird . . ."

He frowned. "The Brothers in Feathers are more than birds. There is much they know that we do not. Some of their senses are far clearer and keener than ours. Remember, he saw the child, the illusion did not hold for him. Therefore, if the outward illusion does not blind him, perhaps the inner one might not either. Would it be harmful to try?"

Such a thought had not crossed her mind. However, with his intent stare on her now, she was forced to consider what he said. Such an attempt could cause no harm she could see. And perhaps—just perhaps—it might provide the key to unlock a stubborn door. Slowly she made answer, though her arms tightened involuntarily around the child as she did so. "I see no harm."

His lips twisted into a ghost of a smile. "But still little good? Well, let us see."

His claw flashed in the sun as he made a small gesture. The falcon took wing, flying from its perch to light on one of the rocks overshadowing Tirtha and her burden.

8

Tirtha sensed the flow of energy issuing from the bird. She would not have believed that from such a small body, and that of a species to which most of her kind assigned neither intelligence nor purpose, this summons—for summons it was—could come. Amazed, she stared at the falcon until she became aware of a second strain of energy joined with that which the black winged flyer controlled.

Even as a man might draw upon one of his fellows for strength and aid, so now did the falcon draw upon the Falconer.

She felt movement before she saw what her companion did; he was bringing forth his weapon of power. Holding it by the blade, he stretched out his hand so that the pommel knob hung steady above the child she held cradled in her arms. The dull gem took on life, within its heart a spark of fire glowed and grew. This was even more impressive and awesome than the light awakened from the rock wall in the valley. She felt now not only a tingle within hand and arm, but through her whole body.

Deliberately Tirtha calmed her mind, set herself to furthering, strengthening, if she could, what the bird summoned. She sensed energy speeding like a dart into flesh, striving to reach to the heart. It sought the very essence of the unseen child whose head rested against her breast.

In and in! The body in her arms twisted in a quick convulsion, so she must tighten her hold to a near bruising grip in order to keep the entranced one steady. There came a thin cry! Of pain? Terror? Perhaps both.

Still the bird raised power, the Falconer fed, the gem blazed.

They sought—surely they could go no deeper lest they carry death with them, while the one who was so sealed away fled their seeking!

Again the small body arched in Tirtha's arms. An invisible fist thudded against her breast, as the mewling cry grew stronger, so that she tried to feel for the mouth in a head that turned back and forth on her arm, to press her hand over it, to stifle any sound that might carry in these dangerous hills.

The gem pommel became so brilliant a ball that Tirtha dared not look directly at it. To whom had that belonged and what sorcery had gone into the forging of such a blade?

Then the falcon gave a croaking cry. Tirtha sensed that it was fast nearing the end of its strength. The body she held continued to struggle. She was able to sense now not just life, which had been near to the borderline of extinction, but overwhelming and terrible fear like a black cloud streaming upward about her to bemuse and stifle her own mind.

There was . . .

In her arms she held a child she could see. Its face was twisted, wrought into an ugly mask of terror so intense that perhaps sanity was lost. Tirtha drew on her healer's comfort, strove to pour down and in the quiet confidence which was a large part of that talent. She made herself picture a wide meadow, bright and open under the sun, a sky untroubled by even the smallest cloud. And through that open land, where fear was unknown, the child she held—yes, now that she could see it she could mind-picture it—ran in happy delight.

Tirtha fought to hold, refine that vision, let it fill her mind and flow outward.

"Nothing to fear." It was a growing rhythm, an unvoiced chant within her. "Safe—safe—no fear—safe."

She was no longer aware of either bird or man, only of the pitiful creature she so held and tried to comfort.

"Safe—no fear—safe."

The open meadow, the flowers she visioned growing to charm the eye with their color, to catch and hold even a most fleeting attention, the cloudless sky . . .

"Free—no fear."

The child's body, which had been stiff, taut, rigid in her hold, began to relax. Was this the relaxation of an outer covering of flesh that had been tried too far and too long—a withdrawal of life essence shocked out of its chosen hiding place? She could not tell.

"Safe—safe . . ." Tirtha strove to increase her flow of assurance, even as she would have with some injured animal, as she had times in the past tried so to heal or comfort.

Those eyes, which had been screwed so tightly shut, slowly opened. Dark gray they were, and with that in them which she recognized. This was blood of her people—the child was one of the Old Race.

The mouth, which had so shortly before shaped those woeful cries, opened a little. There came from between bitten lips, where flecks of dried blood had gathered in the corners to mark the small chin with a dribbled stain, a sigh.

Tirtha dared now to try to reach the child's mind directly. It was free and it was still sane! She had hardly dared hope for that!

With a joyful cry of her own, she embraced her charge closely, crooning a wordless murmur of relief and thanksgiving. Then there shot into her own mind, so sharp and clear it might have been spoken aloud by the child, a touch her fumbling attempts could never have produced.

"Gerik!" Fear flamed with that name as a fire might rise when fresh wood is laid onto its blaze.

"There is no Gerik here." She summoned words. To answer mind to mind was no skill of hers. "I am Tirtha and this . . ." For the first time she looked to the Falconer a little at a loss. She had never asked his name, knowing well that they did not yield such to those outside their own kind.

"I am Nirel, little brother," he answered for himself, speaking to the child. There were runnels of sweat down his face, gathering in large drops to drip from his chin. He had sometime during that battle swept off his helm, so the child who turned his head could see him plainly.

Little brother? Yes, it was a boy she held, which surprised her. For so legendary was it that such power of illusion could only be summoned by a woman, Tirtha had been certain she had carried out of that carnage a small girl. He was young, but perhaps older than his size would suggest, and his body, hardly covered by a short, tattered shiftlike garment, was brown and wiry. The dark hair of the Old Race had a slight wave where one longer lock fell across his forehead, near touching his level brows. What looked out of his eyes, though, was nothing of a young child.

"I am Alon." He spoke clearly. "I . . ." The shadow was back on his face, and his hands reached for the front of Tirtha's jerkin, clasped it so tightly that his nails cut into the soft leather.

"Where—?" He had turned his head against her, hiding his face so that his words came muffled.

Tirtha chose to ignore what might be the true meaning of that question.

"We are in the hills," she replied calmly.

His shoulders hunched a little as he gave one convulsive sob. He held to her for a long moment and then turned to look at both of them once more.

"They are all dead." It was no question but a statement of fact, and Tirtha found that she could answer only with the truth.

"We believe so."

"They said they came from Lord Honnor; they showed his seal rod to Lamer, and so the gate was opened. Then *he* laughed and . . ."

Again that body convulsed and Tirtha answered with a tighter grip. But it was the Falconer who leaned forward and spoke.

"Little Brother, there will come a time for blood payment. Until then, look to the days ahead, not the hours behind." Such words he might speak to one of his own kind and his own age. Tirtha felt a rising indignation. Did he believe that a small child could be so comforted, if comfort was what he intended by that somber advice.

Only it would appear that he was right, for Alon met him eye to eye. His small face wore an intent, serious look and there was almost the same communication between the two of them as existed between bird and man—one Tirtha could not even sense.

"You are a bird man," the boy said slowly. "And he—?"

He loosed his hold on Tirtha, raised a thin arm to point to the falcon who now looked as if it wished to sleep, its yellow eyes half closed, its wings tight held to its body.

"In his own tongue he is called Wind Warrior. He is a flock chief and . . ."

"One of the Learning," Alon said softly. He spoke directly to the bird.

"Brother in Feathers, you are a great fighter."

The falcon unlidded its eyes, gazed down, uttered a single small and very soft sound deep in its throat.

Now Alon turned his head once more to look directly up into Tirtha's face.

"You are—are like Yachne, no?" Again a shadow frown crossed his small face. "She has the Calling in her; you—you are different. But you are of the Blood."

Tirtha nodded. "Of the Blood, but one born in another place, kin-brother. I am from overmountain."

He had moved, not to free himself entirely from her hold, but rather to sit higher in it. She helped him so he could be more comfortable.

"Overmountain," he repeated. "But there is evil . . ." He glanced up, then stared at her. "No—the Dark ones—one can *feel* those. You are not of the Dark, kin-sister. Are you from the east where there is the clouding? Yachne has tried to read the throwing stones many times, but always there is the Dark between. There are the prowlers who come down from the hills, but they are not like Gerik"—his lips met tightly together for an instant—"for Gerik is a man, and he has chosen to serve the Dark of his free will!"

"Overmountain from Estcarp. There is little evil there in the way you know, kin-brother," Tirtha answered as gravely and with the same tone the Falconer had used. "But my kin were once of this land, and now I return for a purpose."

He nodded. His growing composure was far from childlike. She wondered if this was natural to him, or whether it had been born of the release of power that had sent him into hiding and so changed his mind, perhaps enlarging a talent. He seemed twice as old as he looked.

"There are such as Gerik patroling." He hitched himself even higher in her hold. "They will be watching, and they hate all of the Old Blood. We kept mine secret, yet somehow they knew."

The Falconer resheathed his strange weapon and put on his helm.

"Then it would seem that we must find a shelter better than this." He got to his feet, held out the wrist of his claw, and the falcon moved onto it.

Alon pushed out of Tirtha's hold, though she kept one hand on his shoulder to steady him. It was difficult to believe that the child who had been so limp and helpless when she had borne him here could now show such vigor. He wavered for a moment, then stood as tall and straight as his small body would allow, though he did not shake off her hand as the Falconer went to bring up their mounts.

Alon looked at the Torgian round-eyed and hesitatingly lifted his right hand. The beast snorted, moved toward the boy one step at a time as if puzzled and wary, the man loosing the leading rein to let it go free. The shaggy head of the horse dipped, it sniffed at the boy's palm, pawed at the ground, and then blew.

"He—he is different." Alon's gaze swung from horse to ponies, then back again.

"Yes. In Estcarp," Tirtha answered, "his kind are horses of war, and they are highly prized."

"He is alone." It was almost as if Alon had either not heard her or else that what she said meant little to him. "The one whom he served is dead; since then his days have been empty. But he will take me!" There was a sharp change in the boy's face. A smile, as bright as the sun Tirtha had imagined when she was pulling him out of this inner darkness, lighted it. There was an eagerness in his voice as both his hands tugged at the flowing forelock of the horse. "He accepts me!" It was as if something near too wondrous to believe had changed his world.

For the first time since she had traveled with him, Tirtha saw the Falconer smile and gained a dim idea of how different he might appear among his own kind. He caught Alon around the waist and swung the boy up to settle him in the empty saddle of the dead man's horse.

"Ride him well, little brother. As the Lady has said, his kind is not easily found."

Alon leaned forward to draw his hand down the curve of the

Torgian's neck, and the horse tossed its head, whickering, taking one or two small steps sidewise as if he were very pleased with both himself and his rider.

With them all to horse and the falcon settled on saddle perch, they headed back into the foothills. Tirtha watched the boy anxiously. Though she claimed hardness of spirit for herself and even in childhood had cultivated a shell to protect both her inner self and the feeling that some important destiny lay before her, she could not believe that so young a child might so quickly lose the remembrance of the raid and of how he had escaped from it.

Perhaps her first suspicion was right—the use of his power had released within him also an ability to accept things as they were. So, as the Falconer had suggested, Alon was able to look forward and not back—yet another protective measure which the talent brought to him without even his conscious willing.

They halted for nooning at a spring, for these foothills were well watered. The boy shared the last of their rations of crumbling journey cake, as they had not tried to hunt along the way. By questioning, they discovered that Alon's knowledge of the land eastward was limited to stories that had come through infrequent contact with either a single small market town to the south or from such travelers as the master of the holding had trusted enough to shelter overnight.

There was a Lord Honnor who claimed rule over part of the land, but, by all Alon's accounts, his hold was a precarious one, his title often in dispute, though he was a man of some honesty—for Karsten —and did his best for those loyal to him. The master of the garth had been one Parlan, not of the Old Race but with a dislike for the perilous life of the more fertile plains where there was almost constant warfare. He had brought his family clan into this foothill region trying to escape the constant raiding he had encountered during the past dozen years or more.

It was when he had been taken sick two tens of days back that the mastership of the garth itself had fallen on his nephew Dion. Parlan was old enough to have served in Pagar's force, being one of the garrison left behind when the fateful invasion of Estcarp had been ordered. A seasoned fighting man, he had suffered a crippling wound in the chaos that had followed the turning of the mountains, and had then taken a wife and the land his lord commander had offered, only to change his mind and move into the foothills when that lord commander himself was treacherously slain and his forces badly routed.

Alon's own relationship with Parlan and his family was apparently

not a close one. He had been added to the household when they had
left the plains, as a very young baby, and he had been told that he
was the only child of a kinsman who had been killed with the lord
commander, his mother slain in a resulting raid.

"It was Yachne who fostered me," he told them. "She—they were
all somewhat afraid of her, I think." He frowned a little. "And she
was not of their blood either. But she was a healer and she knew
many things—she taught the maidens weaving and the making of
dyes. So Parlan got fine prices for their work in the market. Also
. . ." He shook his head. "I do not know why, but he often came to
her when he was in trouble and she would sleep, or seem to. Then
when she wakened again, she would tell him things. But always she
sent me away when she did this, saying this must not be told or
understood by men. And when I asked her questions, she grew angry, though I cannot understand why."

"Because she dealt in witchery," returned the Falconer.

"And perhaps because she believed, as most do"—Tirtha herself
had only today revised her own beliefs in that direction—"that the
talent is only a gift for women."

"The talent?" Alon repeated. "When I was frightened, then—
what did I do? They said that they would have a hunt and that this
was a fair way to bring down their hare." He shivered. "Gerik's
shield man tossed me out into the field and I ran, and then . . .
then . . ." He looked questioningly to Tirtha. "I do not know what
happened. There was a dark place, but it was not of the evil, that I
know—rather it was like a house, strong-walled to hold me safe.
Somehow I found that and hid until I was called, and that calling I
could not stand against."

Tirtha found it ever more difficult to think of him as the child he
looked. Now she asked abruptly:

"How old are you, Alon?"

Again he frowned. "I do not know, for Yachne would not tell me.
I know"—he glanced disparagingly down at his own small body—
"that I am too small. Frith, who seemed close to me in age when we
were little, grew; he was near half a head the taller. They called me
'babe in arms' when they wished to tease me. It seems that I do not
look like the others. Even Sala who was only ten stood above me. I
think I can count for myself near twelve years since we came from
the plains."

Twelve years—perhaps more! Tirtha, startled, looked to the Falconer and read a trace of the same amazement on his face. The small

body she had carried was certainly that of a child who looked hardly half that toll of years. Perhaps there was more than the blood of her own race in this one. There were stories of strange matings to be read at Lormt. A long-lived elder race might well produce a child whose development was very slow and whose seeming childhood much prolonged. The Old Race was long lived, and they retained a semblance of late youth into scores of years, in fact until they were near death. But this very prolonged childhood was new to her.

Over the mountains from Escore—if the servants of the Dark had thus wandered, perhaps other blood had come also. It could be that Alon had less human blood in him than appearances warranted. If that were true, his self-caused retreat, even from sight, could well be a natural thing.

By evening they found a good camping place. There was a moss-and-turf-covered ledge projecting from a rise of ground, sided in part by an indentation that was close to a cave. Tirtha, seeing on the down side a covy of hares, loosed three arrows in close order and descended to pick up the bodies, while Alon, for the first time since he had mounted the Torgian, displayed fatigue, sitting on one of the saddles the Falconer had stripped from their beasts, hunching his shoulders against the rising evening wind. His scanty clothing certainly gave him little protection against it.

They pulled stones together and lighted a fire at the back of the half cave, broiling the joints of meat over it, to avidly eat dripping bits to which Tirtha added some of her powdered herbs. Comfortable warmth radiated from the back wall of stone. The Falconer rummaged in his saddle bags and brought out a pair of under-trousers which were far too large until they were tied around Alon's waist with a doubled cord, the legs turned up and laced tight. There were no boots to pull over them, but at least they kept the saddle pad from chafing the boy's inner thighs, which were already red. Tirtha covered the marks with salve before he drew on the improvised leggings.

He sat by the fire eating hungrily, wiping the grease from his fingers with a tuft of grass before he turned to the Falconer.

"Lord Nirel . . ."

"I am no lord, Little Brother," countered the other. "We do not use the lowland titles, we of the Eyrie." Then he paused, for he must be remembering, Tirtha knew with a flash of insight, that the Eyrie and its brotherhood had long since vanished.

"I think then," said Alon, with his head a little on one side, "that I shall call you Swordmaster Nirel, for you are surely one who is that.

But you wear more than one sword at your belt . . ." He pointed to the strange weapon. "And I have never seen the like of that one. Though Master Parlan had old comrades come now and then to visit with him, and many of them carried weapons which they cherished and in which they had great pride. What is that?"

The Falconer drew the dagger-sword. Now the gem in the pommel was darkly opaque—even the firelight could raise no gleams from its inner part. It might have been as dead as any lump of metal.

"I do not know, in truth, Little Brother. It is a gift from Wind Warrior, and it holds within it that which I do not understand." He extended it closer into the firelight so that the flame lit the inlays on its blade. "I think that it is not only very old, but that it is a thing of Power, perhaps even like the Axe of Volt."

It was apparent that Alon had never heard of that fabulous weapon. But now he held out a finger not to touch, but to sketch in the air just a little above, the symbols on the blade as he passed each one in a sweep from hilt to point.

"This picture"—he paused above one near the end of that line— "is like unto a thing which Yachne wore beneath her robe on a chain about her neck. It was a secret thing, I think. I only saw it the once, and she quickly hid it again. Did this come from overmountain, or is it falcon power?"

"The Falconers do not deal with any power," came a somewhat repressive answer. "Nor is this out of Estcarp, as far as I know. It must have been borne by one of Estcarp's enemies, for we found it where a mountain fall had trapped and killed those who were the invaders. Though why one of Karsten would have carried a thing they would have deemed cursed—that is also strange and hard to believe."

"Yes, it must be very old." Alon swept his hand up the length of the blade, this time toward the hilt, as if he could, by the very gesture, read something of what it was and for what purpose it must serve its possessor. "But it is not for the letting of blood—none has ever stained it."

He spoke with an authority that made them both stare. Then he gave a little self-conscious laugh. "If Yachne were here, I would have a clout across the mouth for speaking so. She did not like me to say what I knew, even when I knew it. But it is true. There is a feel to a thing that has killed; it clings to aught which has let blood. I do not sense it here. Yet in its way this is a weapon."

"Rather," Tirtha interrupted, "I would call it a key of sorts. For it was through this the Falconer brought you—or he and his falcon—brought you back to this world. It is a power thing, and it answers to them, whether they claim the talent or not."

Alon blinked. "In time it may do even more. I should have Yachne's learning, then perhaps I could take it in my hands and see. It is strange, but inside me now I feel very different, as if there is something before me that is all new, standing ready for me to discover it. I . . . I am no longer Alon, the always-babe, but another—one I do not yet know, and yet whom I must speedily learn."

9

For three days they drifted westward. There were no trails in the foothills, though once or twice they chanced upon indications that they did not travel through a deserted country. There were signs of old campfires, unhidden, and hoof prints of horses stitched soft earth. Still the falcon, scouting aloft, reported only native animals.

The last of the supplies they had brought overmountain were gone. Tirtha's bow kept them in meat. There must have been little hunting hereabouts for years, since the pronghorns and the hares were easy to bring down. Alon also possessed knowledge of the wild. He triumphantly dug up fat roots which, when roasted in the fire, broke apart to be tasty and filling.

More and more the older two came to accept Alon as an equal in spite of his childish appearance. Tirtha's careful questioning produced more of his relationship with Yachne—plainly a Wise Woman of such talent as would have placed her high in Estcarp.

"She was"—Alon frowned slightly as he tended the fire on their third night of encampment—"not of the kin Parlan claimed, nor was she, I am sure, even of the blood they knew. She had been many years with his household, for she came with his mother when she was a girl first handfasted to his father. She was old, yet always she looked the same without change. And it was she who went alone to find me when I was left kinless, bringing me back to the household. Also"—his eyes darkened oddly, as if to hide part of his thoughts—"she was not there when Gerik came. She had gone seeking a rare herb which she thought would draw Parlan out of his fever, or so she said. Had she been within the walls I do not think Gerik could have entered. Yachne"—he nodded, as if to underline the importance of what he said—"could read the Dark Ones. Twice she told Parlan to send away men who came to him seeking shelter, and one of them was a long-time comrade he would have trusted."

"And this garth master always listened to her advice?" the Falconer asked.

Alon nodded once more. "Always. I think he was even a little afraid of her. Not that she would do him or his any harm, but because she knew things that he did not understand. Men always seem to fear what they cannot find a direct reason for." Again it was as if someone far older sat there, licking grease from his fingers, wearing the outward appearance of a child who must be protected from the rigors of the world. If Tirtha closed her eyes and listened only to his speech, she built up in her mind a far different Alon, always to be slightly startled when she looked directly at the boy again.

"She was—is a Wise Woman," Tirtha said now. "Such are always to be found among our people. But if she returns and finds the garth as it now is, will she follow us?"

One possessing the Power could well use the trance (as she herself had attempted) and trail them as easily as if they had left all manner of open markings behind. She saw the Falconer stir. His frown was twice as heavy as Alon's had been. This man could accept her, Tirtha, since she had dealt with him after the established custom, claimed his services by open bargain. But that he might ride with a true Wise Woman whom his kind held close to hatred—no. Nor would she herself welcome such a one who might read her and her mission as easily as one would understand a fair-written scroll.

For a long moment Alon apparently considered her question, his head a little atilt in the same fashion as the bird would hold *his* feathered crest when appealed to. Then, slowly, he shifted his gaze, past Tirtha, past the fire, out into the dark.

"I do not feel her," he said simply. "When I try, there is nothingness. Yet I do not think she is dead. Perhaps, knowing that the garth is gone, she has followed some plan of her own. She is a secret person." Now he looked back to Tirtha. "I could tell many things about other of Parlan's people. I knew when they feared, or were happy over some matter, or when they were about to sicken. But with Yachne you did not know. There was always a barred door past which you did not go. I think that she aided Parlan not because she held any liking within her for his clan, but rather as if there rested between them a debt she was paying. Perhaps it was so with me also. Though I also believe that she found in me some future use . . ." He appeared now to be thinking aloud rather than trying to answer any of Tirtha's yet unspoken questions, turning over ideas which had long puzzled him.

"You would know if she were near?" The Falconer asked that sharply, in a tone that was meant to arouse, bring a quick answer.

"Yes. Even if I could not find her directly, I would mind-touch her inner wall."

"Good enough. I think"—the man regarded the boy measuringly, those odd yellow sparks plain in his eyes,—"that you will tell us if you sense such." He might have meant that for a question, but it came forth more as an order.

"Yes." Alon's answer was brief. Tirtha, at that moment, was in two minds whether they could rely upon it or not. She knew that there was nothing of the Dark in this child. Still, that did not mean that he would consider himself committed to their own quest. They might claim a debt for saving his life but she had no wish to do so. Those who weighed and balanced such acts were tarnished by the doing. One gave aid freely when it was necessary. There was to be no payment returned, save by the desire of the debtor. In so much, in spite of all the hardness of her life, she held to the ways into which she had been born. Nor did she believe that the Falconer would argue differently. The sword-oath he had taken made his road hers as long as their bargain held.

She shifted restlessly. To head on guideless, as they had been doing, was folly; she must know more concerning the direction in which their goal lay. In order to do that, she must dream or else evoke another trance. Only such dreams had eluded her now for days. Her sleep was deep and heavy at night. If she had walked in strange ways, she carried no memories back into waking. To try once more the herb-induced trance, with perhaps this Yachne somewhere about . . . The entranced one was always vulnerable. She had been reckless when she had attempted it before and certainly she had not been in command, for she had not been led to Hawkholme—rather to Alon.

Tirtha had come to suspect that it had been the force of the power Alon had employed without willing it that had drawn her own talent and that led them to the garth. Any gift so much greater than her own small one could bend her to another's will when she was in the disembodied state. Also, Alon had spoken of the Dark spreading eastward. To be caught by a strong evil will . . .

Yet to continue to wander aimlessly—that achieved nothing. She looked to the boy across the fire now, her eyes narrowed a little. There was one way—yet she shrank from discussing it, from even considering it. All her life she had fought for her independence, for the ability to order her own existence as much as any living creature might in an uncertain world. To surrender in even this need came very hard. She looked down at her calloused brown hands, clutched so tightly on a fold of her cloak that her knuckles stood in sharp relief. Will fought need within her until at last that same common sense which she had clung to during all her plans triumphed.

"I must use the trance." She spoke as sharply as the Falconer had done in his questioning of Alon. "That need may not be delayed any longer. I seek guides, and those I can only gain in that fashion. But one entranced, without protection, is in danger. My—my talent is limited. Therefore, when I go seeking, there could well be those of greater power to take and bind me to their will."

The Falconer's frown was dark, his mouth a straight slash across his face. Tirtha knew that with every word she uttered, she aroused opposition in him, brought to the fore all the dislike he had for such as she was. Only his oath bound him, but in that she had a foundation. Alon was watching her with a similar intent stare, but with none of the resentment that the Falconer radiated. His attitude was one of excitement and interest, such as any ordinary boy might show before a feat of action.

"I need your help." Those were the hardest four words she remembered uttering in years.

The Falconer made a quick gesture of repudiation, using his claw as if, with that symbol of grim loss, such a negation of what she had asked was thereby made the stronger. Alon, however, nodded briskly.

Now she looked directly to the man. "This is a thing you wish no part of, that I know. It is not bound within your oath." In that much she would yield to him. "But I have seen what you and your bird brother can do, and so I ask of you, not aid in my going forth, but another kind of help—protection against what might well net me while I am in that other state."

It was Alon who answered her and not the Falconer, and he did not speak to her but to the man.

"Swordmaster, this Lady asks of you protection. She says that you are not oath-bound to give it after the fashion in which she must now have it. Perhaps that is so. I know of sword oaths and shield men only what I have heard in tales and accounts of the old wars and troubles. Perhaps it *is* against your own beliefs that you do such a thing, but this is not of the Dark. Therefore a man does not break his innermost allegiance if he follows a path that helps, not harms. I do not know how great an aide I can be in such a matter." He now addressed Tirtha directly. "I think there is much, very much, that I must learn concerning myself. But what I have now"—he held out his hands as if he were offering her something as invisible as he himself had been when they first found him—"is at your service." Once more his eyes swung to the Falconer as if he waited.

The man had drawn from its sheath the weapon of power, then rammed it back with savage force. His rage, controlled with an icy strength, was visible to them both. He spoke as if he would bite each word drawn from him and answered harshly.

"I hold not with witchery. But also I am indeed oath-bound, though you"—he looked flame-eyed at Tirtha—"have said that in this that is not so. However, the boy is right—one does not give half oaths if one is of the blood. What would you have of me?"

She felt no elation. To have him believe that she had in a manner forced this might even endanger what she would do. For their wills must be united lest there be an opening for the Dark to twist one against the other. Tirtha leaned forward to pinch up dust, as much as she could hold between her thumb and forefinger, her eyes on him rather than on what she did. She saw his gaze narrow.

"Twenty days we agreed. However, if I will it and say I am now satisfied, then our bargain is dissolved even as . . ." Her hand raised, about to toss what she held into the air.

He moved the swifter. His fingers imprisoned her wrist in a hard grip, holding her hand fast so that she might not loose the dust and so break their bargain. She did not believe that it was altogether the firelight that made his face seem flushed. Surely his eyes were fully alive with anger.

"Twenty days I said, and in all ways I do my duty—on shield oath."

"It must be done willingly." She disliked this inner struggle between them, wanting none of it. Let him ride off and be rid of her and all witchery. "For one to hold back even in thought will open doors. I do not know what may threaten, only this is a dangerous land. What I would do is as perilous as if I rode disarmed into an outlaw camp. Help—must—be—given—willingly."

He dropped his hold on her, settled back. "You know best your needs," he returned tonelessly. "I shall endeavor to aid as you wish. What is it you desire of us?"

"I must go again out of my body," Tirtha said deliberately and slowly. "Perhaps that power, which you and the feathered brother share and which Alon has a portion of, can in a manner follow me and so protect my return road so that none else, or no alien will, can make of me a tool or a weapon."

"Very well." He turned his head a fraction, gave one of those small chirruping calls which summoned the falcon. The bird perched on his claw wrist where it rested on his knee.

"I cannot tell you against what or how you shall stand guard," she continued. "Nor do I know if this thing is even possible. But fasten your minds upon the wish that I may succeed in what I strive to do. I hunt a guide to Hawkholme that we may head overland to where it once stood. Keep in your minds that name and the wish that I, in vision, may travel swift and sure over the countryside between where we are and that place. This"—she lifted her hands a little—"is all I can ask, for I do not know how else to bind us together."

"Go, we shall follow." It was not the Falconer who had given that firm promise, rather the boy.

Tirtha took from her belt pouch the potent herb and tossed it into the fire. She saw the Falconer again draw his weapon of power, drive the point of the blade into the earth before him. She leaned forward and inhaled deeply the smoke which brought with it a strong smell of spice and other goodly odors.

There was no going into dark this time. Rather she was enveloped by a blaze of blue light so strong that she nearly retreated, then warmth and strength reached out to surround her. She moved as firmly and with such purpose as she might have walked on a road in Estcarp.

The light accompanied her. She looked up to see a globe of blue (the blazing pommel of the weapon?) spinning with her into the place of otherness. Then that light began to fade as she moved on into a grayness.

Though Tirtha had no impression of foot touching ground, there was land about her, solid looking and as real as any they had covered in their passage through the foothills. The darkness of trees, massed together, arose on one hand, while to the right stood a bare escarpment of rock across which ran a notable vein of black. This was one of the marks to remember, that much Tirtha understood.

The veined wall began to sink lower and lower into the earth as she left the heights behind. Now that distinguishing sable marking disappeared; it was only a ridge of rock she followed.

Hawkholme—even as she had told the others to do, so did she now hold that name firmly in mind. Her one fear was that she might be whirled into the repetition of her old dream and not learn the way, only arrive within that hold, to relive once more the final action.

Tirtha was out of the hills. Open country lay beyond and to her right. To her left the wood thickened into a forest, a growth so tangled that she did not believe anyone could force a pathway through. When she turned her head slightly to view it, she saw a flickering movement that was stealthy and yet continuous. Within that screen of entwined limbs and vines and brush, something paced at her own speed, spied upon her.

She caught glimpses now and then of a pallid grayness but with no distinct form, which slid easily in and out, the thickness of the wood offering it no opposition. Tirtha would have kept to the open, yet what she had summoned up by her will drew her toward the wood in spite of misgivings.

Always that which paced there watched. Tirtha sensed a malignant threat, but she determined not to try to learn more. All her concentration must be centered on reaching Hawkholme.

Even as she set her will so determinedly, Tirtha turned a fraction to head straight for the wood. Here the underbrush appeared less interwoven. There were faint indications that there had once been an opening, that perhaps a long overgrown road had run in this direction. The lurker was still there, yet it did not manifest itself to meet her, rather it followed the same procedure, heading into the undergrowth parallel to her own path.

At intervals the old road was more open. She sighted once or twice a tall stone set on end, as if to mark her path. There were other objects farther back, emitting a pale and ghostly light. She sensed essences there of things that were totally alien, rooted or imprisoned where they stood. Against these the girl hurriedly raised mind barriers, for she felt the touch of a demanding desire reaching for her.

This wood was a place of menace. Even were she here in body and not just in essence, she would have found it so, that she knew. Yet what she sought lay beyond it, and there was no escaping the journey.

How long it would take to traverse the sinister forest, she had no way of knowing. Tirtha had the impression that such a journey was no short span.

However, there came at last an end, where the overgrown trail opened again on meadow land. Here were fields which had once been walled, those stone barriers crumbling now, yet their lines plain to read. Through them curled a stream nearly of a size to be proclaimed a river. On the other side of that . . .

A vast surge of emotion, which she could not define, gathered within her, such as she had never felt before. Even from afar she could see that the defenses the builders of this hold had planned had failed in the end. Strong walled towers, a mighty keep had been raised upon a mound, at the foot of which washed a side channel of the river which had been diverted to ring around the hold. There were the splintered remains of a bridge—now only broken timbers—across a stretch of water to the gap that formed the entrance.

In all, this was a larger and more formidable hold than she had thought, although the huge hall of her dreams had argued it was part of a major building. The clan that had wrought it must have been a strong and well numbered one—and one with enemies, for the whole scene before her suggested that defense had been highly important.

Tirtha had found her goal. Now she deliberately set about relaxing her will—that will which was still bearing her onward toward the ruin. There was no need to travel farther.

The blow came like a blast of winter's wind against an unclad body. Deep and numbling cold cut at her. Tirtha had not believed pain could be felt by one in her present state. How wrong this thing out of nowhere was proving her! She fought, strove to free herself from that agonizing icy horror which battled to keep her prisoner. Now, her will cried out, now—if you can hear me, sense me, aid me —bring what power you have to draw me back!

Had the other two indeed followed her, did they know that she had been so taken? If she had no aid, she was lost, for that cold ate into her will, tearing it apart as a wild wind shreds a cloud.

"Come!"

She could not cry that aloud, but her whole self shaped itself into that plea. Was she being driven back into the same limbo that had held Alon when they found him?

Warmth—a faint glow of warmth. The cold pressed, but there was warmth, and somehow she could draw it to her little by little, hoard it within to keep cold and death at bay. The strand of warmth gave an upward surge, grew stronger.

The cold had reached for her, had sought to compel her onward toward the ruin just when she had striven to break the compulsion she had used to bring her here. It wanted her inside. Now she wavered—if an essence could waver. The drag forward, the chilling against the warmth being fed into her. Her will awoke from the effects of that first, numbing, near-fatal blow. Back—she fastened not on Hawkholme, rather on her memory of their camp.

Think of Alon—the warmth grew! The Falconer—a thread more of freedom gave her strength; the Falconer—it was his face that filled her thoughts now—a face bearing a terrible set concentration like a mask laid over the man she had grown to accept as a trail comrade. Within his eyes those yellow fires flared high. She could see only those eyes and the fires in them—warmth against the cold—the OTHER who willed her to Hawkholme in a state which it could use. Yes, warmth!

Fire rose about her; tongues of blue flame formed a defense wall. Abruptly the assault of the cold ceased. The fires lingered for a moment, died, and she was in the dark.

Rain—she lay out in the rain—water ran down her face, into her open mouth. She heard hurried breathing, fast, shallow, such as a near-spent runner might have. She opened her eyes—there was a blaze of half light around her head, so that she quickly closed them again, feeling that somehow she had been cut adrift and caught up in something that she could never hope to either escape or control.

"Tirtha, Tirtha!" A call, faint at first and then very strong. She was once more aware of her body, of stiffness and pain. The warmth that had aided her return to life slowly traveled from her head down her entire length.

"Tirtha!"

She dared to open her eyes once again. There was Alon's face, one side of it strangely blue. His eyes held fear; then it faded and he smiled—laughed—as if a burden had been lifted from him.

Tirtha saw that other form kneeling by her, in his hands the sword, tight gripped, its pommel ablaze and the blue light bathing her from head to foot. Increasing strength followed the warmth, flowing into an emptiness she had not realized was there until it was refilled. Cautiously she lifted her head. Almost instantly an arm was thrust beneath her shoulders, bracing her higher. She felt the small, chill touch of that claw against her cheek for just an instant.

Alon squatted on his heels directly before her, his expression one of eagerness. The Falconer, because he supported her, she could not clearly see. He had laid aside the sword. Its output of energy had faded; there was only the faintest glow from it now.

"I—am—back." Her lips, as they shaped those words, were stiff. In her own ears her voice sounded hardly more than a whisper. "You brought me back."

For it was from the two of them—no, the three (she must not forget the feathered brother she had sensed as part of her rescue)— had come the warmth, generated within themselves to combat what had lain in wait for her at Hawkholme.

Lain in wait? Tirtha for the first time thought clearly. She had not only the ruin to find, but there was an unknown terror there—one determined to have what? That which she sought herself and still could not name? Logic told her that that might well be the truth. So . . .

She moved her head, her shoulders a little, though she did not try as yet to pull free from the Falconer's support. Perhaps she needed that strong arm behind her to strengthen her—even to remind her— of what she must say to these two, of the decision that was hers to make and about which there could be no choice, for the very honor of the Hawk.

"You found the way?" Before she could speak, Alon's question came.

"I found the way."

"Then we can go." He glanced over his shoulder as if he were ready to saddle and ride at once.

"Not 'we'." Tirtha had herself in hand now. "This is my quest only." She looked directly to the Falconer. "I release you—take Alon. There are those overmountain who will give him shelter—the Tregarths—for they know that power does not always run in the same channels. From here I ride alone."

He regarded her with that same level and angry glance he had worn before when she would have broken their bond in full ceremony.

"There are twenty days—no less."

Tirtha sat upright, and he moved away from her quietly. The falcon gave one of its soft cries and fluttered to his claw wrist.

"I lead no one into that. . . ." she declared sharply in return, determined this time to have *her* will in the matter.

10

Yet strong as she thought herself to be, Tirtha did not have her way. The Falconer was stubborn, determined to fulfill his bargain. Though she ordered him twice to use that sense of duty by taking Alon overmountain, swearing that she would be satisfied, that this would set the balance straight between them, he refused. Tirtha wondered if she must slip away from her companions, only she could not be sure whether the stubborn man would not attempt to track her. It was Alon who confirmed that suspicion when they were alone the next morning, the Falconer having taken the water bottles down to the stream.

"He is single-minded and that rides hard with him," Alon observed. "These bird men are trained to what they believe is their duty. Thus he would pursue it and you to the end. You cannot shake us off, Lady." He smiled and gave a small laugh.

Tirtha was not to be beguiled from her own sense of right. "There is danger waiting at Hawkholme. Did that not already strike at me?"

"And did you not then beat it?" he interrupted. "Yes, it waits, but *you* do not draw back because of it. Neither shall this Swordmaster allow any foreboding to lessen his intent. Nor"—he paused for a second or two before he continued—"shall I. There is in me"—his hands went to heart level at his breast, touching the wrinkled smock Tirtha had washed in a stream—"that I must learn to master and live with. Yachne would not teach me. Did she," his face screwed up into a frown, *"fear* me?" He asked that not of Tirtha but of himself, as the girl was well aware. "Yet there was much of the power in her —one could feel it always. And I am not Wise. I am not—what then *am* I?" Again he spoke to Tirtha. "Have you seen my like before? They tell me many tales of Estcarp—that the old knowledge was treasured there, not lost, forgotten by the Old Race as it was here."

Tirtha made fast the latching of her saddlebag. "I have not seen any male before who has commanded the Power. The Witches who rule in the north say such a thing is unnatural, and therefore perhaps of the Dark."

Alon was on his feet in one supple movement, to stand staring at her, wide-eyed.

"I am not . . ." His protest came sharp and quick.

"Do you think that I do not know that? The Dark Ones cannot hide what they are to any of our blood. Also there is one man, Simon Tregarth, who has something of the talent. However, he is not of our blood, but an outlander who came through one of the Gates. It is also true that his two sons command strange forces, and they carried them and their Witch sister westward into Escore so that they broke the old curse to open that land to all of our race again.

"Though perhaps to no peaceful purpose, for there were many evils loose there, and now they war. Those of the Old Race, who followed the Tregarth calling to the east, fight against many Dark perils. There have been scores of stories during the past few years, perhaps twisted in the telling as such often are. Still we hear of battles won and lost, a country rent by the will of things unlike human kind. It could be that Escore blood has ventured westward here." She sat with her hands clasped loosely together studying Alon measuringly.

"You said that you were son to one this Parlan knew," she continued.

"I said"—he was quick to correct her—"that that was what was told me. The truth is that Yachne brought me to Parlan's clan and told such a tale. So I was accepted, for the man she named as my father was blood-brother by sword oath to Parlan—and it was true he was dead, his lady having vanished also after the battle, and was thought to be slain during the retreat that followed. That was Yachne's story, but"—he drew a deep, long breath—"can one believe it? There are the Gates. Those I have heard of—even of Tregarth's coming—and of that which the Kolders used when they entered this world and strove to make it theirs. Could it be that I am also such an outlander?"

His eyes were large, wide open, and there was that same eagerness in his face which he had shown the night before when she had asked of them their aid in farseeing.

"You have the look of the Old Race outwardly," Tirtha observed. "Yet you have also power—and the measurement of how much is something I cannot make. I have only a scrap of the talent. I can heal a little; I can farsee when entranced; and I can dream. I am not your Yachne. Also perhaps I am now one who is walking straight into such danger as cannot be reckoned."

"Still you must go to the Hawkholme," he said slowly, and she did not need the ability to read minds to guess that he longed to ask her the reason for this journey.

Odder still was the feeling within her that, for the first time, she wished to share her secret. As if this small boy, with his oddly mature speech and apparent understanding, had a full right to know what had driven her for so long. However, there was no time for such a sharing, even if she had been willing to break the cautious silence of years, for the Falconer returned at a pace quick enough to set the bottles he carried swinging from his claw, his hand on the butt of his dart gun.

"We ride." He swung past them to where the ponies and the Torgian were picketed, making it plain that he meant a hasty departure. Tirtha and Alon asked no questions, rather hastened to saddle their mounts. When the Falconer took the lead, he swung north, leaving the stream, holding his pony to a trot that was the best pace for such rough country.

Tirtha pulled level with him. "What have you seen?"

"We may have escaped notice." He had resumed his helm and now the falcon took wing, ascending into the sky in ever widening circles. "But there were fresh tracks on the other side of the stream."

She thought furiously. What she had done the night before, drawing the other two into it also? If there were any hereabouts with the faintest trace of talent, they would have been alerted as quickly as if she had purposely marked a plain back trail or set a signal fire. Perhaps her action had been foolhardy, wildly reckless.

"Outlaws?" she asked. Most drifting through this country would certainly be men from the plains, not those generally receptive to whispers of the Power. Their passing would be by chance only.

He shrugged. "What can one read from tracks in the mud? There were two shod horses of a larger breed—the rest were ponies. A party of six I would say. They headed south and east."

South and east—that was the direction they themselves must take. Tirtha had sensed in her trance journey that what she sought was not too far distant. Perhaps that ridge with its black veining might be only a day's journey on. However, if they had to detour, it would add to the leagues of travel while their supplies were very low, and they might not have time to hunt or garner any fresh spring plants.

"How long since, do you believe?" she asked.

"Since sunrise."

His curt answer offered a little relief. Dared she believe that what she had wrought last night had nothing to do with this near meeting? The evidence could point to another camp not too far away—or maybe pursuit! This Gerik—what motive could drive him to follow them? Tirtha could think of one lure—Alon. If the outlaw had guessed that one of the Old Race with unusual powers had slipped through his fingers at the massacre—would that be prod enough to set him following? Gerik—who was he? Was he an outlaw? Or shield man of some ambitious noble now raiding and fighting over the remnants of Karsten? She waved to Alon, bringing him forward until the three of them rode abreast.

"Who is Gerik? Does some other stand behind him?" She shot the questions quickly, saw the Falconer turn his head as if he understood the line her thoughts had taken.

"He is a raider," Alon answered slowly, "who has come only in the past year into this country. His men—they are . . ." The boy's face was pale, he moistened his lips with tongue tip. Tirtha knew well that she was forcing him back to memories that he had been setting firmly behind him. Still they must know all they could.

"His men . . ." Alon straightened a little in the large saddle. One of his hands rested against the Torgian's neck as if he drew strength and courage from contact with the animal. "They are . . ." He turned his head farther to look directly at Tirtha and the Falconer. "I know it now." There was a quick lift in his voice. "I thought that they were only what Parlan called the scum—those blank shields no lord would allow to ride under his banner, murderers and worse as some of them were. Only now I understand—there was a real Dark One among them!"

Tirtha's hold on the reins tightened, and her mare near came to a halt. The Falconer's hand, which had hovered near his dart gun ever since they had ridden forth, closed upon its butt.

"And Gerik—he was the one?" Somehow Tirtha kept her voice steady.

Alon shook his head. "I am not sure. Only that he is evil, but . . . No, I do not think that he is anything but a man, a true man, though there was in him . . ." His puzzlement was becoming distress. "When they hunted me, I was too afraid. Now that I am here and know more, I realize that I feared not death alone—though that was a part of it—but something beyond, which was worse."

"Could they have learned"—the Falconer's mind followed the same path Tirtha's had chanced upon—"that you held control over Power?"

"I do not know, but then I did not know it myself. It was the fear of them that, I think, broke some barrier in me."

"There were times in the past when barriers against power could be and were induced in children." Again Tirtha recalled her researching at Lormt, which had sometimes wandered into side lanes away from the main search she had gone there to make. "Perhaps it was so with you, Alon."

His distress was open to read. "Then could it have been *me* Gerik sought? Did I then bring the death—the . . ."

"No." Only the Falconer's mouth could be seen below the half mask of his helm. It was set and stern. "Do not think that is so, Little Brother. This Gerik was a raider, and by the looks of it, that garth was worth plundering. Also he may have had some old quarrel with the clan master."

Alon's face cleared a little. "He had with him a man whom Parlan had warned off two moons ago, Yachne telling him that the man was dangerous, even though he had come with a message from Lord Honnor, and that was a true message as we learned later. The stranger had been with my lord for a full twelve moons and served him well. It was after that Parlan fell ill, and Yachne went forth to hunt what would relieve him. But the same man rode with Gerik, I saw his face clearly. He was not of the Dark, the full Dark."

"But you have said at least another was," Tirtha persisted. "What manner of man was he?"

Again Alon's face was haunted. "I cannot tell. I do not remember, truly I do not. I only know that there were some who would hunt me in the meadow and that they wanted to . . ." His voice broke, and he dropped the reins, raising his hands to cover his face.

Tirtha was quick to understand. "Put it from your mind. If it is meant that you should remember, then it will come to you at the proper time. Do not seek it now."

He dropped his hands again. Once more that shadow of an age beyond his stature and his outward appearance crossed his face.

"I shall not seek such inner hiding again." That came as a promise and a firm one. "But I do not have full memory either. Perhaps, as you say, that shall come to me."

Tirtha looked to the Falconer. "Gerik seeks us, do you think?"

His head tilted back a little on his shoulders, and he did not answer her. The bird was winging in, settling on its perch. Once more she listened to the twittering exchange between the two of them. Then the man turned from the feathered scout to speak to them both.

"There is a party moving slowly southward. There are six, and one of them is strange." He hesitated. "My brother cannot explain in what manner save that, though this one wears the appearance of a man, within the body's shell, he is not as we are. Still neither is he Kolder nor one of the dead-controlled who once served Kolder. For that breed is well known to us of the Eyrie that was. This is something else, and it is wrong."

"Out of Escore?" Ever since their encounter with the thing in the night, Tirtha had been alert for any other evidence that the monsters said to run with evil in the west were patroling into this country. The wildness of this torn land, the chaos into which its people had been plunged, both reasons might well draw evil. The Dark reveled in such circumstances by all the old accounts.

Or—suddenly another thought crossed her mind—what of that which she had encountered, the presence manifesting itself as freezing cold, at Hawkholme. Could that also summon? If so, she must not lead her companions there. Though she did not realize it at that moment, Tirtha was glancing hurriedly from side to side as might a hunted one seeking some path of escape.

"There is something. . . ." Alon's hesitant voice barely broke through her preoccupation with her own alarm, but his next words did. "Lady, you carry a sword and on it there is a symbol. . . ."

She must have centered her gaze on him so suddenly and sharply that she disconcerted him a little, for he faltered, and it was the Falconer who cut in with a question before she could speak.

"What is this about a symbol, Little Brother? The Lady is Head of Hawkholme, the last of her blood. What she carries is the House sword. What do you know of that?"

"You are a Falconer, Swordmaster, and your bird rides with you," Alon replied. "But the bird which is like unto that on this Lady's sword, that I have also seen—and before our meeting."

"Where?" Tirtha demanded. On some piece of loot taken at the fall of the hold, tossed about from one thief to another through the years?

"There was another man who came just before the Moon of the

Ice Dragon, when the thick snows fell and closed all the mountain ways. He guested with Parlan for ten days, exchanged his mount for another. On his left hand he wore a ring of metal, which was not gold nor silver, but rather it had a reddish look, and it bore a carving like that on your sword hilt. He had the habit of playing with it as he talked, turning it around and around on his finger, and so one noted it."

"What was his name?" Tirtha demanded.

"He gave it as Ettin and said that he was a blank shield from past service with the Borderers, one who thought of returning to Karsten. He . . ." Alon's puzzled look was back. "I do not think he was of the Old Race, for he was fair of hair and had blue eyes."

At the sound of that name, Tirtha had drawn so sharp a breath that she realized she had caught the attention of the Falconer. The dead man they had found who had worn the hawk crest—he had been a stranger, but this one . . . So many years, could it be true?

"You know this man who wears a lord's ring?" Suspicion was certainly back in the Falconer's voice.

"There was a child, years ago. The Old Race weds sometimes with the Sulcars. And there were Sulcarmen who rode with the Borderers, though their first allegiance is always to the sea."

"And the lord's ring?" Once more he was challenging her. Tirtha sat the straighter in the saddle, met his gaze level-eyed.

"There could be no such true ring. Hawkholme's lord wore one of its like on his hand when he met death within his own walls. His younger brother, who was apart when the attack came, never possessed it. Perhaps it was loot fallen into Ettin's hands. He might claim it, but its wearing was never for any half blood." Her chin was high, and she spoke with force. "Of the true House, I am the last— nor would I have come into Karsten had it been otherwise."

With his helm on, his face so masked, she felt, as always, at a disadvantage—even though the Falconer's expression was never easy to read. He could believe her or not. If he chose to brand her liar (and did not his kind think in their innermost minds that all her sex were?), then she could declare their bargain broken and so be rid of the burden of leading him and Alon into dire disaster. For surely he would take the boy with him to save him from further contamination by one who was tainted like her.

However, what he faced her with now was a question that had undoubtedly been eating at him from the very start of this venture.

"What has Hawkholme to offer anyone?"

In other words, Tirtha knew he meant—what did it have to offer a lone woman who ventured into an act of sheer folly in seeking out a ruined and despoiled hold where perhaps no one had gone for more than the length of her own lifetime.

This was it—the moment when she must share part of her confidence or be defeated before she began. How much would he believe —that she had indeed been compelled by dreams to seek out a heritage, the nature of which she herself did not know, save that it was of the utmost importance and that it must be found?

"There lies in Hawkholme that which I must find." Tirtha chose her words carefully, with no talk of dreams that had pressed so heavily upon her that all her life had led to this journey. "I *must* seek it out. Only it would seem that there are others who would have it also. I do not know why I must do this," she felt constrained to add, though perhaps it was self defeating with such a listener. "It is laid upon me. Have you of the Eyrie never heard of a geas?"

Almost she thought that she saw his lips begin once again to shape the word "witchery" as they had done so often before. Yet he did not say it when he spoke after a short moment of silence.

"There was told to us the tale of Ortal. . . ." He might be drawing something from deep memory. "Yes, I have heard of a geas—and of how such may be laid upon one, allowing no freedom until the deed is accomplished. Ortal took ship in the days of Arkel, who was the sixth Master in the Eyrie, because he offended one with the Power, and it was set upon him to obey, and no ransom offer from the Master could break it. It is a hard thing that you do then, Lady."

That he would accept so readily her explanation of what brought her south was a relief.

"Then you know why I must ride. But again I will say to you, Falconer, and to Alon, this binding is not for you, and you should not follow me. I do not know what lies now in or about Hawkholme, but it is no pleasant or easy thing that I must do."

He gestured with his claw as if to silence her. "Perhaps this Gerik is a part of what would prevent your accomplishing your task. We ride . . ." Without another word he pulled ahead a little, and she thought it better not to trouble him with any new protest at this time. That he was a strongly stubborn man she had known from their first meeting. It could well be that he now believed his honor was engaged, which would seal their companionship tighter than any bargain formally struck.

"This Ettin"—she turned to Alon, for he continued to ride beside
her as the Falconer drew a little apart—"he was a young man?"

"He looked so. He did not talk much, but he had guesting man-
ners, and Parlan took a liking to him. He tried to tell the stranger
that to ride alone to the south was a danger for any man, but his
answer was always that he did as he must do. He had a fine mail
shirt and a plain helm such as the Borderers wore, and his sword was
a good one. But he had no dart gun nor any bow such as you carry.
He was a good man, I think."

She remembered a slender, fair-haired boy who had grown so fast,
who had ridden with a small border company of patrolers when he
was not far out of childhood—for there were few children along the
fringe land. They learned early lessons which carried them into playing the parts of men and women. She and he had met twice under the
roof that had been her first home, or the roof that had sheltered her
from birth, but they had not known each other well. Kin of part
blood they were.

How had the Hawk ring come to Ettin, and what had led him to
attempt this lone journey ahead of her? Was he also dream-led? Was
there a power playing with them and perhaps with others also, such
as that stranger whose mail had borne the Hawk emblem and who
had died of wounds in the wilderness? Him she had never seen, nor
had she heard of any of her House elsewhere in Estcarp. The Houses
and Clans of the Old Race were tight knit, holding together the
stronger because all else had been torn from them. If there had been
other survivors of Hawkholme, then through the years—as refugees
poured over the mountains and thereafter joined the Border legions
—such would have drawn together, for there had been much passing
of names and messages among all who had fled and were seeking the
fate of kinsfolk.

The gravel-paved valley sloped upwards, and the Falconer waved
back a signal to dismount, so that they advanced on foot at a slow
pace, leading their animals, the bird taking once more to the air. At
last, leaving the three beasts to be rein-held by Alon, the girl and the
man crawled on their bellies to look down a far slope.

Nearly beyond eye distance traveled a party of riders, seemingly
with no desire to hide their presence. To the east Tirtha sighted the
landmark that had been so plain in her trance—the cliff with its
black bands. She pointed to it.

"That is the first of my trailmarkings."

"How do they ride?" He lifted the claw in a slight gesture toward the knot of men proceeding easily at a distance-eating trot.

She considered, then had to speak the unhappy truth. "They ride in the same direction as we must go."

In her own mind she no longer doubted that their destination must be the same as hers—Hawkholme. Was Ettin one of them? No, if he had been among the raiders at the garth, Alon would have known him. Nor could she believe that he, being who he was, had been drawn into any service of the Dark.

The Falconer studied the ground before them, in particular the fringe of trees to the east.

"With those for cover, and warnings from the Brother-in-Feathers," he said slowly, "we follow."

Tirtha thought of the sinister wood that would form the second stage of their journey. It was fitted perfectly for ambush, so she spoke of it while the Falconer listened. He glanced at the sky. The sun was well west, near time for a night camp, though it must be a dry one, and they might go hungry.

"They do not ride as if they believed any watched them. Men do not go openly through such a land as this unless they have reason to think themselves beyond pursuit."

"Or else," she commented dryly, "they set themselves as bait to draw those they wish to take."

"Yes, there is that. But what Wind Warrior can do, he will, and in this open country he can see if they are joined or if they have any contact with others. You are right concerning the danger of the wood ahead. There even his sight cannot serve us, so we shall have to go with full caution. But for now, let us try for those trees and there take cover until morning. Or perhaps even wait out the coming day and move on at night."

Night was when the Dark held its greatest power, and Tirtha did not forget that, with those ahead, perhaps, there rode a servant of evil. On the other hand, perhaps the others believed that any such travelers as this party of hers would not dare a journey in darkness. There were so many different things to think on. Suddenly she was tired, as worn as if she had tramped for days along an endless highway. She wanted rest, freedom from this burden, this geas, which had been thrust upon her and which she must continue to bear because of the blood that had been hers from birth.

11

They took cover in a fringe of trees, traveling slowly, while the falcon, in short flights, kept an eye on the party ahead. Those others continued to move in the open as if they had nothing to fear and a definite goal awaiting them.

It was the falcon, also, that brought from two of its ventures small hares, lean at this season, but still food, though they must eat the flesh raw, chewing at strips shaved from the carcasses. Tirtha, long since having learned that one could not be dainty during hard travel, accepted thankfully, even though her stomach was queasy.

They camped that night where the black-veined ledge descended into the earth. Ahead they could sight the forest, dark and threatening to the east, displaying even at this distance the thick weaving of its outer wall, a warning threat.

The party ahead did not attempt an entrance into the forest, though they had changed course to camp on land edging it. Nor did they hide their camp, for the wink of their fire was bright.

Making a last ascent into the dusk-curtained sky, the falcon circled toward it. When the bird returned, it eagerly reported to the man. He listened, though he himself was now only a blot of darkness Tirtha was hardly able to distinguish.

"One of their party is gone," he reported, when the bird was done. "Wind Warrior believes he has entered the wood. That holds danger. Perhaps he goes to treat with what dwells there for a safe passage."

Something which *they* could not do, Tirtha thought bitterly. Or else the rider had been sent to set up the ambush that she suspicioned might await them. Her shoulders drooped. There was no question that she must go on, but why must she take these two with her, to add to her trials?

It was Alon who broke the silence, following upon the Falconer's translation of the report.

"You said"—he spoke to Tirtha—"that there were the remains of a road leading through the wood to your Hawkholme land. Then once men must have ridden it safely. Did not the Old Race have their own guards, not all of them men?"

"Guards—if those ever existed—" she answered out of a dull sense that she faced the impossible and could not hope for better, "who were of no service on the Day of the Horning. Hawkholme fell then, and that was many years ago. Any guards of my clan are dead or long since swept away."

To her surprise the Falconer said slowly, "There is this—only the mountains' fall brought down the Eyrie. For we in turn had safe-guards that were greater than men with sword and dart. Still . . ." His outline moved; she thought that he was putting out his arm, and she heard a small rustle of sound. Perhaps Wind Warrior was settling on his favorite perch, that metal claw. "Some of what we had re-mains there. Otherwise the Brother-in-Feathers would not have come to me. His kin remembered across the years. Do not dismiss too quickly what our little brother suggests. There might yet be something that will answer to your blood even as Wind Warrior came to me."

She gave a bitter bark of laughter. "There is nothing to aid and everything to stand against me. I say *me*—for I will not have the two of you on my conscience, knowing that I may lead you into what may be worse than any death by steel. Alon has already tasted of what this Gerik can turn against one. None of us has any knowledge of shield-building by ritual or appeal to Power. That forest is bad. What waits beyond is worse."

Unseen, her fingers moved in age-old signs, warding off evil fate. Some signs she had always known, some she had learned with diffi-culty, but these gestures carried with them no authority at all. If she were like Yachne, perhaps, Tirtha could stand against the Dark; but she was not a Wise Woman, certainly no Witch.

"To think of defeat is to summon it." Out of the dark Alon's voice was that of a man's, save for its higher pitch. "You would not have been called unless there was a chance."

"What if," she retorted between her teeth, "I was brought hither to satisfy some purpose of the Dark—a sacrifice? How can I swear that this is not so? There were forces in Karsten that always hated and feared my kind. In the past some of them linked with Kolder. Perhaps now they strike bargains with another power."

Her depression was like a thick cloud. She had never so mistrusted the future. Before, the need for the quest had upborne her through much trouble, nor had she been visited by such feelings of despair and helplessness.

Fingers caught at her moving hands, wrapped about them tightly, holding with a fierce grip.

"Swordmaster"—Alon's voice sounded as sharply as one summoning another to battle—"your sword! There is a shadow striving to engulf her."

Tirtha struggled to free her hands from the boy's hold. He—they must go, leave her now! There welled up inside her such a wave of darkness as she had never known. This was not the icy evil that had struck at her during that farseeing. Rather it appeared to be a part of herself, born out of her own fears and doubts, out of every disappointment, hardship, and past danger she had fought. It welled up, filled her, was sour in her mouth, invaded and routed coherent thought. She wanted nothing but to be free of it—of this other self—to find peace, peace forever and ever, all struggle gone.

She felt, through that dreadful fog, pain that was not this new and frightening pain of body and inner essence, but physical pain. Tirtha struggled to win free—to be herself.

"Hold her—the sword—take it . . ." A voice thin, far away, meaning nothing.

Let her be free—at peace! She could not think; she was filled with fear and despair that clawed within her, tearing down, crushing.

"Hold her! She is invaded!" Again that voice. The words were meaningless. There was nothing left for her. Dark—into the Dark—let her go into the Dark. There lay peace, rest, a refuge.

She saw nothing but threatening shadow arising from a depth in her she had not realized existed. Therein crawled all the harshness of her life, all the self-denials that she had made. Now she was alone with the worst that dwelt within her. To face it was breaking her so that only—only death . . . Death—if that would come at a call! Tirtha felt an ache in her throat as if she shouted aloud to summon the end. What she was now was as monstrous as anything that could come crawling out of Escore to run through these hills. *She* was the monster, the evil, she polluted the world—she. . . .

Within that shadow she writhed in a torment worse than any torment of body, for torture of one's body could end in death. For her there would be no death, no peace, no. . . .

"Tirtha—Tirtha!" The voice was very, very far away—so thin that she could hardly hear it. Nor did she want to. There could be no one else in this evil world she had made for herself. She had fashioned this horror, unknowingly perhaps. Still it had grown out of *her*—let it not engulf anyone else.

She could not drive the murk from her mind, still she was dimly aware of other warmth.

"Tirtha!" A voice not so faint, possessing more depth, stronger, even more demanding than that other one. She strove to turn, twist, to outrace the voice.

But she was held. Her body lay against another's, immobilized. For a second or two—the length of perhaps a heartbeat—that realization pierced through the emergence of the *thing* to which her inner spirit had given birth.

Tirtha strangled on a cry, begging for release, lest this other presence be tainted, befouled, lest he suffer because of her.

"No." So emphatic was the denial that it broke through to her. "No, this is not of you, you are not so . . ."

She thought that she whimpered as her strength fast drained away. The shadow was winning; it was possessing the last remnants of her, devouring all she had believed once that she was or could be. That belief was built on rot within her.

"Tirtha!" Again that summons.

Then like a sun rising into the cloudless sky on a fair day of spring when the renewing of life could be believed in, the heart know a stir of joy and well-being, a spark of light rayed through the fog of evil about her. Larger, stronger grew that pinpoint. She was aware of another strength that pushed into the murk of her own failure.

Slowly, steadily it pushed. There came a sharp innermost thrust that pierced directly to the heart of what she now was. Death? If so, welcome.

Once more there whirled through her mind all that she had done, all that she had made of herself until this hour. However, the light followed, fought against sick self-contempt, her deep debasement of spirit. That portion of her confidence, which had been defeated, beaten into the ground, stirred. Slowly, oh, so slowly, a part of her answered the light, was nourished by it. Her thoughts no longer drew pictures of all that had gone wrong in the past—the least of those actions weighing against the good in her.

Again Tirtha strove to ask for help as she had done once before, only this was for help against her own being, a prayer that she be strengthened to face what she was and accept all her faults. The warmth which held her fed that need for comfort and strength of will, even as did the light.

She sighed, and the shadow no longer pressed in so tightly. Yes, this she had done and that, she had been harsh and cold and wrapped within herself, but she was no longer so utterly alone. There was a presence with her lifting her up and out, and out. . . .

Tirtha saw the blur of a face close to hers, another beyond. She lay within a firm hold, while both her hands were imprisoned in another grasp, so tightly that her flesh was pinched and cramped. There was dark about the three of them. However, not that terrible inner darkness that had captured her without warning; this was the natural dark of the night. The Falconer held her, supported her, as he had when she emerged from the trance, while Alon knelt, her hands in his.

"I . . ." She tried to speak, to tell them. It was the Falconer who laid his sword-calloused hand across her lips.

In his claw, as it came about her shoulder, rammed well into the grasp of that cold metal, was the weapon of power. Light shone from it—lighter in color, not blue, but a golden-white—to illuminate all their faces. He had thrown off his helm, was unmasked, and as she looked up into his face, it was no longer impassive. Tirtha could not have said what the strange expression she saw there meant, save that he was more moved by some emotion than she had ever seen him. The flames in his eyes were steady while he watched her searchingly as if she were a land—a gate—that must be defended from all comers.

His bird, which she believed would never leave him, perched on Alon's shoulder as the boy knelt before her. The avian eyes flamed with a fierce light, and the head turned at an angle to survey her with a predator's steady, unblinking gaze.

Alon's small face was nearly ashen in spite of the warmth of the color from the weapon's glow. His lips were pinched between his teeth, and there was such strain in his face as she believed he might have shown had he once more confronted Gerik's men.

"I . . ." She turned her head, slipped the Falconer's hold from off her lips. "I was . . ."

"In the Dark." The man answered her somberly. "This attack . . ."

Alon interrupted him. "You met that which only the Full Dark can summon."

It was her turn to protest. "Not from without." It was difficult to find the proper words. Her mind felt benumbed, beaten and sore, as might her body had she come through, survived only by inches, some battle. "It was inside—inside me."

Alon shifted a little, settling back on his heels. "You even tried to use your sword—against yourself." He had dropped his hold on her hands; now he motioned to what lay between them—that old, worn blade that was her talisman. "What possessed you would have made you self-slain."

"Possessed . . ." Tirtha repeated his words. She had heard, had read of possession. That had been the worst and greatest weapon of the Kolder. Was this how they had possessed men's bodies—turned them into their dead-alive servants? No, that had been done in another way—by the machines that had been destroyed in Gorm, so completely broken that no living man could hope to puzzle out their dread secrets. Yet now she said the only word that had once fitted such a state. "Kolder."

The Falconer shook his head. The expression she had not been able to read had vanished. His features were again set in the somber mold they had always worn. "Kolder is gone. This is another matter."

Tirtha roused herself, feeling that she must explain, must make them understand for their own sakes what she had learned within that shadow—that she carried in her the seeds of dire things, and the longer they companioned her, the more danger for them. All the truths and memories that shadow had used to weigh her down into despair still lay in her mind. This last crime she would not have added to the score to be balanced against her.

"It showed me to myself—what I have been, what I am. I beg you —go, if you have any compassion for me, you have no reason to do more than wish me well and ride. Grant me this much: that you will not be drawn into darkness because you think it your duty to follow where I must travel. Let me go alone; so take such an added burden from me."

Alon's lips parted as if he would speak, but it was the Falconer who answered first.

"Would you play *its* game then? I think, Lady, that you have too much courage to allow yourself to be so misled. Look you to what has happened. We are yet afar from Hawkholme, and yet something which has great witchery seeks to separate us. Therefore it fears. For only against what we fear, do we begin battle or launch a surprise attack. We do not know even the nature of this enemy. However, it would seem to me that when we unite, as we have done twice now, we provide it with a problem: strength it fears to face.

"In Karsten in the long ago the Kolder worked so; deep was their intriguing, their possession of Yvian and others near him, which led him to drive forth your people. And the reason for that was that Kolder could not take over one of the Old Race. The Old Race had to die because they could not be bent to another's will. To seek to divide when there are allies united in strength is a very ancient move of strategy. If we ride hence, and you go on alone, then *it* has won. Do you wish such a victory, Lady? I think not, that is not in you. This enemy seeks to strike through your sense of duty, would set upon you the illusion that you already serve evil and so will lead you to open a door for it."

Tirtha watched his face, intent upon his words, and she knew that he spoke in all sincerity. That part of her which had been awakened through his efforts, through Alon's—the belief in herself, was now strengthened. She was as one recovering from an illness who feels the touch of returning health. There was good council in what he said. Suppose she had succeeded, and these two left her at her demand?

It might not matter that she went on to oblivion save that, though she in herself did not count, what she must do had strong reason and purpose. As Tirtha faced that thought, another clear flow of energy surged into her, bringing with it the will to banish the last of the shadow.

Also, breaking their bonds with her now might not save the Falconer and Alon. Alon was the one to point that out.

"They will search for us, even if you send us from you, Lady Tirtha. We have been one. If they take you, then maybe they can still compel us to them—or it—because of that very fact. We have made a choice. . . ."

The girl shook her head a fraction. "I have forced one on you," she corrected.

"Not so," was the Falconer's quick denial. "I have long thought that perhaps we are all under a geas—that you came to me in Romsgarth not by chance but by purpose. I was minded to ride that very morning for the coast. My comrades were dead; I felt but half a man. There was nothing to hold me to the hills. Yet against my own planning, I returned again to the market because"—for the first time real puzzlement crossed his face—"I cannot tell you why. And see, already I am more of a man, once more a warrior with a feathered brother, such as I had never hoped to be again. That, too, was not chance. Wind Warrior was waiting for one he believed would come."

"And I would have died," Alon said softly. "I think you yourself this night touched on the same death that would have taken me. But you and the Swordmaster and Wind Warrior, you brought me to life and awakened in me that which I had never understood, so that I had only a half life before. Can you say all of this was by chance alone?"

Tirtha moistened her lips with tongue tip, staring first at the Falconer in whose arms she still rested, then at the boy, who was certainly more than he seemed to the outer eye—at last to the bird on his shoulder. The wall she had built around her for years had cracked.

"I do not know what must be sought at Hawkholme," she said, "but it is of importance to more than me. I have come to believe that my clan were guardians of something of great value, which must be found. They say that very ancient powers are awake and move in Escore from which our blood first came. Did those of my House bring with them some weighty symbol of force, some treasure, which is needed now in the war that rages there between the Dark and the Light? If only I had more of the talent . . ." Her old regret was heavy in her voice. "Perhaps had I been trained and not had to forage for myself, garnering bits and pieces I have not the wit to use, I could foresee as well as farsee. I am not a Wise Woman."

"You do not know yet what you are," the Falconer interrupted her. "Make no statement that you are not this or that. But this I know." He looked straight into her eyes. "Our bargain has changed, Lady. There are no twenty days of service. No, what lies between us now shall continue to the end, whether you will it or no. That is the way that things must be."

He used her with a gentleness she did not expect, had not known that one of his schooling could summon, wrapping her in her cloak, settling her with one of the limp saddlebags for a pillow. Then he held the power sword in the air. Its light had faded to the smallest glimmering, hardly more than the flash of a night-flying insect. But by it she could still see the blur of his face and believed that he was staring upon what he held.

"This came into my hand, even though those of my blood trust not in things that are of witchery. Yet it slipped into my hold as if it were made for no other man in this world. That is another sign that I am one in this quest. I, too, have a geas laid upon me to bear this where it must go, wield it as it must be used. I do not know, but perhaps he who was Nirel has died, and I am someone else. If that is so, then I must learn who. Now, Lady, I set it on you to sleep, for you have come through such a fight as would exhaust any warrior. And the feathered brother, though he hunts by day, is an excellent sentinel, so we need not keep watch and watch. Tomorrow we face perhaps other trials, but those are for the morning and one does not look ahead for the evil that may lie in wait."

She was indeed tired. His voice had softened, lost that harsh bite it so often carried. Now it seemed a flow of reason, carrying her easily with it, sliding into rest, which was not the dark peace she had sought, the nothingness of non-being, but rather that which renewed both body and spirit.

Alon, the blanket that had been rolled behind the Torgian's saddle wrapped around him, settled down so that she need not even reach forth a hand more than a palm's width away to touch him. And she heard movements through the dark that told her the Falconer was also seeking rest. What had happened tonight, Tirtha still did not understand. But she was too weary to seek an answer; there would be time with morning light for that.

There was warmth on her face when she opened her eyes again; a patch of sun lay across her cheek, having found entrance between two overhead branches. It required determination and will for her to pull herself up and allow the cloak to fall away. For a single moment of surprise and confusion, she thought that for all their talk the other two had obeyed her and gone their own way, for there was no one in sight. Then the evidence of the saddles to one side, their bags lying beside them, was proof that they had not left. Near her was a broad leaf on which rested two long white roots so recently washed free of earth that stray drops of water lay upon them. Beside them a water bottle sat upright.

She recognized the roots as ones Alon dug now and then. Eaten raw, they were crisp and slightly biting to the tongue but palatable. So she ate and drank, finding that she was near famished, and then wobbled to her feet, leaning back against the trunk of the tree under which she had lain. There was a swishing in the brush as Alon pushed through, his face lighting as he saw her.

He came across the small open space into which they had edged their camp to catch one of her hands, holding it in both of his.

"Tirtha, it is well with you?" His eyes sought hers and satisfaction grew in his expression. "You slept—ah, how you slept."

She looked at the sun and suddenly felt guilty. "How long?"

"It is midday. But it does not matter. In fact, the Swordmaster said that it was a good thing. For he thought us best here until those others are well into the wood. Wind Warrior has gone to settle on one of the trees at the edge of it and watch what they do, look for any guards that may be on the prowl there. Swordmaster is hunting—he put down snares and caught two meadow hens. Also he believes that we dare light a fire if we keep it under cover here."

Alon made a small face. "I do not like raw hare; this is better." He loosed his hold on her and briskly set to work with the bundle of sticks he had dropped when he first sighted her, laying them with care, choosing only the driest, those least liable to give forth smoke.

When the Falconer returned, he had two plump birds swinging from his belt. Also he told her he had found a small side dell in which the ponies and the Torgian had been put on picket lines and were grazing well.

"We are a day late," she said, as he plucked the birds skillfully and impaled them on sticks, to be set to broil at the pocket of fire Alon tended.

"Time not wasted," he reassured her. "It is best to have those well ahead. We shall take the trail tonight. I would not cross the open in the day. And there may be something of a storm later to give us cover." To her eyes, he seemed his old self, impersonal and intent on what he conceived his duties. She was well content to have it so. Her own shell of independence seemed to her at this moment a cloak she did not want to discard.

12

The night was moonless, cloaked by clouds from which fell a drizzle, searching out every opening in their clothing. Tirtha had insisted on mounting the Torgian, bringing Alon with her under what protection her cloak could afford. They kept as much as they could to ways that trees overhung, giving them whatever shelter possible. Wind Warrior reported at dusk that those they trailed had taken to the woods and that they had left no sentry or spy behind.

The three still had no assurance that they were not seen, or sensed, and what lay ahead might not lead to an ambush. Thus they moved slowly, the Falconer as scout. He fell quickly into a pattern that Tirtha was sure he had long ago often followed.

It must have been well past the mid-hour of the night when they at last approached the bush-veiled entrance into the old wood road. In this dark the forest was even more overpowering with its thick shadows, and for the past hour or so, Tirtha had kept doubly alert, striving to pick up any sense of being under observation, such as she had known when her vision had laid open this passage. She dared not, of course, probe too deeply, lest she rouse that which might, so far, have been unaware of their coming. It could well be an entity able to detect a farseer.

The boy in her hold had ridden passively enough, making no sound, during those hours when they had traveled so slowly and cautiously toward their goal. But as the Falconer headed his pony into that near-masked opening of the forest road, Alon stirred, his voice came as a whisper, hardly more than a breath.

"This is a place that lives. . . ." He spoke as one who did not quite understand or, if knowing, could not find proper words to make plain his warning.

Tirtha bent her head so that her lips could not be far from Alon's nearest ear:

"Are we watched?" Her whisper was as low as she could make it.

"I . . . I think not . . . not yet," he returned.

Her own eyes swept from one side of the trail to the other, seeking that wisp of thing that had entwined itself among the trees during her vision of this place. That, she was certain, had been of the Dark, also of a nature far removed from a common existence with those who called themselves human. Let *that* come upon them in its own place and—she disciplined her thoughts, refused to allow fear to rise the higher.

Ahead, the Falconer was hardly to be seen. His bird had joined him at the wood's edge to ride now on the saddle perch. However, if Tirtha could not follow them directly with her own sight, it appeared that her present mount had no difficulty in keeping up with the lead pony, just as her own mare crowded in behind. The three beasts drew as close as they might in such a narrow way without being urged.

There was a glimmer of pallid, faint light on her right. Tirtha's heart beat faster for a succession of thumps until she located the source as one of those stones that marked the road they must travel, as her vision had shown her. She did not like that glow; it carried some of the pallid obscenity of the night fires given off by certain fungi she had seen—loathsome, evil-smelling growths, by tradition nourished by the bodies of unburied dead.

At least the rain was partially kept from them by the overhanging branches of the trees, so she could push back the hood of her cloak, affording her a clearer sight of the way. Then Alon moved in her hold. His hand closed about one of her arms tightly, before his grasp relaxed a trifle. She took that as a warning.

Yes!

What she had thought to face ever since they had headed into this shadowed forest was coming. As yet perhaps it had no more than vaguely sensed them, or maybe it was only making sentry rounds. But Tirtha's skin crawled as she felt the deadly cold spreading before it. Like that monstrous thing which had sought mindlessly to get at her and the Falconer back in the mountains, so was this not of her world. The impact of it was like an openhanded blow.

Whether the Falconer had picked it up also, she could not tell. Yet here the trail widened out a fraction so that the Torgian, without her urging, matched pace with the pony. Thus she dared to loose part of her hold on Alon and put out her hand in turn to touch the man's arm.

He did not return her touch. Still Tirtha sensed, as she had never done before, that he realized what message she would send to alert him and that he was already aware of the prowler. They might still retreat, get out of this place overwhelmed by the shadow. Yet that would solve nothing, for the geas held fast for her, and this was the only road to what she sought.

Their mounts plodded ahead. There were more of those glimmering stones, some set sentrywise along the trail, others to be glimpsed back in the woods. Tirtha, tense in the saddle, sought with what skill was hers to pick up the skulker in that place of utter blackness.

It was like seeing a distant flicker, visible for one second, gone the next, only to show again. This did not register in her eyes, rather in her mind. Whatever creature skulked here was far removed from man or animal. She heard Alon draw a deep breath, a fraction later his whisper reached her again.

"Think of light—of good . . ." His words trailed away, leaving Tirtha for a second uncomprehending. Then she understood. Fear was so often the first weapon of Dark Ones. Perhaps the three of them could indeed draw a curtain between themselves and this thing by bringing to the fore of their minds all that was right and natural, good and clean, within their own world.

She strove to build up a mind picture of the fields of Estcarp where she had labored only last harvesttime, swinging a sickle with the skill she had learned, gathering to her armloads of sunwarmed, fragrant grain. Here were the brilliant eyes of the field flowers making splotches of color—scarlet, yellow, against the gold. Sun lay warm on her shoulders, and there was still the taste upon her lips of apple squeezings which a serving maid had brought in leathern bottles to satisfy the thirst of the reapers.

Sun, color, the gold of grain ripe and ready for the harvest. There was the piper who sat cross-legged on the wall toward which the harvesters were working their way, and the trilling of his instrument roused hearty voices into song. She could feel the sun, taste the apple juice, hear the pipe song even here in the dark. Nor dared she break the web she so strove to weave, though the temptation to do so pressed ever on her.

The trail that had been so narrow at the entrance widened out. Now and then a hoofbeat raised an echo of sound, as if, under the blanket of last season's leaves, there lay an ancient pavement.

So they came into what was a clearing, though ragged-walled, with an outgrowth of brush seeking to reclaim it. Those unhealthy stones were hereabouts in thick company, a number of them set on end to the north to form a rude barrier. But it was what lay in the very center of that way which held them where they were on the edge of this opening.

Lying crosswise on a patch of bared stone were two staffs or wands —wood that had been stripped of bark and shone bone white. Between them, positioned with care to form two sides of four squares, were skulls. These were old, greenish, as if overgrown in part by some vile lichen, and each had been braced to lie face up, the eyepits, the gaping jaws turned toward the sky.

Skulls, yes, but of no normal living thing Tirtha knew. The general shape *was* human in part, save there were heavy ridges of bone above the eye sockets. It was the jaws and lower sections that were the strangest—long cruel teeth sprouted still from the bone there, teeth that must have protruded far out and down from the flesh that had once lipped the mouths. Also there was a forethrust of the jaw line itself which hinted at a muzzle.

Like the thing on the mountain. Tirtha's memory flashed the picture of it as she looked upon this carefully wrought warning, if warning it was.

She was aware of movement to her right. The Falconer was no longer sitting quiet in his saddle. A flash of light through the air . . . Into that display of wood and bone whirled something that came to life in the night with a flare like that of a torch hurled into dry brush.

Point down it struck, straight into the crossing of the staffs, metal biting into the wood. From that point of contact there burst a true flame which ran out along the lengths of the staffs, bringing light to bathe them all.

Was it only a sorcerous illusion, or did those greened skulls open yet wider their fanged jaws as the flames reached out eagerly to lick across each they passed? Had she heard a wailing afar in the distance, or if not in earthly distance in another place? Had that fire, which looked to be here and now, touched also into a world that lay beyond one of the fabled gates? Tirtha only knew that she felt— heard, sensed, she was not sure which—a moment of torment, and then a wink out of a life or lives which had no being in this time and place.

The skulls took fire, each exploding with a burst of sound that she heard. Already the staffs were but lines of ash laid upon the ground. The Falconer urged his pony on, leaned from the saddle to hook his claw about the hilt of the dagger knife which he had so thrown, drawing it out of the ashes that the hooves of his mount had stirred into nothingness.

"Well done." Alon's voice came, not in the faint whisper he had used since they had entered the wood, but as if there was nothing to fear now.

"How"—Tirtha ran her tongue across her lower lip—"how did you know?"

This was witchery, and he had always turned from it, shunned it as she would a manifestation of the Dark. Yet she had seen him now take on the practice of a Warlock.

Alon came to sudden life in her arms, plunging against her lax hold and so leaping forward to the ground.

" 'Ware!" The alarm came out of him in a child's voice. Still there was a man's urgency in that cry.

Tirtha swept back the folds of her cloak. The Torgian had moved up beside the Falconer's pony, and the mare crowded in against the two of them. Alon reached up and caught a handful of the coarse mane of that smaller beast, drew himself up on the riding pad. The falcon mantled, screamed a challenge.

She drew her worn sword. They had somehow gotten into a defense position, the three of them facing outward, the rumps of their mounts pressed together, each fronting a separate portion of the wood about them. Was the destruction of the warning—or the spell —leading to outright attack?

They came out from the strange stones afoot, shadows flitting from shadows. Smaller than men, yes, and carrying with them a stench that Tirtha had come to associate with creatures of the Dark. She saw flames of eyes turned toward her, yet it would appear that, though they now ringed in the three, they were not ready for an outright attack. Instead they fell into a shuffling circle around about the riders, staying out of range of steel.

The Falconer had his dart gun. Tirtha wondered why he did not put it to use, pick off some of those moving creatures. The targets they provided were not so difficult that his aim could not have removed them as they passed him in that circling.

Her sword was little enough defense, yet she slipped from her belt sheath her hunting knife, reached out to press it into Alon's hand. It was all she had in the way of an extra weapon.

From her left there was a glow. The weapon of power which the Falconer had retrieved before the emergence of these night crawlers was ablaze. She could not see that he had armed himself otherwise. Perhaps he had come to depend upon this strange arm more than he did on the weapons he had always known.

Their shaggy attackers—if attackers these were indeed—made no sound save by the shuffling of their feet as they kept their circle moving. Though they stood upright and had only four limbs, they were certainly not of her race, nor of any that approached the human blood. They wore no clothing. The glow from the weapon revealed, as they passed, squat bodies covered with a thick growth of such coarse hair or bristles that they might have had fine roots instead of natural strands sprouting forth. The round heads were marked by no visible features, save eyes that were pits of red fire, and were set directly on their wide shoulders. Their overlong upper limbs dangled so that their claws nearly brushed the ground, though they held themselves upright as they scuttled about.

The circle which they wove was not an even one. They pressed closer toward Tirtha and Alon, kept a farther distance from the Falconer. In him they might believe that they had a more formidable opponent. Why they did not launch their attack puzzled Tirtha. She began to believe they were only a delaying device, and the real strength of those who held the wood as their domain had yet to show itself.

For the second time, the falcon screamed. Those of the haired things nearest it at the time wavered. It would appear that they liked that sound no better than the sight of the sword-knife which blazed ever higher with its own light.

Just as silently and swiftly as the beast things had appeared from the stones there emerged another. This was no hair-coated shuffler. Instead he strode into the foreground, the shamblers breaking their circle to let him enter, before resetting their ring.

Tirtha surveyed him steadily. He was truly human in the size and proportion of his limbs and body, and he wore mail, leggings and boots, and a helm. At first glance he could have been any border rover or perhaps an outlaw more cunning and with better luck at looting than most.

Unlike the Falconer's helm, this one's helmet did not hide the features of the wearer, nor did he have looped about his throat twin veils of silken-fine chain mail which afforded battle protection for the men of Estcarp.

His features were well cut, regular, and of the cast of the Old Race, though the eyes by which he regarded the three were not normal. Rather they held a tinge of red like those of the shambling creatures he commanded. Though he wore a sword, as well as a dagger, he advanced empty-handed, the long fingers of his hands oddly pale in the half-light. There was no badge on the breast of his mail coat. However, on the center ridge of his helm was fastened a carefully wrought, hideous creature which might be a snake with stumpy legs, or a lizard of misshapen form. This had specks of gems for eyes—sparks that caught the light strongly to reflect it with unusual power.

He did not speak, rather examined one after another. When that level and measuring gaze traveled over Tirtha she was hard put to hold herself steady. Accompanying it was a lapping, a pulling at her mind, an attempt to empty her of all she thought or was or would be and do. She resisted, experiencing a recoil of surprise as if he had not thought to feel any resistance.

For the third time, the falcon screamed. The man stood halfway between Tirtha and the Falconer, his attention having passed on to the latter. What would he meet there? Was the Falconer also inwardly armed, or did he lack her own protections? Yet the weapon was his, and no one of a lesser breed could have it fit his hand so well.

Still silent, the man from the forest took another stride to the left until he fronted Alon with his compelling gaze. Tirtha twisted about in the Torgian's saddle to witness that meeting. There had been no change of expression on the stranger's face, in fact no expression at all. For all his partaking of any of the emotions of the living, he might well have been one of the infamous dead-alive from which the Kolder had fashioned their armies. Yet this one was very much of a power, and what dwelt within that outer covering of mankind was to be distrusted, perhaps even rightly feared.

He gave the boy only one long, searching stare. Then once more his attention shifted to Tirtha herself, and for the first time he spoke:

"Welcome, Lady, to that which is rightfully yours." His voice was surprisingly gentle and courteous in tone. He might have been greeting a guest at the door of a holding, the plate with bread, salt and water held ready for the sealing of the guesting bond.

She found her own voice, glad for the breaking of the silence that had covered much.

"I make no claims on this land," she returned. "This is no rule hold of mine."

"It is of the Hawk that was," he returned. "Though the years have dealt hardly with it of late. And do you not"—he made a light gesture with one hand to the sword she had bared—"carry the Hawk's weapon by right of blood?"

How he knew this (had he picked it out of her mind though she thought she was closed to his probe?) was a blow, but Tirtha believed that she had not allowed him to guess he scored against her.

"Hawkholme lies beyond. I make no claims, wood lord. If the years have wrought a difference, then let it so abide. Rule you as you will."

To her amazement he bowed gracefully with the ease of one who had been born to sit in a hall's high seat.

"You are gracious, Lady, and generous," though if she was not mistaken there was clearly a note of mockery in that. "To give freely what cannot be held might seem to some to be a superfluity. I do not believe you deal in such. You seek Hawkholme, but you are not alone in that. I think"—for the first time there was a curve of his well-cut lips as if he smiled—"that it might be amusing to see how you will deal with *them.*"

"And who are *they?*" the Falconer demanded.

The stranger's smile grew a fraction wider. He shook his head.

"Such a valiant company." His mockery was at last open and it had that in it which stung, though Tirtha had long ago schooled herself against any serious acceptance of her quest. "Such a very valiant company! And who can say whether the Greater Powers may not be amused enough to allow you, in your time, some advantage. I think I shall step aside, since you, Lady, have been so gracious as to invest me in my rulership, and allow this game to be played to the end without me. It"—now he glanced at Alon and his smile faded a fraction—"might have certain aspects that do not appear openly at present. So . . ." he swept her a second bow, then gestured. The haired things broke their circle, opening a way before Tirtha, who faced that gap in the wood where the path led on again. "Pass, Lady. And when you come into your full inheritance, remember that what you have surrendered was by your choice, and you have made a bargain. . . ."

"I have not!" she caught him up. "There is no oath-swearing between us, forest lord. No oath-taking nor giving. I have said only I do not want what you have claimed. What I seek lies elsewhere. But you are not sworn to me, nor am I turf-enfiefed to you!"

He nodded. "Cautious, yes. As well might you be, Lady. I will concede that we are not oath-bound. I owe no shield service and come not before your high seat."

"Be it so." She said the old words denying fiefship with emphasis. No pact with the Dark. Perhaps in even accepting this much from him, she was making a mistake. But it was true—even if all Hawkholme hailed her as liege lady, which she did not expect—she wanted no rulership over this dire wood.

"Yet"—the Falconer urged his pony a step or so closer to the stranger. He had not sheathed the weapon of power, and in what appeared a half-involuntary motion, the man from the forest raised his hand as if to shield his eyes from the shine of the weapon. "Yet, still you have not answered me. Who are they with whom we shall deal?"

The forest stranger shrugged. "To you I owe no answer, Swordsman. You have chosen your own road. Ride it or leave it as you will. What you find on it is none of my affair."

"Still," Alon's childish voice broke through the antagonism that Tirtha could almost see forming between the two of them as a darker and even more ominous shadow. For there was something in the

Falconer that answered to this other as one drawn sword rises to meet another when the battle is enjoined. "Still, since you have told us some, do you deny us the rest?"

He sat quietly on the mare, a child looking thoughtfully at the man. Tirtha watched the two of them. With every hour they rode together, she was surer that Alon was more than she could understand, that he was no son of the Old Race, but something different and perhaps far older and longer tied to the Power.

The features of the forest dweller lost their imperviousness. He registered cold anger now. Still it was anger strictly curbed, one that might consume but could not be released.

"Seek you also . . ." His voice had dropped, it held almost the hiss of the scaled ones in a slight slurring of the words. "You are not yet a commander of the Great Lords! Nor do you command *me!*" With that he turned and was gone, as if his will alone had wafted him from their sight. The haired ones scuttled back into the shadows, leaving the three alone.

Tirtha made no comment, falling in with the Torgian behind the two ponies, which now paced abreast down the wider trail leading out of the clearing. She was disturbed more than she wanted to admit, still she made herself face the fact that those she rode with were certainly not what they outwardly seemed. Alon, she had accepted from the first as a mystery, for his introduction into their company had come through such a feat of the Power as she had never known. However, the Falconer, whom secretly she had dismissed as a dour fighter with perhaps pain of body and mind behind him, but one so narrow of belief that he would or could have no part in any life save that he had been bred to—what indeed was this Falconer who had named himself and still was a man divided? One who strove inside him (of this she was somehow sure) to unite two vastly different ways of thought. He carried his weapon of power, and he had used it this night as one trained in at least the lesser mysteries. Yet he clung to his role of fighting man, and he had fronted the man of the wood openly to demand an accounting as would any blank shield on escort duty.

No, she was faced with many puzzles and perhaps two of them, which might yield difficulties in times to come, were the innermost natures of those who companioned her.

Why should she now question them when she must also honestly question herself? She was no longer sure either of Tirtha or what Tirtha might do or become. All she was certain of was that she must

reach Hawkholme. What would chance thereafter? Her dream had
never led her any farther than that single room somewhere within
the ruined pile in which had been hidden that casket. She did not
even guess what it held and what she would do with it thereafter. She
was sure that the forest man had been right in his mockery. They
were riding on blindly into perils that could be far greater than any
this wood held.

It would seem that they had passed the worst the forest could
offer. The withdrawal of the forest lord and his crew—the granting
of an open road to them—ended her foreboding, the need for listening which had held her since they entered on this forgotten road. He
had released them—for what? Trials which he undoubtedly thought
much worse and which would give him a perverse pleasure (even as
he had admitted) to see them meet. She had no doubt that he firmly
expected a sure and final defeat for them from such a meeting.
Knowing that, her old stubbornness arose, and for all her realization
that there was little in the way of preparation she could make against
the unknown, Tirtha rode on with a straight back and high-held
head, sword still in hand, threading among more thinly spaced trees
and the shaggy brush that marked the other side of the wood—
morning and Hawkholme lying before them.

13

Sun banners overspread the east when they left the wood. The Falconer halted behind a last screen of brush between them and open
lands stretching to Hawkholme. The hold stood as Tirtha had visioned, stark amid desolate fields from which there had been no
harvest for many years, though there was a straggle of blighted
greenery rising raggedly now to greet the spring. No breaks showed
in the walls of the hold, though the moat drawbridge had been destroyed.

The Falconer dismounted at the same moment his feathered scout
winged out into the morning, rising so high that its black body was
but a dot against the heavens.

"We are here, Lady. Is this not your Hawkholme?"

"It is the place of my vision, of the dreams." For the first time she mentioned them. Since he had chosen to ride the full way, then perhaps the time had come to be frank with him. She nodded toward the distant hold which had the appearance of a grim fortress. Those who had built it must have had good reason to believe that a time of trial would come.

"Within that lies what I must claim. I do not know why, but it is set upon me to do this."

His eyes, through the slits of his mask helm, were full upon her, measuring. However, it was Alon who spoke.

"There is that which waits." The boy shivered as his face turned toward the fortress.

Instantly, he gained the Falconer's attention.

"Gerik?" the man demanded, as if he believed that Alon's sight was as keen as that of his questing bird, could even pierce those fire-stained walls.

Again Alon shuddered. That horror and terror, which had before thrust him into deep inner hiding, might once more have reached out to touch him.

"Him, and the other, the Dark One. They wait. Also, they have that . . ." He shook his head from side to side, raised one hand to his forehead. "I cannot see . . ." There was a touch of fear in his voice. "Do not ask me."

"Close your mind!" Tirtha ordered. Here was the same problem that had existed in the night-haunted wood. Any use of a talent might well draw upon them attention they did not want. She turned to the Falconer.

"If there is an ambush within . . ." She need not carry that further; he nodded in turn.

"Yes." His head swung from right to left, as he surveyed the land before them for possible concealment. Then he gestured to the left and, remounting, led off, still within a fringe of wood, keeping it between them and the open. Tirtha had already sighted what must be his goal. The river, which watered the land before them and which, in part, had been diverted to fill the moat as one of the defenses of Hawkholme, had been bridged not too far from where they had emerged from the forest. A small ruined building stood on their side of that now-broken span. Tirtha was reminded that in Estcarp's far past shrines to unknown and long-forgotten powers had been so erected.

Certainly the tumbled walls of the small building gave forth no warning of any evil. Its stones were not of that loathsome gray-white such as stood in the wood. She longed to test by thought-probe, but knew she dared not. The Falconer held the point of his sword-dagger toward that possible shelter, and his attention swung between the stone rubble and the hilt of his weapon. He must have come to depend upon its efficiency for ferreting out traces of evil. However, the pommel remained opaque and lifeless.

They were favored in that the river here made a northern curve so that the ruined shrine stood not too far from their present screen. A river running from the east—Tirtha considered that. Where lay its source? There was the dim line of bluish heights across the eastern sky, the sun now above them. Beyond that barrier—Escore. A river born in those heights or even running through them from beyond—what might it carry out of that wild and Power-ridden land?

Why had her kin settled so close in the early days? Had their ties with the east been stronger than those generally nursed by others come to settle in the west, those who deliberately willed out of memory all thought of Escore? She knew the formal history of Karsten well enough—that the Old Race had settled the land, living quietly and without incident until the coming from the south of the invaders, those of a younger race with whom their predecessors had no ties, and from whose company they had withdrawn, farther back into the interior of the duchy. There had followed no intermingling of blood with the newcomers. And as their own numbers had never been many and they had kept aloof, they had gone without strife until Yvian and the Kolder had turned the country blood-mad against them. Was Hawkholme one of the very earliest holds in Karsten? Had its lords kept alive ties with Escore, the ancient homeland?

Tirtha was startled out of her musing when Alon pushed the mare to a quicker trot, sidled past the Falconer, and reaching the edge of brush, slipped from the pony, to drop to hands and knees in last year's brittle weeds. Then he went belly-flat, crawling so into the open, heading for the pile of rocks that marked the end of the broken bridge. A moment later she understood.

To ride into the open would certainly be to court notice from Hawkholme. They could not believe it was without sentries on watch. Wind Warrior was aloft, but who knew what eyes those inside might possess, just as keen and farsighted.

They could tether their animals here; there was rough grazing to keep them satisfied. Tirtha dismounted, stripped the Torgian of his gear, looping the straps of her nearly flat saddle bags over one shoulder, seeing that the Falconer was doing the same.

Once they had the three beasts on lines—the fastening of which the Falconer tested well—they, too, crawled to where Alon squatted behind a breastwork of fallen rocks, staring at the fortress. The protection was not much; the roof of the small building had vanished, but at least they had the best cover possible hereabouts.

Though Tirtha studied the distant ruin of the holding with strict attention, she caught no sign of movement there. She had half expected to experience again the cold attack that had struck at her in vision. Perhaps it attacked only in vision, and the next assault would come in bodily form. She knew so little, could only guess at what might lie ahead.

Alon did not move or look around as they joined him. He was as frozen in his place as he had been enwrapped in the catatonic state in which they had first found him. Except that he had not retreated into invisibility. Now Tirtha crept up cautiously, dared to put an arm about his thin shoulders. His utterly silent watchfulness she found disturbing.

"What do you see?" she asked, determined to break through this abnormal absorption.

"I see. . . ." He shook his head. "It is not see, Lady, it is feel— here!" He raised a small, grubby hand to plant its thumb between his eyes. "There is trouble, anger, someone is very angry. That is the one who, if he were not so angry, would be searching for us. But now he thinks only of this thing which feeds his rage. He . . ." That long set stare with which he regarded the fortress ahead broke as he turned his head a fraction to glance at Tirtha. "He causes pain to another, seeking to learn a secret, one that other does not know. Aieee—" Suddenly the boy clapped both hands to his ears as if shutting out dire sounds neither of his companions could hear. His face screwed into a mask of mingled fear and pain. "It is evil what he does—evil!"

The Falconer reached out his single hand, and with a gesture Tirtha would not have believed his breed capable of showing, he touched Alon very gently at the nape of his small thin neck, rubbing the flesh almost caressingly, as one might soothe a small trembling animal. The boy turned, drew out of Tirtha's loose hold, to fling himself into the man's arms, hiding his face against the tattered cloak across the Falconer's mailed breast.

"Little Brother"—the Falconer spoke in a voice that Tirtha had never thought to hear—"break that tie, do it swiftly! Yes, there is evil, but it does not touch you."

Alon raised his head. His eyes were closed; from under their lids, tears streaked down through the dust and grime on his thin cheeks. "It does, it does!" Now his hands became fists, and he no longer clung to the Falconer, rather pummeled him vigorously. "It is pain for all of us when evil strikes at the Light!"

"Well enough," the Falconer answered. "But we do not spend our own strength heedlessly. There is evil there, and without a doubt, we must face it sooner or later. Do not let it fore-weaken you, Little Brother. You have that within you which is ready for the battle when it comes, only it must not be wasted."

Alon stared up into the half-masked face, then smeared one hand across his own. "You are right," he said slowly, once more that odd note of seeming maturity back in his voice. "What strength one has must be saved for a time when it is most needed. I . . . I will not . . ." He fell silent as if whatever promise he would make was to himself. Then he detached himself from the Falconer and looked again to Tirtha.

"They have not thought of us. I think that they are sure we could never have won through the wood. They believe themselves—for now—safe!"

"They are indeed singularly lax," the Falconer observed slowly. "Why have we seen no sentry? And if they expected the forest to stop us, then why did we so easily win through?"

"Perhaps because of what you carry." Tirtha indicated the weapon once more within that inadequate sheath at his belt.

"Or perhaps"—there was a lightly sharper note in his voice—"because you made pact with that forest runner."

Anger such as she had not felt for days flared in her. "I made no pact. I have not come here to reclaim any lordship. If he wishes that ill-omened wood to rule, then it is his. You heard me deny all fiefdom over it! Also, from what he said, he has no close ties with those ahead. I think it would suit him very well if we finished each other off without any meddling from him."

"A safe and trusty plan for *him,*" admitted the Falconer dryly. "It remains that, if we are not expected, this is the time when we should move."

"Across the open fields, crawling over the remains of the bridge, fording the moat." Tirtha reckoned up the utter folly of such action. To her the problem facing them was a nearly insurmountable barrier.

"In the open day, perhaps not," the Falconer conceded. "We have the night; also we must not go into action without rest. Alon," he addressed the boy now, "Wind Warrior can tell us only what he sees. Can you perhaps let us know if there is any hidden move toward seeking us out?"

The boy did not reply at once, nor did he any longer look at the two of them, rather down at the dirty hands locked together about his knees. He appeared so small, so childish, that Tirtha wanted to protest. Talent—Power—he might possess that beyond many Wise Ones, but drive him too far, and he could once more escape into that other existence. And perhaps a second time they could not draw him back.

He raised his head at last, and still not looking around, he answered in a low voice, "I dare not hold on them—on what they do there. I can—cannot! But if they seek us through any ensorcelment, yes, that I shall know—of a certainty I shall know!"

"We ask no more than that. Also, we shall watch by turn. You, Little Brother, and you, Lady, must rest first. I await Wind Warrior, for to me only can he deliver his report."

Tirtha shared her cloak with the boy, and they curled up together, her head pillowed on the saddle bags, his on her shoulder. She carefully kept in mind that she would not dream, for it could be that even dreams might alert whoever ruled in Hawkholme now.

She roused out of what turned out to be but a light doze often broken, though Alon seemed sunk far into the depths of a heavy sleep. Her shoulder was numb under the weight of his head. There came again the soft sound that had disturbed her. The Falconer and his bird, their heads close together, were exchanging twitters. Then the bird quieted down, to settle on one of the stones, apparently done with its tour of duty. The man took off his helm and wiped his forehead with the back of his hand, leaving a smudge of stone dust there. He seemed to sense that he was being watched, for he turned his head quickly, and his eyes met hers.

Cautiously Tirtha slid away from Alon. The boy sighed, turned on his side, and curled up. She left the cloak huddled over him and pulled herself up to join the man.

"Well?"

"Not so well. There are broken roofs yonder, so Wind Warrior was able to see more than we had hoped. The party—those we followed —are there. But they met with others who had a prisoner. The boy" —he glanced at Alon and then quickly away—"was right. They have been using their captive foully. Perhaps they believe him the one they have been seeking."

Tirtha's teeth closed on her lower lip. He need add no details. She had seen and heard much of how outlaws handled those they amused themselves with or would pry information from for their own purposes. What they had looked upon at the garth as this Gerik's doing had made very plain what tricks he thought worth the trying. But there was something else in the Falconer's words.

"The one they have been seeking," she repeated. "You believe then they have been waiting for me?"

"For you or another with the Hawk blood. There was the dead man, and he whom Alon told me of, the one who wore the Lord's own ring and you said was half-blood. Why should you all be drawn here?"

Why indeed? She considered that. In her pride she had believed herself to be the only one of the kin so summoned. There might well have been others; even a half-blood would answer if a geas call came strong enough. It might be that someone, or something, had indeed summoned any who had enough of Hawk blood to answer, and that these had all been burdened by the same command. If so, the one this Gerik amused himself with now was kin, and his blood debt would fall on her.

"Yes," she said softly. "Though it was my belief that I was the last of the true blood—the full blood—yet it could be so."

"What do you know of that pile over there?" A jerk of his head indicated the ruined holding.

"I have seen part of it in dreams." The time had come when she must be utterly frank with him. "The great hall and a secret place beyond it. Therein what I seek is hidden or was hidden. I do not know"—her frankness swept her on as days earlier she would never have believed possible—"*what* I so seek, only that it must be found. That is the geas laid upon me."

"Little enough." His tone was flat. "You have no other knowledge—none of its doors or how it might be entered?"

She was forced to shake her head, resenting that she must seem so stupid in his eyes. Why had her dreams *not* given her more? To her this ignorance seemed so utterly defeating that she knew again some of the soul-darkness that had struck her on the way.

"There is that which you found with the dead."

Tirtha started, her hand went quickly to her belt pouch. She had forgotten that bit of over-written skin. Now she pulled it out with desperate eagerness, smoothing the scrap upon the nearest flat surface.

Together they bent over it, but still the lines there made no sense. If it possessed a secret, Tirtha could not connect it with the ruined hold. There was no indication of a wall or passage, anything that looked to be a guide.

"Ritual perhaps," she said at last. Nor did he deny her identification.

"Yet it had a meaning for the dead."

"Which perhaps died with him." She rerolled the page, set it once more within its container. No, there was no easy way for them. This venture depended upon their wits and strength alone. She slipped the container back into her belt pouch.

"Wind Warrior sees with other eyes," the Falconer spoke musingly. "He is of the old stock, one keen-witted beyond the others remaining of his lost folk, or he would not have come to me. However, he was never battle-trained, and he cannot supply us now with such information as would point out any weaknesses in what defenses they may have."

"Since he has returned," Tirtha said, "why do you not rest, leaving the watch to me? You cannot take all sentry duty upon yourself."

He did not refuse. Though she knew well that his sort made no complaint, his body was human, and she could guess that he needed sleep—even desired it—that he might be better prepared for what lay ahead. When he had settled himself, discarding his helm and drawing his worn cloak about him, Tirtha moved into a position where she could stare directly at Hawkholme, wishing that she dared use a trance to reconnoiter, though she realized the fateful folly of that.

The sun was warm. She tugged a little at the fastenings of her jerkin. A breeze lingered over the river, and the constant murmur of the water could be lulling. Tirtha sat up the straighter, strove to plan. The curling of the flood about the remains of the bridge piers attracted her attention from time to time. Where the stones had fallen from the broken span, there were pile-ups of captured drift. Not long ago the water level must have been higher, fed by spring storms wild and strong enough to tear small trees, as well as brush, from collapsing banks, sweeping such along. There remained enough force to tug loose pieces of that wreckage which caught on the broken piers, sending them tumbling on. In fact, Tirtha began to watch the rush of water with more care. The current was apparently still to be reckoned with.

The river curved below the bridge, where rocks broke the surface, standing foam ringed, with more drift jammed among them. Beyond that the water ran between banks where bushes were still half buried in its swollen abundance. Well within the range of her sight was the artificial cut made to feed water into the moat.

Surely, with such a force of running water at hand, there must have been drains from the fortress into that cutoff. And even as Tirtha studied the rippling of the current, she could see some of the debris caught among the rocks being pulled loose from time to time, to be whirled or bobbing and tossing in the water. This could just be their way. . . .

By the time dusk arrived and she had awakened the Falconer, allowing Alon to sleep on, she had a plan, a shaky one and risky enough, but was not their whole venture risky? He listened to her suggestion, and half to her surprise and feeding her pride, he agreed.

"To enter below the rocks"—he studied the scene carefully as she had been doing all afternoon—"yes, it is possible. Also it would appear the only way one might gain that place without being sighted. Masked by drift, it is possible."

"You can swim?" She knew that while she was no mistress of water ways, she could handle herself well enough, using floating branches as a screen to make the attempt.

"We have served as marines on the Sulcar ships," he replied. "None go to sea with those warriors unless they are able to take care of themselves mid wind and wave. The mounts we must leave behind. To attempt to tow them through the water, no."

"Falgon will go. . . ." Alon's voice startled them both. They turned as one to look at the boy.

"Falgon?" questioned Tirtha.

"Him whom you call the Torgian—he has made bond with me," Alon returned simply. "And if he goes, then so will the ponies, for he is strong, and they will follow where he leads."

Tirtha was not surprised. The Torgians were noted for choosing masters whom they served until death. "It might not work," she cautioned. "We seek a way into the hold, perhaps through a drain, some small passageway, which a horse could not follow."

"Yes," Alon returned. "But he will wait nearby, the ponies with him. We shall need them later."

"And you shall wait with them." Tirtha was inspired. She had no wish to take Alon into what might well be a trap. It was hard enough to bear the burden of leading the Falconer into battle. This boy-child

—no, let him remain with the horses and relieve her mind that much.

"No, you shall need me." He spoke with authority, an odd compelling authority, which stifled any protest she might have raised.

So, when at dusk they made their way down past the rocky stretch of river, Alon, as well as the three mounts, were of the company. They squatted by the water's edge, working as quickly as they could in the dark, fashioning narrow rafts of drift on which they piled most of their gear, including their clothing. The falcon had taken off, heading toward the main tower of the waiting ruin, as they stepped into water cold enough to wring gasps from them all. Then, having waded out a few steps, they abandoned themselves to the steady pull of the current, their shoulders supported by the rafts, kicking their feet to steer them straight.

Thus they reached the entrance to the moat. Here a fall of stone had nearly dammed the entrance, but they scrambled over it. On the other side the Falconer tested the depth where the water washed directly against the walls and found it no more than knee-deep, though stagnant and evil-smelling, so they redressed hurriedly. Alon stood and set his hands on either side of the Torgian's head. Then he released the animal, which turned to climb the nearest bank, the ponies following. The beasts were gone before Tirtha could send Alon with them. Luckily it was a dark night, with the beginning of rain, and the animals, with near-human intelligence, picked as silent a way as they could.

Above, the building showed no lights, nor had they, during all their drifting with the current, sighted any signs of life. Did those now holding the place believe that, in the prisoner they had taken, they had the one they had waited for? Tirtha found the lack of any sentries suspicious, but there was nothing they could do except go on. With the Falconer moving in the lead, they began a search along the wall for an entrance into the hold from the moatside.

They were dwarfed by the rise of the walls above, and the stench of the mud they stirred up by their passing made Tirtha sick, though she had had only one scant meal that day. To all outward evidence they rounded a deserted building, and Tirtha kept a tight hold on her thoughts, did not try in any way to sense out what might be above. She saw the dark shadow that was the Falconer stop short, set both his hands against the slimed wall, his head at an angle. She, too, looked up.

There, just above them, was what they had been seeking, a rounded opening. Alon pressed close to the man.

"Up! Let me see."

The Falconer caught the boy about the waist, lifted him until Alon's feet were on his shoulders and Alon's arms and chest above the lower rim of the opening. Alon stretched out his hands. By straining her sight, Tirtha could see them against the opening, moving back and forth.

14

Alon set one hand against the edge of the opening; with the other he thrust inward. Tirtha heard a rattle and was alarmed lest the sound carry. It was plain that Alon worked to loosen something within the shadow of the opening. The Falconer braced his body closer to the slimed wall, holding steady. There came another sharp *ping* from above. Alon swung down a dark bar that Tirtha hastened to catch.

It was metal, foul smelling, flaking off rusted bits in her hands. She let it slide on down into the sludge about her feet where turgid water swallowed it up without sound. Alon was at work again, and it was not too long before a second bar, torn from its setting, was freed, dropped, and likewise disappeared.

They might be striving to force entrance into a totally deserted building, and the very fact that they heard nothing, saw no sign of any guards, was to Tirtha a source of continued uneasiness. Those within might know very well that their prey was coming to them, resting at ease, needing only to wait. Yet what other recourse had she and her companions?

A third bar was freed. Then Alon dropped down from his perch to report in the thinnest of whispers:

"There is now a full opening, and I felt within. It is a foul place, but it is clear. There are even hand holds on the walls. Perhaps the lord here once planned a way of escape for a bad time."

"That could be true," murmured the Falconer. Tirtha could also understand the logic. Had this moat not been half dammed off from the river by the fallen wall and if, instead, the water in it had been up over the old markings they had felt as they had come, the opening would have been below the surface, completely masked. A determined or desperate in-dweller could well use it secretly. However, she eyed this particular door to Hawkholme with little favor. This opening was narrow, it was good that they had gone short of rations recently, and that she had always been thin, with few curves to plump out her jerkin or leggings. She wondered if the Falconer could force entrance, but, like all his breed, he was wiry, not thick of body.

"I go first," Tirtha declared firmly. "But how will *you* reach it?" She looked to the Falconer; he could give her a hand up as he had Alon, but who could do the same for him?

"There will be a way." He spoke with such confidence that Tirtha knew he was sure of his own ability. He caught her quickly under the arms to lift her, steadying her body against the wall until she thrust her hands into the mouth of the drain. One arm scraped across a broken space from which Alon had loosed a bar. She groped frantically within, seeking those holds Alon said existed. Then one hand, digging deep into noisome, crusty filth, hooked into what was manifestly a loop. A moment later she discovered its twin on the opposite side.

Tirtha was grateful for past hard work in the fields. What she had learned on Estcarp farms gave her the strength needed. Had she not had those years of hard physical work behind her, she could never have fought her way up that hidden ladder where the stench near choked her, her hair and garments rendered sodden and thick with foulness. Her cloak she had left bound to her saddle, and she was glad of that, for its folds would never have allowed her passage. As it was she felt the harsh rasp of stone against her leather garments, with now and then a painful scrape on her skin.

Luckily the way was not straight up but slanted. And Tirtha discovered, once inside the hole, she could feel ahead for each hold, drawing herself along more easily than she would have believed possible, though it was a worm's progress. The nastiness of the foul encrustation choked her, so that she could only hope that the exit lay not too far ahead.

In the dark she could move only by touch. Also the stench grew even thicker, though this drain had been abandoned for many years. Finally, her hand hit against a solid barrier and she could have cried out in her dismay. Holding on with one hand, she clawed along that surface. The drain took an abrupt turn here.

The long slant, up which she had worked her way, ended in a

right-angled space. Above that there seemed to be nothing but solid roof. She refused to let herself panic. She ran first one hand and then the other back and forth across the barrier. Her third such try brought success. She knocked loose a solid cake of encrustation, enough so that once more her fingers hooked into a space that felt carved to receive just such a grip.

First she bore down, dragging with all her might, to no purpose. Must she believe that, if there had ever been an opening here, it was now impossible to move? A last desperate try made her shove instead of pull. There was a grating sound. So heartened, Tirtha changed hands again quickly and put all the effort she could into a full side-wise push. Stationed so awkwardly, able to work only with one hand, she fought stubbornly. There was a give, the barrier moved, though with a louder grating that winged her heart to a faster beat. She held on for a wild moment, five fingers gripped on the sliding panel, the other hand flailing out into an open space. Then she was able to hook that hand over an edge and pull herself up with a wrench that took what seemed the last flare of her strength. Her head and shoulders rose into clean air as she flopped across the edge of a stone bench onto the floor of a narrow chamber in the heart of the wall itself.

A cool rush of night air struck at her as Tirtha pulled herself around to face the fissure in the wall through which that welcome breeze came. This must be the upper floor of the main dwelling chambers wherein the family had once had their private apartments. She scrambled to her feet, feeling about her. Her outflung hand broke a remnant of charred wood, as she stumbled into a narrow hall. The far end of it showed faint light, radiating from far below. Sighting this, Tirtha crouched, trying to still the gasps of air she had been drawing into her lungs, as if such sounds might betray her to any keeping vigil by that distant gleam of light.

Sounds from the wall chamber marked Alon's arrival in turn. The boy moved out to clutch at Tirtha's shoulder. They leaned against the wall together, intent upon the far end of the hall, until the Fal-coner joined them. With him came light, dim and wan yet visible. The pommel of the power weapon was awakening.

Again Tirtha left the other two, to slip along that wall. She passed yawning caverns on her right where more burnt wood marked doors to chambers, but those were not important. She had to reach the Great Hall. Only from there could she trace the steps to be taken for conclusion of her mission. And surely the Great Hall would be the one place where their enemies within would be.

Corridor's end gave upon a staircase circling about a center core, winding steeply downward, the steps narrow wedges of stone. There was a groove cut in the wall about this formidable coil of descent, perhaps to provide a hand hold.

At the foot of the spiral was a lamp in a niche, a basin of stone with a wick fed into it through a hole in the loose lid. The light it gave was limited, but that any here had seen fit to light this stair at all was a warning, one that Tirtha thought it well to heed. She hesitated at the top of that well-like way. Only one person at a time could descend, and if a guard waited below, out of sight . . .

She became aware of a soft rustle and glanced back. By the eerie light of the Falconer's weapon, she saw that the bird which accompanied him was again perched on the man's shoulder. Its head was extended well forward as it also stared down.

The presence of the lamp bothered Tirtha. Since they had come into the upper hall, the place had been utterly silent. Though these walls were thick, much of the interior had clearly been destroyed by fire and sounds should carry. Such quiet only meant to her that the three of them were, in spite of Alon's earlier reassurance, not only expected but that a trap awaited them. She edged away from the stairway, then wondered if that was exactly how she was expected to reason—that the lamp below was set so as to make them take another path.

A hand caught hers, startling her, pulling her down so that she was on a level with the boy.

"*He*—he is here. . . ." There was fear in his voice.

His grasp on Tirtha tightened, held with frantic force, pinning her to the fire-stained wall. If he should lapse now into that state of withdrawal . . . Terror was building up in him to such an extent as to awake panic in Tirtha herself. By his very touch he fed it to her. She caught at him, strove to shut out of her mind any dread of her own, to return only what strength of spirit she had to offer.

Somehow their alarm must have spread in turn to the Falconer, perhaps through the medium of the bird on his shoulder, for he swung up between them. The dim glow of his sword rested on both woman and boy, its pommel pulsating with the light that was both a warning and a solace against the spread of the Dark.

Alon's involuntary shudders shook Tirtha. She could see his face, a vague blur turned up to hers. Then the light swept over him. He had closed his eyes tightly, his mouth was twisted as if to utter a noiseless scream. However, as the thin glow of the gemstone touched him, that expression of witless terror receded, even as she, also, felt a warmth rising within her body.

They had more than one weapon, these enemies who made their den in Hawkholme, and perhaps the strongest could not be seen or heard. They who invaded must seek action, for to remain cowering here was to open gates to this other, more deadly form of attack.

If she had only had better preparation! Those dreams—they seemed now to her to have been more deceptive than helpful. There must be a way through this ruined stronghold, yet she could only blunder and hope and perhaps fail.

No! Again that insidious thing which attacked through mind and emotion had struck at Alon through one kind of fear, at her with another. What of the Falconer—what did it strive to reach in him? For the impression grew in Tirtha that the thing lairing here with its servants might indeed need to reach them by devious means, that it shrank from physical attack. Why? The Sword—yes, it could be that weapon of power which had spun about them its small light. Perhaps, because it had come into the Falconer's hand from the first, he was now the best armored of the three.

She heard again a rustle of wing as she deliberately pushed closer to the man so that her shoulder rubbed against his.

"I must," she said in the lowest whisper she could manage, "reach the Great Hall. It is only from there that I know my path."

He did not answer at once, but neither did he draw back from that contact between their bodies as she thought he might. As she had tried with Alon, perhaps in the same way he sought now to reassure her. Even as she thought that, there was in her, this time, no answering surge of rebellion. The three of them *were* locked into action which they must share; upon each other they must depend until the very end.

Again came a rustling of feathers. Tirtha could see by this faintest of lights that the falcon was mantling, bobbing its head, stretching its neck forward, not toward the stairwell from which they had retreated, but toward the other end of this hall. The Falconer swung in that direction, holding the sword in his claw, for he had drawn his dart gun in one sure movement, and had as usual taken the lead, walking with a scout's care that Tirtha tried with all her might to equal, drawing Alon along with her. The reflection of the powered gem appeared to exert a soothing effect on Alon for though he clamped fingers tightly in Tirtha's belt as an anchorage, he opened his eyes, pacing beside her in the wake of the man.

What they came to was the ruin of another staircase. Its core was stone, but that had once been covered with wood, and paneled walls must have once enclosed it—now burnt away. So again the descent would be a perilous one. Still, there was no lamp below, while the roof stretched high above their heads, for they had issued out of the mouth of a hallway which was on one level of what must have been a towering chamber.

The falcon winged out into this open space of which they could see so little. Now the Falconer began to descend the stairs, one step at a time, his helmed head turning slowly from side to side, as if he sought to hear the more clearly since he could not see. There was no change in the quality or strength of the light given off by the sword. Oddly enough, as Tirtha and Alon began their own halting descent some two steps behind the Falconer, the boy appeared to have fully shaken free of his fear. In his small face his eyes looked larger than before, as if his sight could pierce the dark.

Thus they came into a vast space surrounding the foot of that ruined stair. For the first time Tirtha believed she recognized the necessary path. She turned to the left, bringing Alon, by his continued hold on her, along, the Falconer falling in at her side. Through the darkness, lit only by the small glow the sword gem spun about them, she guessed what lay before her, as if her dream had once more enclosed her.

This *was* the Great Hall. In Tirtha arose an excitement that fear could not touch. Because she had won this far, what had drawn her here was strengthening, taking over within her. She strode, not crept, confident of where she went.

The dais with the chairs of honor had stood there. She could not see them; doubtless they had been swallowed up in the fire or hacked wantonly to pieces by those who had overrun the hold. Now she must turn this way, behind a screen. . . .

So sure was she that a screen stood there that she put up her hand lest she run into it. Yet there was nothing but a wall. The Falconer, as if anticipating her request, held the sword up and forward. What she sought lay beyond, of that she was certain. Almost roughly she loosed Alon's hold, ran to that wall, swept her grimy hands back and forth across it. Her fingers left trailmarks in dust and ash, but she had no luck this time. There was no possible hold she could discover that would open for her like the door in the drain.

It lay here! She knew it. Tirtha strove to command her impatience. She closed her eyes—this might be the most dangerous thing she could do, but she must throw open the gate of memory to the dream, command it, as in the past it had commanded her. Only so could she come at what she must take into her hands.

The great hall—piece by piece she labored to draw it out of the nothingness and ruin about her. Just so had the lord sat, and his lady, between the two of them on that table the casket. Then had come the alarm. The more Tirtha pulled and drew, the clearer the picture became. She could feel those others she had not seen clearly in her dreams, their rise of emotion, fear and excitement, determination, dread, above all a flare of courage that was like a lighted torch in the dead dark.

The lady—Tirtha did not know it now but her own hands were up breast high before her, cradling the invisible at the level of her heart. Behind the carven screen—now the wall—a wall once paneled in wood carving, fancifully wrought, painted and gilded here and there. Only it was not the wall that was so important. She did not raise a hand now to its surface. Instead she advanced the toe of one worn boot, planted it firmly on a pavement fashioned of many small colored stones in strange and angular pictures. So by instinct she sought out one of those fitted stones slightly larger than the others, and upon it she bore down firmly, with as much weight as she could bring to bear on such a small surface.

There was resistance. She tried again, the need for speed lashing at her. Once, twice, three times. Surely it would not refuse her entrance now that she had come so far!

The wall moved. With a thin screech of sound as if metal crossed metal long ungreased and near-rusted in place, a passage opened. From that shone light—blue, faint, but still light!

Tirtha threw herself forward. With the opening of the door the dream vanished. Still the summoned vision had served her well. This was the secret place, and before her must lie what was being guarded —which those of her line were pledged ever to protect until they were released from a very ancient bond.

Beyond lay a small room, and though time had wrought some ruin within, the wrath of men had not reached here. There were tapestries on the walls. At the stir of air which entered at her coming, they moved. From them fell patches of paper—thin fabric, like dead and dried autumn leaves. What she had come for stood as it had been left —on a narrow table of stone jutting forward from a wall of which it was a part. The top of the table was deeply incised with symbols, which had once been brightly painted but were now dulled and dusty. They were words of Power so old that no one among those who served what rested here could any longer understand them. Tirtha, looking upon them, knew that these were Names here that, were they spoken, could destroy the walls about her, change perhaps even the running of time as men knew it.

Within a concentric circle of those Names stood the casket. It was of the same silver metal as the sword that had come to the Falconer, and from its surface arose the diffused light filling the room. Tirtha put out both hands. With widespread fingers she drew in the air above that waiting treasure signs issuing from buried knowledge as old as the land on which Hawkholme stood. Then, between her two palms she felt the weight of the casket as she lifted it, to hold against her, even as the lady had borne it hither in her dream. Lifted it and turned . . .

The scream was that of a war cry, given to waken and alarm. Over her head swooped the falcon, out from the dark behind them. One of the bird's feet was now a stump from which curled a thread of noxious smoke. At the same moment Alon and the Falconer were both hurtled inward toward her. They did not bear her to the floor, as perhaps they might have done had there been more room. Rather, they threw her backward so that her spine hit hard against the shelf table, bringing a pain so sharp and terrible that Tirtha lost control over her body and sank to the floor, folding over the casket which she still held.

There followed a crash, and she heard another scream—not from a bird's throat this time, but from Alon she was sure. The pain that filled her brought darkness, and she sank into it as an exhausted swimmer sinks into a sea he can no longer battle.

"Tirtha! Lady!" Moisture on her face, a burning within her lips. She strove to see who called, but all was a haze that swam back and forth, making her ill so that she quickly shut her eyes. Pain filled her. When she strove to move, to crawl away from the fire which she felt as if about to consume her utterly, there was no life in her body. Her hands—no, she must not loose—loose what? She could not remember. But, save for the pain that burned, her body was as the dead.

"Tirtha!" Again that call. She sought to escape it, to find a way to flee both the pain and the demanding voice. Only there was something that compelled her to open her eyes once more.

The haze this time separated itself into two parts, one large, one much smaller. Tirtha frowned and squinted, trying to see the better. Faces—yes, Alon—slowly she fitted a name to the nearest—and

Nirel—yes, that was his true name—Nirel. She thought she repeated both, but perhaps she did not, for she could not hear her own voice. It was such a struggle to try to hold on to this contact that she would rather they allowed her to slip back into that place of darkness, of peace.

"Holla!"

The force in that call was as terrible in her ears as the scream of the injured falcon. It offered no rest and it held her here.

"Hawk's brood!" A second time words rang through the very air of this place, a torment added to all the rest she bore.

"Give unto the Dark Lord what is his and all shall be well."

Yet that was no true promise or bargain. Even through the waves of pain that beset her, Tirtha knew that much.

"By Harith and Haron, and the Blood of the Hawk Brood"— Tirtha did not know from whence came the strength to draw intelligible words out of her, making her voice firm for that moment— "only to the Appointed One do we resign our guardianship. The hour is nigh. . . ."

"The hour is nigh in truth," roared the voice out of the air. "Treachery begets treachery. What is of the Dark shall return there, be it bound as might be. To all sorceries there comes an end, just as there is an end to time itself. Render up what was never of the Light."

Deep in her something else stirred. He who was without, he could not enter, he dared not take, save by the permission of the true blood. And she—*she* was the true blood. This must not end in Hawk defeat —only in death. And against death who may fight?

Her mouth worked. Tirtha strove to fight the dryness that filled it so she could shape words once more.

"This I hold—I of the Hawk—and if death is the portion of that holding, then let it be so."

"Aaaaghhh . . ." That came as a wordless howl of fury, dying away in an echo, as if he who had voiced it had withdrawn to a far distance.

Tirtha looked again to the two with her. She lay flat upon the floor in the heat of her pain, and she believed that her body was so broken she could not long be contained within it. Perhaps that purpose which had drawn her here would strive to hold her so, even in this agony. Now she gazed first at Alon and then at Nirel who held close to his breast the injured falcon. The bird's eyes were dim, and its head sagged forward. It was dying—more blessed than she might be, Tirtha thought fleetingly.

"I ask pardon of you," she said, first to the Falconer, for he had truly been outside this dire pattern before she had deliberately drawn him in, and he had lost much already. "This is an end my dream did not foretell, but there are many times unexpected changes in life's weaving. Give me a comrade's passing farewell even though I am what you deem the least—a woman." She did not wait for any answer. In fact she shrank from gazing longer at him, since she did not want to read refusal in his eyes. Instead she spoke now to the boy.

"Your pardon also, Alon. Though I did not willfully draw *you* into this venture. Perhaps that, too, was another fault in the weaving for us. I have failed, and by my nature, you both are caught and with you the brave bird. If there is any truth in the old stories, perhaps lives so oddly bonded here shall be later led to understand the why of such geas-setting. I think we shall not issue forth from this place alive. The secret I hold is not for those without. For that I must thank the Power which I never could summon."

Her words came slower and lower as pain lapped her round. She looked once more to the Falconer. His face was again only a blur.

"Leave in my hands," she said, "what I have taken up. That I must guard as best I can until the end."

15

Alon reached across her, his hands out, not to her but to the Falconer. Into that hold the man relinquished the limp bird, which the boy drew as protectingly to him as Tirtha kept the casket. The Falconer arose from where he knelt, and she saw him, through the pain that held her, turn slowly, gazing about, sweeping off his bird helm to see the better, while he still clasped the sword within his claw. From it issued a wan light to vie with that from the casket.

Tirtha closed her eyes, ready to surrender, yet death did not reach for her as she hoped. The Last Road might lie before her, but something held her back from that journey. Alon murmured to the stricken bird.

Bird?

Tirtha blinked. Now her injury built illusions. There had been a falcon in Alon's hold. Now a shimmer covered that huddle of black feathers, as if one misty picture were fitted over another. What Alon nursed was not the same—rather a strange thing with gray-feathered body and large open eyes banded round with scarlet feathers. This other bird raised its head high, though behind its shadowy form she could see still the drooping crest of the falcon. Its bill opened as if voicing a challenge or cry of anger.

Alon's eyes had closed. Now they flickered open, appearing large in his thin face. He stared down at what he held as if he, too, was aware of change.

The Falconer, seemingly alerted by what he sensed rather than heard, swung swiftly around, to stare at boy and bird. That doubled misty outline faded in and out, sometimes blotting out the falcon, at other times losing the gray bird. There might be a struggle between the two, one life force striving to impress itself upon a weaker one.

Alon shifted the bird, leaned closer still to Tirtha. She gained a measure of strength to dispute pain, to clear her mind. For that this had important meaning, she was sure. Perhaps some act might follow which, even if it could not save her, would carry to an end what the geas demanded of her. Guardianship was not enough, though it had been faithfully held to the last of the Blood to whom the task had been given. There was more, and if events were out of her control, yet all was still not swallowed by Dark mastery. Did the Falconer nurse some suspicion of unknown danger? His sword swung into place above Tirtha's body from the other side, its point aimed at the bird that struggled from one form to the other.

The gem in the pommel flashed, emitting waves of light to encircle the bird. The bird became whole, complete, not dead but vibrantly alive, a species unknown to Tirtha. When its beak opened once again, its cry could be heard, as fierce as the call of the falcon it had replaced, yet with a different, even wilder note. Its head darted forward on a longer neck than the falcon had owned, a sharp bill struck at Alon's fingers—struck but did not break skin. Instead the head jerked back, to slew about at a nearly impossible angle to view the boy.

It did not threaten such attack again, but it beat its wings, and Alon loosed his hold, so that it fluttered forward and down, coming to perch on the casket still resting between Tirtha's numb hands.

There it again elongated its neck, its be-ringed eyes approaching her own.

The bird spoke—this was no cry or twitter, but a recognizable word. She had heard of birds trained to mimic human speech. Yet this was no mimic. Whereas the falcon had communicated by its own twitterings, which only the man could understand, this one, arisen out of the other's death, uttered what they could all distinguish.

"Ninutra . . ."

In the sway of Tirtha's mind, where pain and the need for holding strove against one another, there flickered the faintest memory. Out of Lormt, out of some legend she had picked up in her wanderings? No, this was another thing, perhaps a blood memory, descending to her from the line of those who had worn the Hawk and kept faith with something greater, not of man and woman at all.

The pain became a raging fire enveloping her, and she recognized that the fire was not entirely of the body, but a sign of Power alien to anything she had dreamed might exist. They said there had been Great Old Ones who had left humanity far behind, made of themselves that which in later days had little touch with mankind. This fire—and within it a face of carven beauty—was utterly remote. Yet the face bore eyes that still lived, looked into this place, considered the three of them, weighed them, before making judgment. The old accounts spoke of adepts who were neither of the Light nor the Dark, who withdrew from quarrels and strivings for power among their kind to seek only new and stranger knowledge. Tirtha did not feel the Dark in this one, nor did she sense any surge of strength the Light might have granted her. Still in her mind remained that face, until Tirtha was sure that she would carry it with her even into the death that must come. To such a one as this, no plea she might offer could reach.

Or . . .

The geas! Had this one laid *that* upon her? Had there been ancient dealings between this One of High Power and those of the Hawk? If so, then she could surely claim, if not for herself, then for the two with her, some aid. Tirtha strove to form that appeal, a last demand that a faithful servant be so repaid.

There was no change in the face she saw, only intelligence and measurement. Tirtha felt more pain—the numbness in her hands and arms was receding—though the rest of her body was only a vehicle for torment, dead to all else.

Her fingers fumbled with the casket, feebly running about its sides, hunting clasp or lock. There was none she could find by touch alone, and her sight was dim. Nor could she lift her head to look closer at what she clung to. It must not be given into the hands of another. The bird still squatted upon it—wings outstretched as if to hide it from view. Tirtha suddenly realized she could not even feel the touch of feathers. Illusion? Yet Alon no longer held the dying falcon—it was gone.

"Ninutra!" The bird raised its neck and head to form a single line, the open beak pointing at the shadowed roof above them. It summoned—surely it summoned! Still, who could reach them here save what prowled without, lacking the secret of the door?

From the four corners of the ceiling in that hidden chamber burst scarlet flame. Between those fiery tongues the air moved, as if all the dust the years had deposited here was drawn in, whirled about, kneaded into mass and substance. Over Tirtha that whirlwind centered and took form. There was a sword—a long-bladed, plain-hilted weapon of a misty-gray—a thing pulled from shadows not of a human world.

The point was above the casket and the bird. Tirtha understood. What lay within the guardian's hold was to remain secret. Yet it was also a focus for the power that had been summoned. There was nothing they could do but watch and wait, for they were only a very small part of another's plan. Perhaps in the end they would be discarded. One did not strike bargains, make pleas to such as this.

There was something about the shadow sword. Even as the Falconer's weapon bore unreadable symbols along its length, so did similar markings appear here. And those in part she recognized. Some of these were written on the dead man's scroll! She marveled at that for a long moment.

Alon, no longer holding the bird, had dropped his hands to lie limp on his knees where he sat cross-legged. His eyes, taking on a kind of luminance, not from those flames lashing over his head, but rather from the Falconer's weapon, were fixed upon that shadow sword, and there was that in his face which no child could know nor feel. He was gathering what he had not yet learned properly to garner, fighting a private battle of his own.

The Falconer stood as might a defender, waiting for a last fatal charge meant to bring down all he would protect. His weapon of power was held point up as if to engage that shadow weapon should it strike.

"Nirel." Into that Tirtha put what strength she had left. "Take the scroll, for it is a part of this, though I know not how."

The Falconer did not move, but Alon, as if he were well aware of what she carried and recognized its value, opened her pouch and pulled forth the metal rod thrusting it upward into one of the empty dart loops on the man's shoulder belt.

Within her mind the face of carven beauty withdrew as by a click of fingers, though Tirtha was sure that what it represented had not yet put them out of mind. Instead she felt, through the stone on which she lay, adding to her torment, a quivering of the rock, a tremor. Again she found voice, this time to cry a warning.

"Away from the walls!" She was not sure in what direction what was coming might strike, and they might all be buried. In that fashion, what she still held would be made safe.

The Falconer threw himself forward. With his clawed arm he swept the boy flat to the floor, thrusting him against Tirtha, while she cringed from the pain the contact caused her. Then the man was on his knees, arching his own body over the two of them. His mailed chest nearly flattened the bird as he tried to protect them.

A second tremor moved the floor. The flames flared out fiercely, still there was no heat in them. Now the shadow sword tilted in the air, though perhaps Tirtha, lying face up as she did, was the only witness. No longer did it hang point down; rather it stretched horizontal, and it grew longer, wider, casting over the three of them a shadow.

The ragged tapestries on the walls swung as they might have had a tempest caught them. Pieces of cobweb-thin fabric tore loose, to settle on the three so entwined.

There came a crash. Behind a fall of the rotting fabric, a widening break in the wall showed, stones loosened, fell outward and away. In the dark beyond, a second wall came into sight. That, also cracked, swayed out, to crash. The light of day flooded in—a day of sullen skies and great bursts of lightning, which sent force whips lashing across the sky. Thunder was war drums beating up an army.

Tirtha saw that opening. They could go, these two, the way was open. In so much had the Power which had brought her here answered her plea. She tried to break her hold on the casket with one hand, thrust the Falconer up and away from her so that he could see that door to freedom and take it—he and Alon. Yet she could no longer detach her flesh from the box. There was movement; the bird swept across her face, though she felt no brush of feather. It passed out from under the hanging sword, turning in the air, sped like a well-thrown lance out into the midst of the storm where its gray body became one with the half-light, gone from their sight.

"Go . . ." Tirtha tried to raise her voice above the violence of the thunder. There came another crash, another portion of that outer wall disappeared. Now there was a strange smell in the air, though it held none of the noisome stench of the Dark. She was sure that lightning had struck very close, perhaps somewhere on the building.

The Falconer levered himself up. The flames that had played about their heads had been snuffed out; the outline of the shadow sword was gone. It would appear that all manifestations of that other Power had been withdrawn. There was an open door to freedom, yes, but one she could not take.

Tirtha was enough of a healer to be sure that her back had been broken and that, even if they moved her (which she believed they could not do), it would only prolong the end for her, in turn putting them into greater danger. Better she had been buried under collapsing walls, taking with her what she was born to guard.

The Falconer was on his feet, pulling at remnants of the tapestry. There were lengths here and there, which, when he dragged them free of the broken walls, seemed stouter. These he smoothed out on the floor, Alon scrambling up to help.

They had at length a padding of four or five thicknesses, as long as Tirtha was tall. She could understand their purpose and knew it would fail. But also she realized now they would not go forth and leave her. Perhaps death would come swiftly when they attempted to move her; she could wish for nothing more than that.

They were done at last. Now Nirel stooped above her. Tirtha bit her lip until she tasted blood. She gathered all her last strength to make certain that she would not give tongue to her agony. He knelt, and she felt his hands slip slowly under her shoulders. There followed such a wave of torment as made all her earlier suffering seem as nothing.

"My . . . belt . . . pouch . . ." She mouthed the words, and Alon must again have heard them first, for she saw his hands swift in their movement. "The . . . bag . . . with"—she had to swallow before pushing the last words out—"the dragon sign . . . put all . . . in . . . my . . . mouth. . . ." This was the last mercy she hoped for. So powerful was this drug one used it with great care. To swallow all she carried was inviting the end. Let it come fast and free the two of them.

Alon had the smaller bag open. He held the mouth of it to her lips, shook free dried leaves that struck her tongue like a spoonful of dust. Tirtha choked, swallowed, choked, and fought to get the full portion down. Rightly, it should be taken as a brew. Swallowed dry in this fashion, she did not know how long it might need to work—she could only hope. Since the portion was far more than had ever been advised for use, she trusted it would serve.

Pain again, but through its piercing agony she continued to fight the dusty mouthful into her throat, swallowing convulsively. Then the world went scarlet with another protest from her broken body, and from that she passed into blessed nothingness.

She became aware not of her body, but of the self that had only before ventured forth in dreams and farseeing. The relief of being free of pain was so great that she exulted in nothing else for a period of time. This, then, was what came afterwards—what mankind had so long speculated might lie at the end of the Long Road—freedom indeed.

Only she was not free. Dimly, through her relief, she felt the tug of some tie. At once she opposed it. Might a geas last past the very fact of death? How could she still be entrapped? Tirtha knew fear and then rage, and her rage was a fire blazing up about that inner self. No! She would answer to no one, to nothing!

Nothing, not even that call.

Call? Yes, from a far distance there was a call, a demand, an urgent command.

Then she knew that she was indeed not free, that her body still encased her. It was immobile, that body of hers—dead—while within it she was hopelessly imprisoned. There was no longer any pain, only the deadness. She was looking up into the sky from which rain fell in great sheets, though on her dead body she could not even feel its beat. It filled her eyes, and so she could only see as through a heavy mist.

Yet she saw and she heard.

"Take it, fool—it is what we have sought!"

"Take it and die, is that the way of it, Lord? You saw what happened to Rudik . . ."

"She is dead. Have you not proof of that by the bite of your own sword?"

"I have also seen Rudik. I do not seek what happened to him, Lord. This is of your desire—do you then take it."

"Fool! Have I not said many times over, to each his own Powers?

This is not of my knitting, and should I reach for it, it will be destroyed and none of us thereafter shall have the good of it. There are laws of the Talents and those may not be broken."

"It was perhaps wrong to shoot down the bird-lover. We might have used him then . . ."

"Not so—you saw his weapon. It was well that your dart struck first, for that was a thing bound to him, and thus the same rule would have held."

"Then use the boy. He has no weapon and he . . ."

There came an angry laugh. "Why must I be plagued ever by the service of fools? The boy—he is perhaps near as great a catch as this trinket box you so fear to meddle with. There will be pleasure for the Great One in meeting him! No—take up that box and now! I have held my hand because I know that you are shortgifted in wits and courage—you ravagers of an undone and ruined land—but need I compel you?"

"Lord, remember you are still only one among us, for all your talk of mighty forces that will come riding at your call. And Rudik is dead, in such a way as none of us here has any desire to follow. There is that other . . ."

A moment of silence and then, "Perhaps you are not so great a fool as you would seem, Gerik. Yes, he is still alive, even after your kind attentions and earnest discussions. I think he has enough of a hand left to do our bidding. He may not be a true Hawk, but there is a part of the proper blood within him, unless that was all spilled during our time of reasoning. So he may be able to achieve what must be done. Get him forth and try! I do not like this storm, there is the smell of Power here, such as is no friend to the Great One."

Tirtha lay within her shell of death and tried to understand. The bird man—Nirel—dead? It would seem so. For a moment she felt a thrust of strange pain, though not from her dead flesh and splintered bones but rather from another part of her. And the boy—that was Alon—him this "Lord" would take as captive to present to some greater doer of Evil. But it would seem that the casket was still hers, or at least within the guardianship of her dead body—and it had already caused death to one who would take it from her. That was true—the guardianship might pass only by right and by free gift, she knew, perhaps had always known in some hidden part of her.

So—one of the Blood? One to take from her even in death if it could be . . . And she had not the power—no longer any command. Again she knew the swelling fire of anger—a rage that filled her world. She could not be foresworn—she was the Hawk and in her hold this . . . !

Still the rain blinded her eyes which she could not close or blink; but she could hear, even as she heard voices now, whimpering sobs of pain, the cries of one broken and vanquished. She saw approaching her three shapes half hidden by the storm, two dragging a third between them. The two, who carried rather than led that helpless one, hurled him to the ground beside her, so he fell out of her range of sight. Then one of his captors stooped and caught a fistful of hair, drawing him up into her murky vision once again.

She saw a face bearing such scars and mutilations as made it a mask of horror, yet that part of her imprisoned in death felt emotion only vaguely, as if it were such a distance from her now that it was one with the helplessness of her own body. The other guard grabbed at the limp and helpless man, seizing an arm down the scorched and beaten flesh of which water runneled. There were fingers on a hand that was fire-shriveled. All but two of them were bent at impossible angles, but the hand was dragged forward above Tirtha, and though she could see only a fraction of movement, she realized that it was being made to reach for the casket, which must still lie upon her breast, perhaps tight in the hold of her dead hands.

The guard dropped that hand. She heard a scream such as could be torn only from one suffering the deepest agony that the Dark might devise. His body arched into her sight, nearly won to its feet in that last terrible torment, then fell back and away. There was silence, save for the battering of the rain and the distant beat of the thunder.

"You see, Lord, even your half-blood could not do it."

There was a sound in answer that was no word, rather a hissing of sheer rage. Then he who had been so addressed apparently mastered his flaming anger.

"Well enough. The puzzle remains. We shall take the dead with us, since no one seems like to master her. Sling her over a pack pony and let us be gone. There are those who can be summoned by the very smell of Power, and we are in debatable land."

"You ride for Escore, Lord?"

"Where else? Get your men together, Gerik, and let us be about our business. As for the cub—I shall see to him. She, at least, will need no guards."

"Lord, my sword-oath serves only this side of the border. We do not ride crosswise into what lies eastward."

Again that snarl. "You will discover, if you try otherwise, Gerik, that your oath is more than you deemed it at its taking. When I speak, you ride where and when it is my desire that you do so."

Once more a length of silence. Tirtha discovered that while she might no longer sense by physical means or judge by what she saw, still she was keenly aware of all about her. That Gerik was cowed was untrue. He was in a little awe of the one he addressed as "lord," but already a wily and subtle mind, well melded with cruelty and ruthlessness, was twisting and turning to find a way free. Murder was the least, perhaps, and the most forthright of the thoughts now in the outlaw's head.

However, for the time being, he was willing to adopt an outward show of being completely under the other's domination. She heard stamping of hooves on stone. Moments later she was lifted, and inwardly waited for the pain to strike—no, she must have been right. Her body had died, and it did not matter how roughly slack flesh and broken bone was handled. She felt nothing save that she was indeed lying across a pony's back and that she had been lashed in place there.

Alon had made no sound. She wondered then if once more he had fled back into that hiding place he had found during the attack on the garth. But he had certainly not become invisible, for they spoke of him as booty to be carried off.

They rode under the fall of the rain, eastward bound. Behind them they must be leaving the dead. She had no idea what might have happened to the unfortunate Rudik, but that the Falconer had found the end of his journey and that the tortured rag of humanity they had brought to rob her had been finished, Tirtha did not doubt.

She hung in her bonds unfeeling, and at length she was able once more to flee imprisonment from the shell of her inert self, sink back into the darkness. Still she was not free. Even in death the casket rode with her, and she came to believe that she would be bound in essence of spirit as long as it existed and was not returned to the one who could claim it by full right.

Was that the woman figure she had seen in her mind—the one the bird had called upon as Ninutra? If the bird had flown free from the keep to summon help, help had not come. Tirtha wondered about what had happened when Nirel and Alon had gotten her out of the destroyed secret chamber. But all that was very far away and had no more meaning for her. She need only wait and hope that that wait would not be long, until the final meeting wherein it would be de-

cided once and for all whether a blood-oath might hold past death
and how strong such a tie would be against the Dark.

Tirtha thought once more of the woman—not to make any plea—
that was no longer in her power. If this Ninutra was the prime mover
who had set the geas into action, then it must be her time and place
and power that would bring the end into view. Surely there would be
freedom thereafter, but perhaps even yet—though she no longer had
a body worth the struggle—a final battle lay ahead.

16

Perhaps time and death had no meeting place; or perhaps it was that,
even though dead, she was still held to the world she knew. Tirtha
drifted between a place where she knew nothing and was at rest and
being remotely conscious of what lay about her. There was the rain
and storm, winds that buffeted the land, vicious strikes of lightning,
though the fury of the unleashed weather led the commanded of this
party to make no concessions. They rode through the worst of it as if
there were clear sky above.

Tirtha's vague touches of the outer world caught strange, floating
fragments of thoughts that were not her own. She did not try to
gather or consider them, yet she knew that those who rode were
certainly not united. There were fears here, anger, dour resentment,
weariness, but above all fear. That emotion gathered force, aimed in
one direction, toward the leader under whose orders they journeyed.

During one of her feeble contacts with the world she was trans-
fixed, caught. Not by any confused emanation from those whose
prisoner she now was, but by a far more vigorous and demanding
force.

"Tirtha!" That came like an arousing shout uttered in her very
ear, drawing her into far keener awareness than she had had since
they had fought that battle for the casket across her body. "Tirtha!"

The call, having found her, fed energy to awaken and strengthen
her.

"You live . . ." That was no question, rather a demand. "You
live!"

Which was folly. Still that bit of her which was able to respond could not say this was not true. She wondered if the fact that she still must fulfill a guardianship, that she had not been absolved of the geas, kept that small ember of life aglow in her.

What sought her—this was not the Great One who had rent open their prison. Nor was it the Dark Lord who commanded here. The Falconer was dead. Alon?

As if she had asked that aloud, there came an instant strong reply —wordless, yet unmistakable. The boy lived, nor had he retreated so far into his inner hiding place that he could not reach her.

"Where . . ." She found it exhausting to bring out even the beginning of a question. Let the dead, or the almost-dead rest; she resented being bound by any will.

"East . . ." It would seem that she need not form a full thought, that Alon could pluck meaning from what was vague even to her. "There is a Dark One—he believes me in his hold. But I have seen the bird twice!"

The bird that had flown into the storm? What had the bird to do with them? Oh, just let her go! Tirtha strove to will herself back into peaceful nothingness.

"Messenger . . . They come!"

She did not care. The fleeting strength that touch had brought was not enough to hold her. She slipped once more into the dark.

Then it was dark and yet not truly dark. Rain no longer beat on her face. Somewhere, not too far away, there must be a fire, for there was a ruddy glow, though she could not turn her head to find its source. She stared unblinkingly upward at rough stone. They must have taken refuge in a cave.

This could have been one of many such camps as far as her slight hold upon the living world could tell. Tirtha lay looking up at that rock. Perhaps the dying, or the dead, dream of life, and this was such a dream. She was content that the pain was gone and that there seemed to be a barrier between her and any contact with the real world or the unreal one.

"Tirtha!" Once again she was being summoned back, she thought, sluggishly and resentfully. "You are awake—I know it!" There was some heat of anger. Alon might have been hammering at a door that had refused to open to him.

"The bird—it is out there in the night! I have heard it call twice. They are coming! This Dark One—he knows it, he will try me!"

There was nothing left in Tirtha to raise an answer. What moved

Alon had no meaning for her. A shadow appeared between her and the fire as a tall shape loomed above her. The shadow leaned forward, so her moving eyes saw a helmed head, a face in partial darkness. A second shadow was now beside the first, someone dragged to her side even as that miserable prisoner had been brought to her to steal the casket—a smaller, thinner shape.

"He's scared into an idiot, Lord. Look at the face on him."

"Yes, look at him, Gerik! This waif you would have hunted for your pleasure has more strength in the smallest finger of his hand than you can summon to swing that sword of yours! Idiot? Ah, far from that. He is hiding—hiding! But there is a trick or two that will peel him out, even as you peel a fos-crab out of its shell after a good steaming."

Hands hard and heavy on its shoulders crushed that smaller shadow to its knees beside her.

"I thought as how he was so very precious, Lord, that none of us was to lay finger on him. Yet you want to risk him . . ."

"There always is a time, Gerik, when one plays for high stakes. I do not think that this one will be risked. He is of another heritage. Among such, like does not prey upon like. It may diminish him somewhat. However, that can be risked for what we shall gain. To transport this other carrion only slows us, and time has become our enemy. We are not the only seekers, and I will tell you, Gerik, you would find some who come searching such as you would not care to face." Laughter, low and heavy in contempt, came out of that shadow. "Now!"

She did not know what he did to the boy he held prisoner. There came no cry out of Alon, nor was there any longer any touch from him to her. He must have retreated into his own refuge.

"Seems like he isn't too quick to answer, Lord!" Gerik said after a long moment. "We could try a trick or two . . ."

"Silence!" The word was sharp enough to stop even Gerik in his covert rebellion.

The two beside her seemed linked unmovingly. Tirtha sensed, very far, the faintest touch against her near-buried self, a lapping of power that perhaps might well have blasted one who accepted or was forced to accept it fully. The smaller shadow moved a fraction, its arms hanging limply from the shoulders and prisoned in its captor's grip raised, the hands extending toward Tirtha's body. That lapping power arose the stronger—exultation fed it.

Then there came a tearing cry, so wild and strange that it might have been a shout a man charging into battle would voice, his nature drowned in a lust for blood and death. Another shadow appeared, over the shoulder of the standing man. She saw it clearly. The bird that had been born from the body of the falcon!

The man at her side stumbled back a step. One of his hands fell away from Alon's shoulder, while the boy sagged forward as one whose full strength had drained away. Now he lay across her, his rain-wet hair drifting over the lower part of her face, as motionless as she herself. Though Tirtha did not believe that he was dead—or dead-alive as she was sentenced to remain.

The bird now perched on Alon's shoulder, twisting forward its long neck so that its eyes were very close to her own as it gazed steadily at her. No, no bird! This was again that head, that face she had seen in her pain back in Hawkholme.

Only for a moment did the bird stare into her eyes, or the face thus look upon her. Then it swung about to confront the man shadow, and from it came once more that sound which was a name, "Ninutra!"

From the man it so confronted, there sounded an answering cry. Or was it a summons for help—a backing for himself in some struggle he now feared unequal?

"Rane!"

He might have laid a goad to the bird. The thing hissed viciously. It fairly leaped from Alon's body straight for the man who had been trying to jerk the boy up again. The blow it delivered was out of range of Tirtha's sight, but she heard a cry of pain, then an oath. He was no longer between her and the fire, and she could hear other cries, not all in the same voice. It would seem that the bird was waging battle with more than one.

Alon remained where he was. She could not feel his weight upon her, his voice reached her in the faintest of whispers, which the cries and sounds from beyond covered.

"They fight. The bird has drawn blood. But the Lord summoned, and there will be more than one come to us. Also there is one who follows. Time is drawing in. Oh, Tirtha, hold—hold, for the end is far from decided."

She guessed that he had used speech lest that which had been summoned, or the lord, having extended his own power to that summoning, might pick up their touch by mind. But she could make no answer. Nor did she desire to do so. This was no longer her battle. It was rather a trap wherein she was held, from which she longed to be free.

The clamor lessened, and then a shadow strode once more between the light of the fire and her body.

"What's to be done with the boy now, lord?"

"See he's well bound and stow him safe." The reply was sullen. "There is too much abroad now to try again."

Alon was lifted off her, taken from her sight, lying limp in his guard's hands. Once more Tirtha was allowed to drift into her blessed nothingness.

What came to arouse her next was pain—a memory of it, or so it would seem, not a part of her. Still she carried it with her as one carries an annoying burden one is ordered to bear. She looked out upon the world, losing her hold on nothingness with reluctance. There was sky above her again—dull and gray, but from it no rain flowed. Her head jerked to and fro so that she caught glimpses now and then of mounted men, mainly one who rode beside her, leading the pony on which she was lashed. She gathered she had been bound to that mount in a strange fashion, face up, probably because of the casket that must still be frozen into position on her breast, making this the only way she could be transported.

More than her surroundings, the girl grew aware of what was awakening inside her. Not only the pain, but also her thoughts were coming alive once more. She had not this time answered to Alon's call, rather to something else—a reaching out from . . .

Warmth—the casket! What she bore was alive? No, that could not be true. It was metal, unless it cradled more than she could have guessed—some sentient power? One could believe anything of the Great Ones and that what she bore was of their earlier possessing, Tirtha no longer doubted. There was feeling within that thing, which rested not far from her heart, to the covering of which her hands were still frozen. Her head bobbed again to give her a quick glance down the length of her body.

Yes! She held the casket as firmly as she had since she had taken it up from its resting place at Hawkholme. The rope, which helped to bind her to the pony, also was looped carefully about her hands as if those who transported her had doubts about her being dead and had thought that she might rouse, to throw the treasure from her, perhaps into some place from which they could not fetch it forth again.

Dead? For the first time her less sluggish thinking began to doubt this. The drug Alon had fed into her at her urging had been a huge dose of what was meant to give healing sleep. Perhaps it had paralyzed her body, taken the pain but left her living. The thought of being forever so enchained was much worse than any physical pain, striking her as hard and swiftly as a sword thrust.

The sky appeared to be lightening a little. Now with the bobbing of her head she sighted a patch of blue. Since she faced the tail of the horse, back the way they had come, she caught sight of what must be the rear guard, a single man who rode as one who was uneasy, turning watchful eyes on the back track. There was no mark of any roadway. This was all open moorland with a round mound or hill here and there. The spring growth was already high and green. She saw a hawk wheel into the upper air, a flock of smaller birds turn sharply, forming a fan pattern against the enlarging patch of blue.

As Tirtha became more and more alert mentally, breaking through layers of shadows that had wrapped her around as a moth might lie encased in its cocoon, she watched the rear guard with greater care. Twice he pulled to a halt, sat looking back over his shoulder. Yet the land behind was so open one could view it for an ever-lengthening distance. Even she—who had no control over her eyes and had to watch those portions the movements of the pony allowed her—saw nothing move there.

Again her interest awoke so that she longed to reach out. Alon? No, she dared not attempt to touch the boy; she did not know how deeply he was kept captive, not only physically, but by the talent of the Dark Lord. Surely that Lord could sense, since he must be very alert to any manifestation of the talent, any attempt on her part to contact her fellow prisoner. So feeble a gift as hers would lie as open to his reading as one of the record rolls of Lormt.

Still—were they pursued? She remembered Alon's whisper of one who followed. The raided garth where Gerik had caused red ruin— could that have set on their trail some band of a lord's following determined on vengeance? Tirtha believed not. Hawkholme lay too far inland. No one would have followed the raiders with such single-minded fury unless it was their own homestead that had been so despoiled, and Gerik had left only death behind him at the garth that had been Alon's home.

There remained Alon and that Wise Woman Yachne who had taken him into the homestead. Why had Yachne tried to protect and hide one who was manifestly not of her race or kind? Had she perhaps foreseen a future in which Alon could be forged into a tool or a weapon of her own? The Power had always been a danger to those who could summon it even slightly—in itself it was a peril. He or she who could accomplish a little began to yearn to be able to control more. If that inner desire became great enough, it corrupted. Such corruption was of the Dark.

Yes, Tirtha believed that one who valued, who craved Power above all else, might trail behind and seek, single-minded, to regain what had been lost. Even though the odds against any success were very, very high. Yachne had been said to be a Wise Woman, a healer of sorts, which meant one limited in talent. However, that did not also mean that the face she presented to the world was more than a mask. She could well have come out of Escore on some business of her own, adopting a lesser role in Karsten than she would play among those with whom she was bred. Alon had been her charge or her possession.

Tirtha had not realized how much her mind had cleared until that faint pain began to increase. Her body, which had been so dead, was coming awake. She cringed inwardly, realizing the torment that lay ahead, carried as she was, if the action of the herb began to fail. The end could be that she would face such pain as that poor remnant of a man from Hawkholme must have felt before the last act his captor had forced him to had released him forever. Tirtha knew some of the disciplines of pain-containing—had used them during her journeys to combat the ordinary small trials of any tramping of the roads, but they had never been meant to cope with such an ordeal as would be hers now. There was no one to aid her, unless she could provoke the lord of this party to finish her off as they had done the Falconer. Perhaps it would come to that, if she could persuade him that the casket would be his after such a merciful stroke.

Only, what she held could not be so easily surrendered. That knowledge was deep in her. Tirtha was still guardian, dead or alive, until released from her bond. A provoked sword thrust would not be the answer.

The rear rider had reined in his mount once more, facing the back trail. He was a brutal looking fellow, clad in rusted and badly mended mail, a pot helm a little too large. Its ill fit appeared to bother him, for he put up a hand now and then to tug it more firmly in place. All the rest of their party that she could not see plodded on, drawing her, in turn, farther and farther away from the rear guard who still sat where he was, his horse's head hanging as if it had been ridden too far and too long.

This was a quiet group. There was no conversation among them, only a snuffle of bit, the whiffling snort of mount now and then to break the silence. Pressing in on Tirtha came their combined feelings of uneasiness, fear. She remembered more clearly Gerik's protests about crossing the border. There were hills between fabled Escore and Karsten, though not the stark mountainous country that formed the Eastern barrier back in Estcarp. Even so, crossing into such debatable land was nothing to be taken lightly. Those of lowland blood, with their hatred and fear of what the Falconer termed witchery, would have little desire to push on.

The Falconer . . . Shot down . . . she had a dim memory of hearing that. He must have brought her out of the crumbling fortress-hall with Alon's help, only to meet death. What had become of his power sword? She was somehow sure that none in this company would dare to claim it. It had come to him, and there were many old tales of weapons that chose their masters—or mistresses—serving no others. Now her memory grew vivid for an instant or two, and she remembered his body arching over her and Alon, keeping from them, or ready to do so, the tumbling walls. A blank shield served his employer to the death—that was the code. Yet it was Tirtha's thought that in the end the Falconer had not lived only by the code, that, woman though she was, he might have forgotten her sex in that moment and viewed her as a shield-mate cut down in battle. She remembered his dark, hollow-cheeked face and what lay always in the depths of his eyes—that strange yellowish fire that could be heightened by anger or perhaps by hidden thoughts she had never understood. He had found peace, which was all she could wish for him.

His falcon, which had so oddly taken on that other-seeming when death finished it—what had been its real end? And who or what was Ninutra?

Even thinking that name opened a new inner path of thought. This time Tirtha did not see a woman's face, rather she felt a warmth throughout her whole body—inward surely, not in her drugged and deadened flesh. While . . .

The air twisted, turned. Could *air* twist and turn? In spite of the bobbing of her head, that constant motion which was disruptive to clear sight, Tirtha detected movement overhead, and it *was* in the air! A gathering of fog—whence came a single patch of fog on such clear a day? Some small cloud might have been dispatched to hang directly over them, traveling steadily with them. Was she the only one who saw it? She heard nothing from those riding about her.

Fog? No, shadow! Only one should not be able to see an airborne shadow at midday! It twirled, lengthened, solidified. The same sword that had hung above the three of them back at Hawkholme was now visible, growing in both breadth and length. They traveled under it, and there was a threat in it.

Not for her; Tirtha had already decided that. This was a manifestation of the same power that had aided them at Hawkholme. Like the gray bird, it was representative of a warning, a challenge. She half expected to hear the scream of the bird, perhaps that name uttered out of the air overhead.

What she did hear was a loud cry that must have issued from the man leading the pony to which she was bound. He had reined in and jerked the pony in turn to a halt. Her head had fallen a little to one side so that she could see his arm stretched upward as he pointed to what hung above them. There were other exclamations. Then came the voice of the one she had not yet directly seen—that Dark Lord who commanded Gerik in spite of the outlaw's will.

"It is a vision only. Are you such as to be frightened by shadows?"

"There are shadows and shadows." Again Gerik spoke, his impudence hardly controlled. "If it is a vision, Lord, then whose? And it has an uncanny look to it. I do not think *that* and your cup-brother would deal well together. You have said that there will be those in Escore to hail us with 'well done' since we bring that dead thing over there with its hell box, and this youngling whom you drag along in spite of the death-coming look to him also. Well, are we not in Escore, or so you have told us? Where then are your friends? Does it not seem that it is those with little liking for you who have found us first? I say"—his voice came a little louder now as if he were approaching the pony upon which Tirtha was tied—"that we have fulfilled our part of the bargain, Lord. This dealing with Powers—leave witchery to them who know it better than we. There are good enough pickings in the Duchy; why should we go hunting trouble?"

It would seem that the only man Tirtha held in sight agreed with that. For he who had led the pony dropped the rope and backed his mount away from the smaller beast. A moment later he was joined by another, who looked much like him and was surely close akin to the one she had seen stop behind them on the trail.

Above them all now the sword had taken on such firm substance that it looked—at least to her—to be a very solid object suspended in the air and of a length that only a man near the height of a foothill could have put hand to, had it indeed been a weapon to be used.

The Dark Lord laughed.

"It is too late, Gerik. As I told you once—though perhaps you did not believe me—those who take service with my lord (and by pledging your aid to me in certain matters, you did just that) are not released at their will. No, not until he has had his full usage of them! Try to retreat—if you can!"

The two men within Tirtha's range of vision looked a little pale beneath the dirt and the wind-browning of their faces. Both turned as one and used the spur. Their small horses bounded forward down the back trail. However, they had only gone a length or two before they slowed and cried out, as beasts do, in an extremity of terror.

Crouched in the grass confronting them was such a creature as Tirtha had never seen, though the thing she had faced in the mountains had been strange and evil enough. This was in its way worse, for it had nothing about it of any sane animal. Rather it was insectile, as if one of the harmless spiders, which wove morning webs in the meadows, had grown nearly pony size in an instant. The thing was furred with coarse, bright scarlet hair, thickening about the joints of its huge limbs into vast masses. Across its head was a row of pitiless dark eyes above mandibles that clicked, while a thick green slime oozed from those threatening crunchers.

The riders were fighting their horses as the mounts whirled, dashed back past Tirtha, carrying their riders with them, away from that creature, which squatted and eyed the party with an intent glare.

"Yahhhhh!" It must have been Gerik himself, the man who had refused to be totally cowed by his employer, who bounded up. He had a heavy spear in his hand, holding it with the ease of one who had victoriously gone into battle many times before, and he must have had iron control over his wild-eyed and now screaming horse, for he was forcing it to carry him straight forward, the spear aiming directly at the monster crouching to close the back trail.

17

The spider creature did not await Gerik's charge. Rather it leaped, apparently willing enough to spike its hairy body on a spear in order to reach its enemy. It was Gerik's horse that reared or dodged. The pony's mad fear gave it an agility never meant for such a stocky body. Losing footing the beast crashed sidewise, carrying the man down with it, but not before the spear pierced the thick abdomen of the monster.

Perhaps it was his example showing that the monster could be attacked or the compelling personality of the man who had led them, which now brought those who had first fled back into combat. They returned into Tirtha's line of vision, spurring toward that mass of animal, monster, and man interlocked on the ground, their swords out, flailing at the heaving red-haired form, slashing at any part of it they could touch.

The downed pony screamed as only an animal in dire pain and fear can do. There had been no cry from its rider. Perhaps the shock of that spill had made Gerik an easy prey to the creature. But the thing itself was in dire straits. Twice it strove to draw itself together for another leap. The dribble of poisonous stuff from its mouth parts ran in a thick green stream. It had lost two legs, hacked off by the frenzy of those who attacked it.

A sword thrust, well aimed, cut into one of those intelligent, mal-ice-filled eyes. He who had been so lucky in that stroke tried again. A stream of the evil green slime sprayed outward, sending him back screaming, dropping his blade, tearing with both hands at the skin of his lower face. He began to run in circles, howling like an animal in its death throes.

Part blinded, lacking two limbs as it did, the spear driven far into its paunch, the thing managed to raise itself from the now silent yet still twitching body of the pony and swung to face its second at-tacker. One foreleg, armed with a vicious looking claw nearly as long as Tirtha's forearm, stabbed out at the fighter who backed, then stood his ground, aiming shearing strokes at the creature. His steel met the claw and rebounded. It would seem that this part was not so vulnerable. Once more that envenomed spray arched through the air from the monster's mouth.

The man leaped back, more lucky than his comrade, as the creature made a jerky move to follow. Then a head and arm, the upper portion of a body, arose from where the thing had squatted over its first prey. Gerik was on his knees. His two hands gripped the hilt of a sword, and he stabbed into the round body now half turned from him. If the claw had been armored well enough to turn away steel, the body of the thing was not so protected. That sword, driven by all the strength the man could summon, sank into the wide back, hilt-deep. There came a fountain gush of black liquid spurting up and over Gerik, who fell, hidden again from sight.

However, the monster did not swing about to savage him. It struggled still to reach the man who had struck it from the front—he retreating hastily. Until at last he broke, turned and ran, while the thing still attempted to leap after him.

At last it toppled, such limbs as remained intact no longer able to support its thick body. Still it was not defeated, for it continued to spray into the air that green slime. Where that fell on the ground, small tendrils of steam or smoke arose, while the air was filled with a vile odor.

It was then that the reins of the pony on which Tirtha was bound were seized, the animal pulled into jolting trot. They were on their way from that battlefield, giving no aid to the man who crawled upon the ground, his ruined face a mask of horror as his screaming became a thick bubbling in his throat. Nor was there sight again of Gerik. The other man who had fought the creature was running, crying out, following behind them. Yet the pony and he who led it gained more ground drawing away from the survivor.

Because of the jolting of the pony, Tirtha could no longer see the battlefield clearly. Nor did she know how many of their party were left. The Dark Lord in command certainly—perhaps he was the one who led her pony—and with him Alon, but were there more? The fact that their captors' numbers had shrunk so drastically might have meant a chance for escape, had she not been in this dead body. However, Alon had perhaps a chance. She longed to contact him.

Pain awakened stronger in her. Perhaps that pain would overtake and hold her a prisoner in another way. Now, however, her mind cleared. Tirtha seemed to be pushed into thinking, to be far more aware of what lay about them, above them. Above them! She strove to settle her bobbing head for a fraction of time to glance overhead. Yes, the sword was there. Perhaps that was what had kept the pony steady, kept it from running wildly from the monster. Had the blade also protected them from attack, or had that been the result of Gerik's recklessly brave charge?

Tirtha fought hard to keep the gray length within sight. Yes, she had not been mistaken. There were symbols on the blade of that overshadowing weapon. Many of them appeared on the skin roll the dead man had carried. She recalled Alon thrusting it into the empty dart loop on the Falconer's shoulder belt. If they had not despoiled the dead, these carrion hunters, then there it still remained. Even were it now within her hand, Tirtha would not have known how to make use of it.

They were passing from the open rolling lands now. She caught glimpses of hillocks rising like steps to greater heights on either side. There appeared no road, but she believed that they were following a trail well known to him in command.

Since she dared not try to reach Alon, and she must, as long as she could, remain master of her body (in which the pain was waking more and more with every swing that the swifter pace of the pony brought about), Tirtha set her mind on the shadow sword continuing to hang above them.

She was sure that this manifestation was not of the Dark, that it answered, in a manner not given to her to understand, the thing she carried. Was the sword a weapon of that woman who had come to view them in the hidden chamber?

Ninutra—though Tirtha did not shape that name with her lips or utter it aloud, yet she formed it slowly, letter by letter, in her mind with all the concentration of one following the intricate weaving of a spell. There were words that went with healing; many of them she knew and had used. Such words in themselves had no power, it was the intonation that counted, the fact that the same phrases had been thus employed for countless generations to build a channel for the healing to pass through, even as a mason built a hallway, choosing the best and strongest of the stones available for his task.

Names were power. There were the Great Names, which no one, without strong safeguards, dared to utter. If this was such a one— well, what had she to lose? Life meant very little now. If what she bore, beyond any will or desire of her own, was tied to one of those ominous names, that gave her a small fraction of right to attempt a summoning.

She closed her eyes. Tirtha's heart jumped, and that she also felt. In so much had she gained control of her body. She could lift and lower two eyelids, sense the beating of her own heart!

Closing her eyes firmly again, she turned her sight determinedly inward and for the second time strove to build that name into something she could visualize.

First there were flames, like those that had burst from the corners of the hidden room. They flared in fierce warning. Warning! What did that matter to one like her, already doomed?

Ninutra!

Her will had wakened. If there abode somewhere a power that could be so summoned, then let it come! She was perhaps a plaything, a tool of forces she did not understand. Yet she was the Hawk —and there existed a bargain out of the past. Tirtha had a queer feeling, as if an inner part of her had swung then, quick as a flash of light, across a wide gulf measuring years of time, only to return again.

Ninutra!

It was not the impersonal woman's face that formed or was borne through those flames which died, leaving a mind-picture, indistinct, yet still discernible. This was the countenance of someone not unlike herself—young, a woman, one of the Old Race. Still there was in her great strength, even though she might be but a voice, a channel, for a greater one.

Ninutra!

Behind the woman hung the outline of the shadow sword. Tirtha saw a hand appear also out of the haziness about that face. Fingers closed upon the sword hilt, brought the weapon to swing outward, so that its point was aimed as if ready for combat. There were two other figures moving, one advancing on either side, to stand with that woman. But of those Tirtha could see so little they were like pillars of smoke and mist.

This much she had learned—there were indeed those who could claim the shadow sword. Perhaps they might be, in their own way, favorably disposed toward her. Yet what lay ahead was of more importance than a single woman of the Old Race who had stood by the word of her blood to the end. For that end, when it came, was not concerned with Tirtha herself, but with greater matters.

The three in the mist vanished; not so the sword. It continued to fill Tirtha's mind with its presence. Those symbols along its blade blazed with angry fire. From it she was drawing something—this much had been granted her—strength to hold firm against the pain of her body, that dead body which could no longer serve her. She would be sustained, for there was yet a need for her, and that she would have to accept.

Thus she lay within her vision, holding to it with all her will, striving to force out of it a barrier against her pain. She was never to know how long that vigil of hers lasted.

The sword began to fade, the symbols were gone, sinking into its more and more tenuous length. Tirtha looked upon empty darkness before she opened her eyes upon the outer world again.

She had indeed been deeply sunk inside herself, for she was no longer upon a pony. Instead she lay upon a flat, unmoving surface, a hard surface, as her body returning to half-life told her. There was light here, thin streamers reached like the flames of giant candles up into the sky. Also with that light was a chill, the miasma of evil. This place was of the Dark, no matter what light played on it and within it.

Beyond the upriding columns of light was a night sky. Tirtha saw the far wink of stars, yet between her and their glitter there was a wavering curtain, as if even clean starlight must be so veiled in this evil place. With a determination that drew upon every portion of the strength she hoped still abode within her, Tirtha strove to turn her head.

Pain answered, but pain was not important; she was mistress of her body, of its pain. She threw pain from her as she would throw some evil thing that unwittingly crawled upon her. Then Tirtha discovered that indeed she could shift her head a fraction, see a little of what lay to her left, enough to know she was not alone.

The light came from pillars of what might have been ice, congealed through centuries of freezing. Deep within them lurked shadow cores. Between her and the deadly cold of the nearest pillar was Alon.

He sat, his legs stretched before him, a loop of rope about his ankles. His arms had been drawn cruelly together behind his back and there lashed. With upheld head he stared straight ahead, wearing the blind look of one so overcome by fate that nothing mattered any longer.

"Alon!"

He did not look to her, the trance which held him did not break. Had he retreated into nothingness? No, something assured her that was not so.

"Alon!" The effort to get out that single word for the second time was almost more than Tirtha could rise to.

There was a flicker of expression across his face. Yet he remained so caught in misery he could not be reached. For a long moment she watched him, unable to summon again such strength as those two attempts to reach him had demanded.

"He is gone, he has left us—with the Dark . . ." Those words came from between lips that hardly moved. But in her was a quickening of spirit. Alon wore only the outer mask of shock and despair —within he was still alert!

"This is a place of Dark. He believed us safe-caged here. . . ." Alon was continuing. "Do not summon. The one who rules here will know it."

Do not summon? Had Alon somehow been aware of her earlier struggle? No, do not even think of that within this place! Caution flashed instantly across Tirtha's mind. There was a Power that made of this a prison—she had no knowledge of its range—but apparently he who had brought them here trusted in its strength of guardianship.

Alon still stared into nothingness, but now Tirtha saw that, for all the cruel straining put upon his arms where they were so lashed behind him, his hands were moving. His fingers did not try to reach the knotting of those cords—that would be physically impossible, bound as he was. Rather, to her wonder, he was smoothing the coils as he might have smoothed or patted the hide of an animal. What he so played with was not woven rope, she noted, her full attention drawn by Alon's actions, but a long strip of braided hide.

What the boy sought to do Tirtha could not understand, but his motions were purposeful, so she did not try again to distract his attention, only watched his struggle to pat, stroke, and fondle what bound him, always giving otherwise the appearance of one completely cowed.

Realizing suddenly that her very attention on the boy might attract whatever held grim rulership here, she strove to lock it out of her mind and was about to follow a second line of defense by closing her eyes so she could be sure she would not turn her head again. Then came a sudden flicker at the joining of those punishing cords.

Tirtha watched what she thought at first must indeed be an illusion, deceptive, meant to tantalize, to bring false hope. If it were illusion, it was a remarkably exact one. The hide loops, which Alon had rubbed and caressed with his fingertips, moved of themselves.

They might have been sleek creatures of the serpent family that had curled into awkward (for them) tangles and were now loosening themselves at their own whim.

Tirtha saw the constricting knots unfasten, allowing the rest of the cords to slide at apparently no other will than a desire within their own blind lengths. They wriggled across the boy's body, slipped away. His arms, ridged by brutal welts, fell forward. Tirtha could well imagine the torment the sudden release of such binding brought him. Yet one hand lying half across his thigh was twitching, and he leaned forward, to bring its fingertips against the second drawing of cords about his angles.

Once more he began that rubbing, that caressing; Tirtha watched his face intently. He retained his unrevealing mask. One glancing at him would say he was under such complete control as vicious handling and fear could force on a young child. There was no movement of his lips—he could *not* be reciting any spell or words of power.

Yet again he succeeded, as the second loop slackened, drew itself out of the tightly drawn knots, and he was free. He made no further move as yet, simply sat loose of bonds. Then she saw his chest arch in a deep breath and his hands come together, as he deliberately rubbed ridged wrists and the grooves on his arms with a dogged determination.

Was there other restraint laid on the boy besides the cords from which he had just released himself? Or could Alon now get beyond these lighted pillars? She could do, say nothing, only watch and wait.

However, it would seem that whatever talent the boy had brought to his freeing had not been exhausted. He continued to sit rubbing his wrists, staring ahead. Save that now there was a quality in that stare which was not one of resignation or retreat. Tirtha's own senses heightened little by little. That she lay in a place which was wholly inimical to her and all her kind, which generated within it a chill she could feel faintly as her body slowly awoke, she had accepted. Yet there was something else beyond. . . .

Alon changed position for the first time, drawing his feet under him, so that he now squatted on his heels. He made no move toward Tirtha, appearing to be still locked in that stare. Yet there was a subtle change, a kind of alertness, as might be sensed in one awaiting a signal.

Tirtha longed to be able to change the position of her own head enough to follow the direction of the boy's continued line of gaze. Only she could not. Alon had stopped rubbing his bruised wrists and arms; now he put out his hands and drew to him those lengths of cords he had in some manner made his servants. He stretched them out side by side. At her present angle, Tirtha could not see what he was doing; she could only speculate.

Once more his hands moved. He was again using his fingers, presumably passing them along the cords. These movements were more emphatic, swifter. She watched as best she might, and at the same time she grew to sense, more and more, that outside the ghastly candle pillars of this cage there was another entity at watch. The miasma of evil which encased this place was like a wall. If a would-be rescuer prowled there, the girl could not know, nor dared she strive to learn.

Alon raised a hand slowly, the fingers moving as if he beckoned. A dark shape obeyed his summons, lifting to follow. Serpent? No, the thing was too thin, it lacked any swell of head she could see, having only a questing tip. The cord! It was taking on a form of pseudo-life, or else Alon had wrought from it an hallucination!

As the boy spread both hands outward in a vast sweep, the cord end remained aloft, stretching up near as high as his own head from the pavement. It swayed back and forth. His hands met palm to palm and then pushed apart. The tip of the cord swung away from him, flung itself toward the line of pillars, then fell completely out of Tirtha's line of vision. Alon's hands continued to move. Not in the wide sweeps he had first used, rather up and down in small motions, as if, though they were flattened out palm down, still he had grasp of an invisible line that fed along the ground. He had risen to his knees, his back straight, so concentrating on what he did that the aura of his intense effort reached her.

All Alon's strength was centered on this. She remembered how once she had asked of him and of Nirel that they lend their energy to support her in farseeing. Could she, in some manner, now back Alon in a like fashion? There was the pain ever pushing against what barriers she had set her inner will to hold. Were she to release that will, strive to add its force to what the boy needed, those barriers could well fall entirely.

Tirtha closed her eyes for a moment, faced firmly what might be the result of such action on her part. Alon was risking much, using full energy on what he strove to do. She could only believe that he was battling their enemy. While Alon himself—she had come to accept that the boy understood more than she could even guess.

She chose. Will could be aimed, and in that moment before she could shrink from the results of such a breaching of her own defenses, Tirtha did just that. She kept her eyes fast closed, but held Alon clear in her mind, as she summoned up a picture of a touching between them, not for any communication that might arouse a guardian here—rather a picture of her own hand reaching out to clasp the boy's squared shoulder and, down that arm and hand, flooding the strength of her own will.

The fire of pain leapt in upon her. Tirtha was wrapped in it. Still she fought to keep mental hold on her vision. Might even pain itself be a source of power? That flashed across her mind and she seized upon it, held it, strove to add the force, not of the torment, but of the power that generated it, to what she had to give.

This was a descent into such agony as she would not have believed anyone could bear. Nor could she even be sure that what she was trying to do met with any success. Had her offering reached Alon— could she spur, energize him further in his strange ordering of the very bonds that had held him prisoner?

Agony filled her, as if her flesh swelled outward, unable to contain the full force of this. There was a burst of fire in her head. Alon was gone, and then everything . . .

"Tirtha!" Then again, "Tirtha."

Into the great nothingness rang that name. Something answered against its will, fighting, and yet unable to withstand the drawing of that voice.

"Tirtha!"

Three was a number of power—an ancient bit of knowledge. Thrice summoned, one could not remain apart. She was drawn—all that remained of her.

Searing pain came, then it was gone. For another had cut it from her even as one might cut away a tattered body covering. Tirtha was sealed against what her body might strive to raise for her punishment. Also that awakening which had begun in the place of the Dark had carried forward. She knew that she breathed, if in shallow gasps, that she heard with her ears, and now she saw with her eyes, for she opened them.

Around her there stood no tall pillars of corpse candles. The scent and strength of the Dark was gone. There was light, yes, but it was the true coloring of the sky at sunrise, while over her blew a gentle wind carrying the scent of flowers. Only more important to her, was the face of the one who knelt beside her. Hands a little browned by the sun—long-fingered, slender hands—were outstretched above

Tirtha's breast, and she knew that it was those hands that barred the pain from overwhelming her.

This was the girl she had seen in her mind vision—she who had held the shadow sword. She was not the Great One who had looked upon them with detachment and no hint of pity, rather this one was a Voice, a priestess. In her the human still abode and was alive in her face and in her voice as she spoke.

"Welcome, Hawk Blood, who kept well the faith. The conclusion of the guardianship is near upon us. We come to an end—and perhaps a beginning—if the Power reckons it so."

"Who . . . ?" Tirtha found a weak word.

"I am Crytha," the other answered readily. It would seem that there was indeed to be a naming of names. "I serve Her whom you have knowledge of, even though that came to you only dimly. She of the Shadow Sword, the Lady Ninutra."

As she spoke that name, it was echoed. In the air over her downbent head appeared the bird that had been born from the dying falcon, or else one so like that there could not be feather's difference between them. It opened its beak to scream. Crytha looked away from Tirtha, her eyes viewing something or someone beyond.

"Yes, it is truly time," she said. "Our ingathering begins."

18

Though pain had been walled away, Tirtha had no strength or power to shift her helpless body. She could only see what advanced into a narrow range of vision. Crytha still knelt beside her, but two others now moved forward to stand, one on either side of the priestess, each in his own way memorable to look upon. One was tall, broad of shoulder, thick of body, as befits an axeman. For the weapon he bore two-handed before him was a double-bladed axe. His helm mounted a marvelously wrought dragon from beneath which he looked upon Tirtha with compassion. Yet his eyes moved from side to side at times, as if they were in a place where constant close watch must be kept.

His companion was younger, more slender, fair of skin, and he held a sword such as was common enough among those who had ridden along the border. He might not be wholly of the Old Race, yet he was plainly human born. It was he who spoke now.

"There comes a rider. . . ."

Crytha made a small gesture. "Yes. But there is more than that one. Rane walks . . ."

The wielder of the axe shifted his weapon as if making sure of its balance. His features lost all softness, his upper lip lifted the way a hunting cat would snarl.

"We are too close to *his* source," he said. "Best we . . ."

Crytha interrupted him. "She cannot be moved." Her gesture was to Tirtha. "This must remain our field of battle whether it appears a fitting one or not. For she also has a part still to play." Crytha got easily and gracefully to her feet. The three of them, Tirtha saw, looked beyond in another direction.

With infinite care she brought her small strength to bear, willed her head to shift. It lay a little raised, as if there were support beneath. Thus she discovered she could see farther, even look upon what still rested on her breast, her hands frozen so tightly to it they might have become a part of it. The casket was still hers.

She raised her eyes from it, to follow the others' line of gaze. So she caught sight of Alon. He was not standing as they did, awaiting what came, rather he raced forward. She heard the high neigh of a Torgian, a cry of triumph from an equine throat.

There were many rocks about. She still felt a chill issuing from behind. Though they may have, through some trick of power, won free of that Dark cage, yet the newcomers had not transported her too far from it. From the amount of debris lying about, she could be amidst ruins of either a temple or perhaps a hold or a village. Between two still-standing heaps of time-eaten stone, marking nearly destroyed walls, Alon dashed. Moments later he returned, fingers laced into the mane of a horse, to the riding pad of which clung a man, his body drooping, his dark-haired head bare, half his face masked by a brown crust of dried blood. Yet no mask could ever again conceal him from Tirtha's recognition.

Within her prison–body, her heart gave a great leap, as if to break all bonds of bone and flesh. She was half—three-quarters dead, yes. But here she saw another dead arise to ride.

The mount followed Alon, rather than being directed by its rider. Though his eyes were open, Tirtha wondered how much he really saw of what lay about him. The Torgian came to a halt, its head down, as Alon smoothed its rough forelock, murmuring to the horse the while. Now the rider stirred, strove to straighten. A measure of intelligence came into his eyes, piercing whatever daze he had fallen into. It was plain he both saw and knew Tirtha. Then his gaze traveled to those three who stood by her. She saw his claw waver toward his belt. He wore no sword now, there was no dart gun in its holster, but the glowing pommel of the weapon of power was still within his reach.

He dismounted, perhaps would have fallen had he not caught at the mane of the Torgian to steady himself. Crytha took a step or two ahead of her companions.

"Long awaited, come at last . . ." It was as if she recited part of a ritual. "Brother of the winged ones, you to whom the weapon, Basir's Tongue, has cleaved and made choice, we give you welcome, even though it be not to your rest but perhaps your bane and ours."

The Falconer stared at her. Now he loosed his hold upon the horse's coarse upspringing hair, raised hand toward his head in an uncertain gesture.

"You—are—the—night—walker. . . ." He spoke hoarsely, as if against his will. "You came to draw me back from death."

"From death?" Crytha said, as his last pause lengthened. "No, you were not dead, Falconer. They left you for such, but while you serve the Great Ones, then death comes not so easily."

"I serve the Lady." There was a tightness about his mouth. Flecks of dried blood fell from his jaw as he spoke. His hair, as Tirtha could see in the ever brightening day, was matted with dust and blood along his skull over the left ear. "This lady . . ."

His claw pointed to Tirtha where she lay. "What would you do with her? Does your Great One claim her, too?"

"She does," Crytha answered promptly. "And you, also, for what you carry."

It was her turn to point, and her fingers did not indicate the sword whose light gleamed bright enough to contrast even with the day, but rather the dart-looped belt about his shoulder. He looked down, his gaze following the line of her finger. Then he reached up slowly and clasped what he had carried out of Hawkholme—that rod with its concealed roll of the unreadable.

"How . . ." He looked totally bemused, as if this were the last thing he expected to find.

"By the wit of your lady," Crytha told him briskly. She crossed to stand before him, holding out her hand. He fumbled, freeing the dead man's legacy, then gave it to her.

The younger man who had joined her had half turned his head, looked over his shoulder to where Tirtha believed might be the site of the cage from which she had been brought.

"There is a stirring . . ." he cautioned sharply.

He of the axe laughed, giving a small flourish of his ponderous weapon. "When is there not, Yonan? Let it stir. It must come to terms sooner or later—its or ours. And I will wager the weight of this"—again he gave a short dip and lift of his weapon—"that the result will not be altogether to the Dark's liking, if at all."

"He who comes is Rane." Holding the tube of parchment, Crytha had moved back toward them.

"Meaning, Lady of the Shadow Sword, that I am too hopeful? Ah, when has it ever bettered a man to foresee an ill end? Such foreboding will sap strength before the contest even begins. And this is a foreseen meeting—what of your Great One?"

Crytha frowned. "You are bold, Uruk. One of the Four Great Weapons may be yours, but that fact does not open all gates for you."

The man, still smiling, made her a half salute. "Lady Crytha, as a twice-living man I have seen much, heard much, done much. There is little left of any awe in me. I have been a god to the Thas, those underground dwellers of the Dark Rule, and I have twice been a war captain. We are facing now a battle, so I ask you frankly, what may we expect in the way of allies?"

It was not the priestess but Alon who answered him. The boy had advanced a little, the Torgian following him, and Nirel, one hand again on the mount's neck for support, pacing along.

"You have us . . ."

Uruk turned his face toward the boy, and his smile grew the wider. "Well said, youngling. Having seen how you broke from Rane's cage and drew this lady with you, I give you good credit as one to stand beside in line of battle. And"—his gaze swept on to the Falconer who met it head up, back straight, with a lifted chin—"any man who carries one of the Four is a shield to the arm, a stout wall to one's back. Welcome, you to whom Basir's Tongue gives willing service. And"—now his eyes dropped to Tirtha—"Lady, you are of the Old Blood, and it is plain that this was a meeting planned out of the time we know and bow to. I know not what your weapon may be —is it left to you to be able to wield it?"

She looked down at the casket between her locked hands. "I do not know"—she spoke for the first time—"whether what I bear is weapon or prize. I only know that of it I am the set guardian, and this geas has not been lifted from me. I think that if you depend upon me for any weaponry you must plan again. This body is dead and I remain in it still only through a power I do not understand."

She heard a breath quickly drawn and saw the Falconer's claw swing forward and then back again against his body. Just the claw, she did not look higher to his face.

"Rane!" The younger man appeared to pay but little attention to the rest of them, his concentration was on what lay behind, which she could not see.

There came a crackling in the air about them, a feeling of Power gathering, sweeping. Not yet at them, rather for him, or *that*, which summoned. Uruk glanced once in the same direction his companion watched, and then he spoke to Crytha. His smile had vanished; there was a sharpness in his voice.

"I have asked—what of your Great One?"

"She shall do as she desires." The girl was abrupt in her reply. She was angered, Tirtha thought, by his question or his insistence upon an answer to it.

Uruk shrugged. "It is true that the Great Ones make it a habit to conceal their plans from their servants. Well enough. If this is to be our force, then make you ready." His sweep of eye passed over them all. "Rane, I do not know in person. In the telling any story grows the greater with each repeating of it. He is a Dark One who has his own strengths. It would appear we are about to test them."

The short sword to which Crytha and Uruk had given a name was free in the Falconer's hand. He stood away from the horse, came to Tirtha after the proper fashion of a shield man serving his employer. She looked up the length of his lean body. The tattered cloak had disappeared, along with his battered helm, his long sword, and dart gun. Now he worked his arm through the useless dart belt, tossing it from him. His hand showed blue as if the light of the sword pommel pierced his flesh.

Tirtha felt a new warmth. Her hands that had been so useless and dead—were they coming alive again? Between them, the casket blazed. Alon had come up on her other side. Even as the other three appeared to draw together into a unit, so were they also forming a common bond. The boy made a summoning wave with one hand. From the ground where Tirtha had not noticed it lying, there arose, swaying back and forth serpent-fashion once again, one of those coils of leather rope. The end of it swooped forward into Alon's grasp. He twisted a goodly length of it about his bruised and blood-stained wrist as if to give it stout anchorage, and then he raised the loose-hanging portion to swing it back and forth.

Uruk's axe was in plain sight, Yonan had drawn his sword, touched its point to earth, grasping its hilt in both hands. But Crytha seemed not to note all those battle preparations. Instead she had drawn the skin of symbols forth from its carrier, letting the rod fall free, and was studying it with care. Tirtha saw her lips move as if she shaped sounds, but there was also a frown of puzzlement between her eyes. Then, with a quick step, she was at Tirtha's side, had stooped and laid the roll of skin on the lid of the casket. Once more back among her companions, the priestess then held out her empty hand.

Mist whirled, gathered, intensified. What she held was the Shadow Sword, save that Tirtha would now swear that blade had real substance and was of the same strong steel as she had seen in many a warrior's scabbard. Along it runes glowed brightly, faded, then glowed again, as they might if they winked in and out of another time and space.

This Great One who might be moved to join with them or not—Tirtha's thought went to her. It would seem that perhaps her active help was not to be counted on. Surely they had come out of the sealed room at Hawkholme with her aid, only then to fall straightway into the hands of the enemy. Or had that been all a part of a plan? Perhaps they were of no value for what they were, only for the services they rendered. Perhaps she and Alon had been deliberately given into captivity that they might be brought to this place at this hour. Tirtha was sure she could not depend on any concern for her as a person, she was but the means of controlling what was frozen into her grasp.

Controlling? Why had that particular word come into her mind? She had no control over the box or what it might contain. Hers was only the guardianship. Yet in her dreams the Lord and Lady of Hawkholme had known . . .

Tirtha looked to the casket. Warmth—the warmth had grown. The scroll fashioned of ancient skin hung across the lid, touched her two hands, for Crytha had left it unrolled when she had put it there. Tirtha struggled to grasp some wisp of thought hovering at the very edge of her consciousness, the importance of which—yes! It was important! Hawk was the guardian—she was Hawk!

But the Great One was not here, unless some portion of her dwelt within Crytha, now armed with the shadow sword. Certainly she was *not* in Tirtha. What could be done, must be done—that would be of Tirtha's doing. She began her own moves, though her broken body lay inert. To use power only a little—that added to one's talent. To be a guardian of Power—one did not remain unchanged! She was left only her thoughts.

She envisioned the casket as it had been in her dream, standing on the high table, open, an equal distance from both lord and lady. What lay within—what must be guarded? An open casket—perhaps now she was fatally loosing what should be bound—but she *would* be a part of this battle, not an inanimate prize for them to fight over.

Two of them—lord, lady . . . Did it then take two, a man and woman, to complete the full pattern? Balance was ever a law of nature, perhaps of witchery also. Witchery—the Falconer had called it that, her own small dabblings in the unknown. Yet he carried now what this axe man out of Escore called a "named weapon," one of four of power.

Two to summon—Alon?

Tirtha did not raise her eyes to the boy where he stood beside her. She tried to shut from her mind, from *her,* the outer world beyond. If they moved into battle, there was nothing at all she could do now to aid and perhaps she could hinder. Therefore let her try this.

It was like feeling one's way along a passage in deep dark, through unknown halls and runways, never sure of taking the right turning. Two and an open casket . . .

"Nirel . . ." Names, true names were of importance. He had given his into Alon's keeping; yet she had been present when that was done. Therefore, whether he had intended it or not, it was also hers, though he might not have gifted it directly. "Nirel . . . Nirel . . ." Three times called—the power lay in such calling.

She did not look to him either. Had she even called aloud so that he could hear?

"Give me"—now she spoke deliberately, with the full power of her thought behind what she would say—"your sword hand."

The metal claw—that was not the man. She must have flesh to flesh, even as it had been in Hawkholme with those others of whose blood she was.

Did he hear? Would he answer? Tirtha centered her thoughts,

concentrated with all the force she could raise. Those dark corridors —yes! She had chosen a way that was open, though to where it might lead she did not know, and there was danger in this. But what could stand as true danger to one who was already dead-alive? Danger to him also, but at this moment they were all in peril, and who could balance one against the other as the worst?

Tirtha still watched the casket. However, she was aware of movement at her right. A shadow fell across the upper part of her body. There was the claw, wedged into it the sword, but stretching out to her breast and the casket was a true hand of browned skin, grimed with trail dust, bruised and blood-stained.

The casket—when they had tried to take the casket from her in the outer part of Hawkholme men had died. To take, yes, against her will, in opposition to the guardianship. This she invited, and she believed that she now held that right. If she were wrong, Nirel would die horribly. Yet if he had any such fear, the steadiness of his hand did not betray it.

His palm fell over her hands where she kept her locked grip. She could not feel the warmth of it against her own deadness or perhaps she could not because of the fire rising in the box.

"Raise!" Her voice rang out commandingly. "Lord of the Hawk, help me to raise!"

She saw his hand tighten over hers. A sweep of his fingers flipped away that roll of pictured skin. As if some breeze which could not be felt caught it, it fluttered up. But her inert hand so tightly clasped in his was moving—yes!

At that very moment there came a roar of sound so blasting they might have been struck deaf. Instantly, a vast wave of darkness followed, washing out from behind where Tirtha lay. Things moved in that darkness. She heard cries, saw quick flames that might have come from axe blades, from swords, even from the lashing of a cord whip.

No, this other task was for her, for Nirel. If he followed his warrior's instinct now and arose to fight whatever had spread from the trap, they were lost! He must not!

The blue light from the sword in his claw still hung over her, joining the glow from the box. And his hand remained on hers! He was slowly raising that lid, even as she had asked of him. Still she could not see what lay within, for the box was so placed that the opening was on the other side.

The lid arose until it was straight up, and the glow from within burned bright and even. His hand remained firmly on hers, holding them so.

Now Tirtha cried aloud: "The time is served, Ninutra—Hawk bond is given."

What loomed out of the dark before her, standing at the foot of her supine body—this was not the woman of the impressive face nor her priestess. This was another. Nor was he . . .

Human in his outward form, or did he wear that as he would wear clothing when he treated with her kind? He was weaponless, nor did he wear mail—rather a tight half garment, which seemed made of reptile skin clinging tightly to his lower limbs, reaching to his waist. It was black, but the edges of the scales glinted with the scarlet of new shed blood. Above it the dusky skin of his torso was smooth, his face awesomely handsome, his head capped with a tight-fitting covering of the same jet and scarlet scaled skin, enclosed at the brow edge by a broad band of scarlet gems. He raised his hands slowly, and Tirtha could see webs of skin as he spread wide his fingers.

He straightened them out flat as if waiting for something to be laid upon them. Nor needed he to voice his demand; he desired what Nirel and she together had uncovered.

"Time is served." His lips did not move, but words rang into silence. For though that black cloud still swirled about, there was no longer any flash of weapons through it, no sound of a struggle.

"I . . . am . . . the . . . Hawk. . . ." It was as if a heavy weight rested on Tirtha so that she had to force out those words with a pause for breath between each of them.

"You die. . . ." he returned, with that same indifference she had sensed in Ninutra. "Your death can be swift and in ease. It can be otherwise. . . ."

"I . . . am . . . Hawk. Lord and Lady—theirs the guardianship . . ."

"Lord?" There was mockery in that. "I see no lord, only a discredited beggar of a masterless fighting man."

"He is what I choose by my own right. . . ."

For a moment Rane made her no answer. He was looking, she knew, to Nirel. And as if she had seen it written on the air between the two of them, she knew what Rane would do, was doing now. He was calling upon age-old beliefs, all the prejudice of Nirel's people, drawing upon their disgust for women which abode within the mind and memory of the man beside her, striving to use such to end this alliance. She could not fight this portion of the battle—it was Nirel's alone. Perhaps it was already lost.

Yet still his hand remained on hers, and the claw-held sword was steady to light that joining.

What *did* Rane raise in Nirel? Tirtha could not guess. Nor could she reach out, she discovered, to aid the other in his fight. Would the fact of sword-oath, as great a bond as that was among his kind, be any armor against such an assault as this?

"Fool, die then!"

Rane's palms turned down. He no longer waited for a gift. His fingers crooked. Through her ran pain—red pain—a fire eating away her body inch by inch. She struggled to keep back her screams, wondering how long she could. Let Nirel release this common hold, and that other—the victory would be *his!*

The fragment of skin with its scrawl of pictured symbols, which had been fluttering in the air above the box, though it could not be wind-borne, suddenly began to twist upon itself. Even through the haze of her pain, Tirtha saw it change. The twisting substance took on a bird shape—not that of the gray bird which was Ninutra's messenger. This one was darker, black of feather as the clouds about them.

It . . . it lacked a foot, its head drooped, its wings beat with such a manifest effort that it could barely keep aloft. But it flew straight toward Rane. Then, with a last desperate burst of speed, it sped into his face as if determined to pluck out an eye, as Tirtha had heard the war falcons had once been battle-trained to do.

The Dark Great One threw up an arm to beat the flyer away. As he did, that claw, so close to her own body, moved also. The sword of power that had been found in a place of death hurtled through the air, crossing over the casket from which, in its passing, it appeared to draw more light—went on—aimed at the dark-skinned breast of him who threatened.

There came a blast of red, of black, if both could be the color of flames. Tirtha was blinded by that vast surge of energy, that upward flare. She felt the pressure laid on a hand coming to life—alive to agony. Nirel's flesh against hers, so tormented and torn, was forcing down the lid of the casket, to seal it again. She twisted under a final upsurge of agony, and at last she screamed in a way that tore at the very lining of her throat.

Dreamy content, a feeling of rightness in the world—what world? Where? She was dead. Could one dead feel the beating of a heart, draw deep breaths of scented wind? There was no pain, there was only . . .

Slowly Tirtha opened her eyes. Sunlight beamed over her head—the sun of early summer. She was stronger, more alive than she had ever felt before in her whole pinched, grim existence, as if she had been truly dead before and only now awakened into life. Her body was whole. Instinctively she used a healer's sense without thinking to assure herself of that. In fact, it was as if she somehow stood above and beyond that body and could see into it. There were no broken bones, no harm. She was healed!

She lay in a strange place—a round hollow filled with red mud that gave off an odor akin to certain herbs she knew. There came a tapping. She looked down. Mud had been mounded over her body, had hardened into a crust that covered her. A bird now perched upon the smaller hump above her upturned feet, and with its bill, it was chipping away at the covering which fell in flakes. A bird? No, a falcon, black and strong and standing on *two* feet!

There was a stir by her side. Quickly she turned her head. Nirel knelt there, even as he had done when they had united to open the casket. There was no encrusted blood matting his dark hair, no sign of any wound. His fine-drawn body was bare, unscarred. He, too, was picking at that which covered her, picking with *two* hands. The cruel claw was gone, he had ten fingers busy at his task.

She gasped and he smiled—such a smile as she thought could never have touched the somber face she had learned to know so well. Then he raised his restored hand, spread, retracted, spread again, those fingers.

"It . . ." The wonder of that or of her own healing encompassed her, and her voice was lost in it.

"It is witchery," he said with such a light gaiety that she wondered if this could be someone else wearing Nirel's body. Then she looked into his falcon eyes and knew that could not be so. "The witchery of Escore. We have been here long, my lady, but it has served us well."

She remembered. "The casket!"

"There is no more geas for the Hawk," he told her, as he pulled away with his new-found fingers a long strip of dried clay. "That witchery has been reclaimed by the one who set it, having once sent forth the casket into safety with those of your clan who swore to guard it when the Shadow fell here in the long ago. It was returned that it might serve now as a weapon in the right hands."

"Ninutra?"

He nodded as he pulled off more of the clay, then clasped her hand, drawing her up toward him. She looked from those entwined hands to him.

"I am still a woman." She forgot Great Ones and their dealings.

"As I am a man."

"And a Falconer?" She could not yet accept this change in him. Dim in her mind was that dream vision, Lord and Lady under the Hawk, closed in a bond she had never known or thought to know, but which might possibly exist again.

He turned his head and chirped. The bird arose from the crumbled clay, gave a cry, alighted on his shoulder.

"In so much as this"—he lifted his free hand and caressed the feathered head which bent to his touch—"do I hold with the old. But now I am a Hawk—did not you yourself name me so, my lady?"

Was there a shade of anxiety in that? Could it be that he looked to *her* for reassurance?

"A Hawk," she returned firmly, and allowed him to steady her on her feet. More than their bodies had been cleansed and healed here. There might lie before them much that was of the Dark—more pain, more needed strength, but neither of them would walk alone again.

"Alon?" For the first time she remembered the third one of their comradeship.

"He too seeks a destiny—that which is truly his."

Tirtha nodded. Yes, that would also follow. Alon in his own way was now free.

"A Hawk," she repeated softly. "And let them 'ware all hawks henceforth, my lord, Nirel."

His arm was about her shoulders where the weight felt right, a part of a life to be. The falcon took wing and spiralled heavenward as together they walked away from what was past and could be forgotten at will.